I0649836

ILLEGAL LIFE:

A NORTH PHILLY STORY

[RE-LOADED]

J. CERRONE

Written & Edited by J. Cerrone Smith

Book Design & Cover by Kyn Mixson

ISBN 978-0-9898111-8-7

Paper-Chase Publications LLC

Philadelphia, PA

Note: Please be advised, this book is a work of fiction. Any likeness to any person, living or deceased, is purely coincidental.

Dedications: To everybody doing what they have to do to survive in the city where I was born: Philly a.k.a Killadelphia, Pistolvania! Keep your heads up. We're gonna make it!

INTRO: (SUMMER 2014)

"I'm so glad to be out that bitch for the summer!" Carl exclaimed with a smile as he approached the front porch of his family's residence on Ninth Street in the Hunting Park section of North Philadelphia. His brother, Will and Will's best friend, Pop, had been sitting on the stoop since they arrived home from school, smoking marijuana and enjoying the warm weather.

"You better stop cursing before Mommy hears you and puts you on punishment, young-boy," Will chastised his younger brother.

"That ain't even cool," Carl groaned. "You don't get punished when you slip up and curse around her!"

"Yeah, well, I'm not thirteen years old either," Will chuckled as he exhaled weed smoke and passed the blunt to his closest friend, Pop.

"So, what? You've been cursing and hustling since you were my age," Carl replied. "That's not fair, yo! Hey, Pop. Pass me the blunt, bro."

"Aw, *hell* no!" Will roared. "What happened at school today? You came home tripping!"

"Yeah, my nigga," Pop chimed in, chuckling. "You're in your bag today!"

"Naw, I'm not in my bag," Carl objected. "It's just that today was the last day of school and I'm going into high school next year, so I'm kind of an old-head now. I figured I might as well start doing what old-heads do. Besides... y'all been smoking weed since you were younger than me!"

"What we did when we were thirteen ain't got nothing to do with this right here, bro," Will shook his head. "You're supposed to do better than me, not try to do the same shit as me! Ain't no point in me being out in these streets, getting money to help Mom, so she can focus on her health and you can focus on school if you're gonna be out here trying to be a G! Just stay in your lane, little bro!"

"Whatever, Will! Why you always tryna play somebody?"

"I'm not tryna play you," Will tried to console his annoyed younger brother. "I'm trying to help you. Matter-of-fact... I got something way better than tree for you. Wait right here for a minute." Will quickly ran up the steps, onto the front porch and disappeared into the house.

"Yo, hurry up and smoke this shit, young-boy," Pop quietly instructed Carl as he passed the small remainder of the lit marijuana cigar to the young teen.

"My nigga, Pop! Good looking out," Carl quietly exclaimed as he carefully attempted to retrieve the remnant of the cigar without burning his fingers. "That's why I fucks with you!"

"It ain't about nothing," Pop replied nonchalantly. "Stop drawing, though. Smoke that shit then toss it before your brother comes back out!"

"Say no more," Carl replied with a smile as he pursed his lips, placed the blunt to his mouth and inhaled before choking while attempting to stifle his urge to cough.

Carl quickly regained his composure and repeated the process. However, the second time, he inhaled too deeply and accidentally sucked the small, heated paper-wrapped marijuana roach directly into his mouth, burning the back of his throat. Carl immediately began to cough violently, his eyes tearing profusely.

"Oh shit! You good?" Pop asked with nervous concern.

"Yeah...," Carl gagged. "That shit burned the back of my throat! Fuck that!"

Pop burst into laughter as Carl's coughing spell died down. Carl finally stopped gagging and began to spit repeatedly onto the sidewalk in front of his home.

"Damn, C! I guess you should have listened to your brother," Pop chuckled as quietly as possible, trying not to be heard by Will so as to avoid being reprimanded for sharing the marijuana with Carl.

"Whatever, nigga," Carl smiled as he wiped tears from his cheeks. "Anyway... what's up with Cannon? I only saw him once since he got out. That's my old-head!"

"Cannon's chilling," Pop casually informed Carl. "He's getting at a dollar and still crazy as shit! You know how my cousin gets down!"

"True. Cannon's a straight-up G," Carl hesitated before changing the subject. "Um... Pop... can I get fucked up off accidentally swallowing that blunt?"

"Ha-ha," Pop laughed, amused. as he turned to examine Carl's facial expression more closely. "You look high as shit off those little two puffs! Damn, virgin lungs!"

"Chill, Pop," Carl quietly objected as his older brother exited the residence with a large bag in hand. "You drawing..."

"So, I figured I'd give you an eighth-grade graduation gift as an incentive to keep up the good work in school," Will began as he walked down the steps of the porch carrying an expensive designer backpack and approached his younger brother.

"Oh snap, Will!" Carl slowly exclaimed. "That's for me? That jawn is tough."

"You already know," Will replied as he extended his arm to hand Carl the backpack, but then drew it back when he noticed his younger brother's red, watering eyes. "You alright, nigga?"

"Yeah, I'm cool," Carl hesitated. "Why, what's up?"

"I'm just asking 'cause your eyes are red and glassy all of a sudden."

"Yeah, um," Carl stuttered. "My allergies been acting up off-and-on all day today."

"Yeah, alright," Will replied suspiciously as he reluctantly handed the bag to Carl and inquiringly glanced over at Pop, who seemed to be preoccupied with his cell phone and was ignoring Will's gaze. "Open the bag and see what's inside."

Will rolled his eyes as he noticed Carl fumble with the zipper of the designer leather backpack for roughly a minute. After growing frustrated enough with his own sudden lack of coordination, Carl sat down on the stoop, placed the bookbag between his legs and unzipped it.

"Oh shit! What's all this?" Carl's bloodshot eyes grew large and his face beamed in excitement, even though his speech was slightly slurred and his reaction time was much slower than usual. "A watch, a gold chain, cologne and a hundred-dollar gift-card from Game Stop? Good looking bro-bro!" Carl slowly stood up and gave his older brother a sloppy, but strong hug to show his gratitude.

"It ain't about nothing, C," Will nonchalantly replied as he hugged his brother back. "Congratulations on finishing eighth grade! I gotta send you off to high school looking fresh and I figured you might as well have some extra shit to help enjoy your last summer-break as a young-boy!"

"That's love, big bro," Carl slowly placed the chain around his neck and struggled to clasp the watch closed around his wrist due to his blurred vision from being under the influence of a small amount of marijuana for the first time. "How you work this jawn, bro? It won't close."

"Here... I got you," Will huffed as he grabbed his younger brother's wrist and quickly fastened the watch's wristband. "Look man... you've been doing real good in school, staying out the way, making me and Mom proud. Don't start fucking up just 'cause you think you're grown now that you're going into high school! I got you all this stuff 'cause I wanted to give you some motivation to keep doing good in school and to stay away from the street shit. You know I'll hook you up, so you shouldn't feel the need to go get it yourself and you can focus on school until you're old enough to get a real job and get legal bread. You feel me?"

"Yeah, Will," Carl agreed as he reached out and grasped his brother's extended hand for a handshake. "I got you, bro. I'll stay out the streets and in the books as long as you have my back!"

"Okay, cool. So that means no more sneaking and blowing tree behind my back, right?" Will tightened his grip on Carl's hand as he stared him squarely in his eyes.

"Ouch! Yeah, my fault bro," Carl acquiesced. "I promise. No more smoking!"

"Alright, bet. Now get your ass inside so you can brush your teeth and shower before Mom gets home for your graduation dinner."

"Ok, I will," Carl agreed. "Thanks again for everything, Will! Talk to you later, Pop. Tell Cannon I said what's up."

"Alright C-Murder! I got you," Pop chuckled as he shook Carl's hand.

Will glared at his friend upon hearing the comment Pop made to Carl. He waited for Carl to finish entering the house before addressing his trusted associate.

"Yo, Pop," Will began. "I know you mean well and all that, but I'm gonna need you to respect my word when I tell Carl something, especially about not blowing tree. I understand he's your young-boy, but he's my little brother. I'm not tryna corrupt him. I don't want him getting caught up in the streets like us."

"I feel you bro, but smoking a little weed ain't never hurt nobody," Pop protested.

"He's thirteen, my nigga," Will quickly snapped. "Plus, I had just said I didn't want him blowing and then you give him the shit as soon as I go in the house? That was disrespectful. Then you called him 'C-Murder?' I don't want Carl thinking being in the streets is thorough and trying to be like us."

"It was just a little-ass roach by the time I passed it to him, though.."

"It doesn't matter, Pop," Will firmly replied. "He doesn't need to fuck with none of that shit. He just needs to worry about school! I understand you don't have any siblings but I damn-near gotta act like Carl's dad half the time. I don't need you fucking up what I'm trying to do to make sure he stays out of trouble."

"Aw, shit," Pop sighed. "Here you go, hopping in your 'I'm so mature and got so many responsibilities' bag again! Look, my nigga... my fault. I was just tryna let my young-boy see what it was hitting for. You know he was gonna find a way to get high sooner or later. I figured it would be better for him to smoke this shit than to get some fucked up weed or some shit that's laced with some other shit from his dumb-ass friends at school. I got you, though. It won't happen again."

"Alright, bet."

"I'ma get up out of here, though," Pop informed his friend as he rose from Will's stoop and shook his associate's hand. "Enjoy the dinner with the fam. I'll see you at the spot in the morning."

"Alright, my nigga. I'll get with you. Be safe."

CHAPTER 1

Will was a tall, light-skinned, good-looking, Black teenager – seventeen years old to be exact, with a low, Caesar haircut and three-hundred and sixty degree waves in his hair. He had a mustache and a goatee, which were thick for his age, and he kept them meticulously trimmed. Will was well-dressed, too – he did not wear t-shirts very often. He preferred to wear Polo shirts, always ironed and starched, of course, with designer jeans and some expensive sneakers or Timberland boots. And of course, he didn't leave the house without donning his long, Herringbone white-gold necklace along with its matching watch and bracelet.

Will's friends often teased him, calling him a "pretty-boy" for how particular he was about his appearance.

"Y'all niggas can talk that shit all day, but the girls love me though," Will would laugh.

It was true – he was a favorite among the females at the school he attended, Simon Gratz High School, in North Philadelphia, as well as with the females in his own neighborhood. Will lived in the Hunting Park section of the city on Ninth Street, right near the park, but he went to school on the other side of Broad Street in Nicetown. Will was very athletic and was a star player on his high school's basketball team, which is why he was able to attend Gratz in Nicetown, instead of a school on the Hunting Park side of Broad Street.

Will had a girlfriend, Stacy, whom he had been dating since the beginning of eleventh grade. However, being a star athlete brought a multitude of groupies with it, and the temptation, Will found, was impossible to resist. In actuality, Will didn't have much time for his girlfriend, the groupies, or even basketball. He was too busy making money. You see, Will had his clothing, jewelry and women addictions to support. Not to mention the fact that his mother, who had raised him and his thirteen-year-old brother, Carl, by herself, needed help with the bills. So, at the tender age of thirteen, Will had decided to do what so many others before him had done – sell drugs. There was no shortage of coke-heads in his predominantly Puerto-Rican neighborhood, and he decided to capitalize on it.

An older Puerto-Rican man named Rick introduced Will to his connect, a guy named Tiny who owned a few bars in the area. At first, Tiny fronted Will just an eight-ball (three and a half grams) of cocaine, under Rick's supervision, and with strict instructions to make sure Will "didn't fuck up!" Will did just fine. Now, at age seventeen, he was flipping an ounce of coke every two days.

Will was doing well for himself – he was earning about two-thousand, five-hundred dollars' profit each week – and he was saving up most of his money to buy his first car. He also planned to move out of his mother's home when he turned eighteen in January. Pop was his partner-in-crime. They were buying an ounce of cocaine every two days for eleven-hundred dollars, breaking it down to points (.1 gram) and selling them for ten-dollars each. They were making one-hundred dollars per gram.

Will had a dilemma, though. A few college basketball scouts had attended his high school games and rumor had it they were interested in recruiting him. However, Will had no interest in attending college. If he was going to play basketball, he wanted to go straight to the NBA. He already did not like school, and the thought of going to college just made him sick.

"Don't nothing move me but the money," Will would state quite seriously. "I need that NBA bread! The only way I'm going to college is if they give me a full scholarship – then I *might* go! But on some real shit… fuck that! I'm either tryna go straight to the league or stay out here hustling! I know I could be a boss one day, if things keep going the way they are with this coke."

"You ain't lying," Will's closest friend, Pop, a short, dark-skinned teenager, replied as they sat in Rick's stash-house, meticulously bagging the ounce of coke into points. "Pretty soon we'll be able to cop some bricks, and then we'll really be paid!" Pop was not only Will's closest friend, but also his business partner in the cocaine business. They had grown up together and were the only two Black guys on their block, other than Will's younger brother, Carl. It was the summer before their senior year in high school and they were both excited to graduate, although Pop cut class a lot to sell drugs.

"Yo, dog, I would've dropped out already if it wasn't for playing ball," Will continued. "I'ma just see how this basketball shit works out. I ain't sweating it, though, 'cause I think the streets is what I'ma be doing for life!"

"You gonna have a short life then, young-boy," Rick interjected as he walked into the room.

"What you mean, old-head?" Will asked as he turned around in his chair to face Rick. "You're twice my age and you said you've been hustling since you were my age. You're still alive and you're good…"

"Man, you have no idea! Watching your back every day for stick-up kids or the cops is no way to live," Rick replied. "I've been doing this shit for years and it gets old. I'm only still hustling 'cause I dropped outta school when I had my oldest daughter and I had to support her somehow. I've done five years in jail behind selling drugs, too. If you're smart, you'll go to college even if they don't give you a full scholarship. I know you have enough money saved to pay for it by now!"

"Well I ain't tryna talk about how much bread I got stashed," Will chuckled. "But I'm good. I definitely ain't wasting it on tuition though!"

"Will, you sound stupid, nigga," Rick said with disappointment as he shook his head. "Don't let these streets run you…"

"Anyway," Pop interjected, "let's finish bagging up so we can make this money, Will!"

"No doubt, enough talk," Will agreed. "We've been bagging up for hours!"

"Alright, my fault, I'll let y'all do what you do," Rick replied. "I just overheard y'all while I was in the other room getting wetted and I was tryna drop some knowledge on my young-boys!" Rick then left the room and went about his business of finishing his PCP-laced cigarette.

After about another hour of bagging up the coke into ten dollar bags, Will and Pop finally finished. They loaded up their book bags with the approximately two-hundred and seventy-five bags and left Rick's stash-spot.

"That's my old-head and everything, but that nigga be tripping sometimes! That's why we need to get our own stash-spot when you turn eighteen," Will vented. "I can't deal with him all the time like that. Shit... I've been dealing with him since I was thirteen and I've already proved myself. I don't need him over my shoulder anymore."

"Yeah, I feel you," Pop agreed. "How the nigga gonna be in the other room smoking wet and then come out talking about how you need to stop hustling and go to college? Ha-ha! That shit is more hypocritical than a motherfucker!"

"Yeah, I know, right?" Will pulled out his pre-paid cell phone as it began to ring. "Yo. What up?"

"Hey baby... why you answer the phone like that?" Stacy asked. Stacy was a shapely, brown-skinned girl who was also seventeen and had healthy black hair with gorgeous burgundy highlights that fell to her shoulders. She was very much in love with Will and had lost her virginity to him. She called and text-messaged him all the time, which irritated him – especially when he was busy handling business. He told her he "needed to focus on getting this money," but she kept at it anyway.

"No reason, ma. I'm just busy handling shit," Will replied nonchalantly. "What's up?"

"I was hoping I could see you today since I haven't seen you in a few days..."

"I can't right now, Stace," Will replied matter-of-factly. "I gotta get on the block and get this money. You know how it is."

"Aw, damn baby! I miss you! And I need some! It's been three days," Stacy whined.

"Maybe later when I get off the block I can come over and bless you! But I just bagged up and I gotta get half these jawns off before I quit for the night."

"Okay... but you better not be dissing me for those groupie hoes I see following you around at school and at your games," Stacy teased, although she was quite serious.

"Now, you know I don't fuck with none of those bitches," Will lied. In fact, he just had two of them over at Pop's house the previous night – one for himself and one for Pop. "I only want you, ma! I'll be over there later."

"Okay baby, that's what's up! What time?"

"By the time I catch the bus over there, probably twelve or twelve-thirty. Will your mom be home?" Stacy lived in Nicetown, on Twentieth Street and Hunting Park Avenue. It was a short bus ride for Will.

"Now you know her crack-smoking-ass will be out trying to get some rock," Stacy replied, dejected. "We'll have the crib to ourselves."

"Okay cool. See your sexy-ass then. Peace baby."

"Bye, baby."

"Nigga, you crack me up," Pop chuckled as Will hung up.

"Why's that?" Will asked, puzzled.

"You playing Stacy like a fiddle," Pop replied. "You treat her like one of these groupie bitches but you been with her for almost a year! She's head-over-heels, my nigga!"

"Yeah I know, right? She be hitting me up like crazy! It's too much! She called me like five times while we were bagging up," Will sighed. "She's a good girl, though. I know she's loyal; that's why I'ma keep her. But I'ma still do my thing. I'ma just let her think I'm not doing nothing else 'cause she would flip!"

"Yeah, like if she knew about those bad-ass Puerto-Rican jawns we had last night!"

"Exactly!" The two teenagers laughed in unison. "The jawn I had had the craziest head-game," Will boasted.

"Not better than the jawn I had," Pop protested as they walked to the corner of Ninth Street and Lycoming Street where they usually sold their coke. All the coke users in the neighborhood knew the duo were always on that corner and knew they could find them there. And when they weren't there, their customers would call them.

"So, dog, anyway, back to what I was saying about getting our own stash-spot," Will started. "My birthday ain't until January, so I was thinking we could put our bread together and rent a room and keep the weight there and bag up there after you turn eighteen in October. That is, unless you wanna get an apartment..."

"I ain't got enough bread for an apartment," Pop confessed.

"You got money saved, though, right?"

"Yeah, but honestly, I be blowing that bread – *literally*! I smoke a lot of weed! And then buying clothes and sneakers all the time, paying all my mom's bills 'cause she don't work; I don't have a lot of money left by the time we need to re-up."

"I feel you on helping your mom out and all that, but maybe you need to slow down with copping all that gear. We need a stash-spot where we can handle our business so we don't have to do the shit outta Rick's crib anymore. We still gotta pay him a piece 'cause he goes to Tiny for us to cop, but if we get our own spot we can go straight to Tiny ourselves," Will advised.

"Yeah, no doubt," Pop agreed. "I'm just tryna keep up with your pretty-boy ass and get the bitches! That's why a nigga needs the gear and the kicks... a nigga wasn't blessed with the 'good' hair," Pop joked.

"Here you go with that shit again, nigga! Naw, but for real, I was looking online at rooms for rent in Nicetown near Stacy, and I saw a couple jawns for like four-hundred a month and we just gotta put down one month deposit. Do you have enough money saved for that?" Will asked.

"Oh, no doubt... I could do that a few times."

"Alright, bet! We're gonna make moves and do that shit in October when your birthday comes, right?"

"No doubt, my nigga," Pop affirmed.

"We can get a table in the room, a TV and maybe even a sofa if it's big enough so we can have bitches over there when we're not handling business."

Their first customer of the day walked up and bought three bags. He was a regular customer, as all their customers were at this point. Will had been selling coke for almost five years and Pop joined him two years in. Will was puzzled that Pop didn't have more money saved up by now. Pop said he could pay for the deposit for the room-for-rent "a few times." What did that mean – he only had twelve-hundred dollars saved? How could that be after selling ounces of coke for three years? Even though he was paying all of his mother's bills, Will thought Pop would have more money saved than that. After all, Will paid most of his mother's bills and bought all of his younger brother's clothes. Even after all that, he still had managed to save over seventeen-thousand dollars, though he hadn't revealed that fact to anybody, including his mother, Stacy or Pop. Since he already had his driver's license, his plan was to save twenty-five-thousand dollars and buy a car for about fifteen-thousand. Then, when he turned eighteen in January, he was going to get an apartment and fully furnish it. Will was excited about his plans and was proud that he had been able to save all that cash in a safe in his room in his mother's house on Ninth Street. As he thought about this, more customers walked or drove up, each buying between two and five bags.

As they stood there on the corner, Pop decided to play some music on his cellular phone. A song by Chinx Drugs, featuring Rick Ross and P. Diddy, entitled "I'm a Coke-Boy" was their theme song. Will and Pop rapped along to the music in unison as they stood there. That was, until the police drove by.

"Oh shit! We're slipping!" Will blurted out. "We forgot to take the rest of this shit back to the crib!" Fortunately, the police didn't bother the teenagers and kept driving by. However, the two young men decided it was a good time to go. They had sold almost half of their product within four hours. It had been a good night and it was time for Will to go see his girlfriend. "Alright, my nigga, I'll get with you," Will said to Pop before he entered his house to drop off his book bag.

"Alright, homey, be safe," Pop replied and walked down the street to his house.

Will walked to Roosevelt Boulevard and caught the bus, taking the short ride to Stacy's block. He knocked on her door and she opened it, wearing nothing but a smile and a negligée.

"Hey baby," Stacy embraced Will and kissed him softly on the lips. "We've been waiting for you."

"Hey sexy," Will replied. "Who's 'we?'"

"Me and my pussy!"

"Ha-ha! Oh, I feel you," Will laughed. "Well let's get it popping, then!"

The young couple made their way to Stacy's bedroom and Will aggressively tossed her on the bed and almost ripped her negligee as he pulled it off. Will grabbed Stacy's breasts as he kissed her passionately for several minutes. Then he turned her around and entered her from behind, thrusting himself inside of her and smacking her butt. After about ten minutes, they had both climaxed and collapsed on her bed. Stacy rolled up a blunt of marijuana and lit it.

"Will," she said and turned to look at him as she exhaled the smoke out of the opposite side of her mouth and passed the blunt to him.

"Baby, do you love me? I mean, do you *really* love me?"

Will exhaled the weed smoke heavily. It was really a sigh, however, and he tried not to roll his eyes since Stacy was staring at him. She asked him this same question every time they had sex. Of course he cared about her; they had been together for almost a year. But he was too young to have a girl who needed so much reassurance. "She probably needs so much reassurance because her father wasn't in her life," Will thought to himself.

"Yeah, baby, you know I love you," Will replied coolly. "Why you keep asking me that?"

"I don't know… I guess I'm just a little insecure. I know all these bitches want you since you get money and you're an all-star ball player. I know I'm not the baddest bitch out here…"

"To me you are! You're fine as hell," Will reassured Stacy. He wasn't lying. Stacy was considered one of the most beautiful girls in their school. But some of the groupies were also just as physically attractive and they were easy to have sex with, which made them even harder to resist!

"Just please don't ever cheat on me, Will," Stacy implored. "I would die!"

"I wouldn't do that," Will said as he took another drag and passed the lit blunt to his girlfriend. He felt bad for lying to her, but he couldn't tell her that he had been cheating on her since day one.

"I know you said you're gonna get your own apartment in January when you turn eighteen, right?"

"Yeah Stace, that's the plan."

"Can I move in with you?" Stacy asked with an innocent, child-like expression. "I can't live with my crack-head mother anymore and I wannabe with you all the time, baby!"

"Maybe… we'll see, ma."

"Just think about it. I'll cook and clean for you and everything! It will be great!"

"Yeah, I'll think about it," Will replied calmly. But in his mind he had already decided against it. "Well, let me get up outta here before your mother gets back," Will said after they had finished the blunt.

"You're leaving already?"

"Yeah, I'm tired, ma," Will forced a yawn. "I'll call you tomorrow."

Stacy got up with a frown as Will got dressed and she followed her boyfriend to the front door.

"Okay, baby. I love you. Talk to you tomorrow," Stacy said as she kissed Will goodbye.

"Alright Stace, I'll get at you, baby." Will walked down the block to the bus stop. "Damn that girl is too needy!" he said to no one in particular.

CHAPTER 2

Tiny's nephews, Jasiel and Jose, were twenty-one year-old, twin brothers and were stick-up kids who lived on Marshall Street near Hunting Park Avenue. Their father was serving a life-sentence in prison for a murder he committed when the twins were toddlers. Jasiel and Jose's mother had died of cancer when they were nineteen, leaving them the house and a fifty-thousand dollar life insurance policy. Wisely, they took their uncle's advice and had used the money to pay off the thirty-five thousand dollars that remained on the mortgage. They split ten-thousand dollars so they could each buy a vehicle for five-thousand dollars – Jasiel had purchased a used Pontiac Bonneville and Jose had purchased a used Chevrolet Impala.

However, they didn't really need two cars because they usually went everywhere together, unless one of them was going to visit a female. Most of the remainder of the money was used to buy guns, bullet-proof vests and a safe for the guns. Since they both smoked wet, or PCP, they used what money was left to get high. Their motivation to buy bullet-proof vests was because Jasiel had been shot in the stomach a few years prior while attempting to rob a drug-dealer in the park who had spotted him coming. The drug-dealer had shot him and fled and Jasiel used his cell phone to call his brother, which had saved his life. Jasiel spent three weeks in Temple Hospital recovering from his wounds. On this particular night, while Will was at Stacy's, the twins were at one of their uncle's bars, which was around the corner from their house, looking for their next drunk victim.

"Yo, bro!" Jasiel said excitedly. "We gotta get a nigga and get a nigga soon, man! The bar's about to close! Did you peep anybody in here?"

"Yeah, man," Jose replied calmly as he pointed across the bar.

"See that big, fat nigga over there? He's drunk as shit and he got all that ice on. I seen him take out mad money last time he was paying the bartender. We gonna follow that nigga to his car and rob that fat motherfucker!" Even though they were twins, the brothers' personalities were polar opposites. While Jasiel was very excitable with a short fuse, Jose was mostly calm and laid-back.

"Ha! I know, right?" Jasiel laughed. "We got bills to pay! The water and electric is due in a week and the cable is due in two weeks. That's like five-hundred right there, not to mention car insurance!"

"Don't sweat that shit. We're gonna get all his shit and sell that shit to the jewelry store. We'll get his cash, too," Jose reassured his brother. On this night, Jose had driven his Impala to the bar and was going to be the getaway driver.

"Y'all good?" Tiny asked as he walked up behind the twins, put his arms around their shoulders and greeted them.

"Yeah, we good," the young men answered in unison.

"Y'all staying out of trouble?" Tiny tightened his arms around their necks as he smiled. He knew the twins had been stick-up kids since they were in their mid-teens and he did not approve of their choices in crime. Tiny would rather that they get into the cocaine business with him. He figured it was a little less dangerous than sticking guns in people's faces, especially since Jasiel had been shot. But Tiny also didn't agree with their decision to rob people for another reason. He felt it was better to earn your money hustling. Not to mention the fact that he suspected that not only did his nephews rob drug-dealers, but they robbed some of his bar patrons as well. Tiny suspected this because, on occasion, he would overhear some of his customers saying they had been robbed at gun-point around the block from one of his bars after leaving. "Y'all better not rob any of my customers, motherfuckers!"

"We wouldn't do that, Unc," Jose lied.

"I wish we could rob that Black motherfucker, Will," Jasiel chimed in. "But you won't let us!"

"You know I've been selling coke to the young-boy for years," Tiny replied matter-of-factly. "You would be taking money out of my pocket! I'ma tell you again... don't rob that young-boy!"

"Alright," Jasiel agreed. "But I can't stand that motherfucker! He's always hustling in our neighborhood and fucking Boricua bitches! He's *begging* to get robbed!" At that moment, Jose tapped Jasiel's arm and motioned towards the fat man they planned to rob – he was heading toward the exit, walking right past them.

"Okay, Unc… we're about to bounce," Jose said as he got up and shook his uncle's hand. Jasiel did the same.

"Yeah, I need to close down this jawn anyway," Tiny replied as he shook his nephews' hands and walked away. Then, as he walked towards the deejay booth, he turned around and skeptically watched the twins hastily exit through the front door. He shook his head before continuing to handle his business and making the announcement for the last call for alcohol. Tiny sensed his nephews were up to no good.

The twins followed the fat Puerto-Rican man, trailing him by a distance of about twenty feet. The man had the feeling that he was being followed and kept looking over his shoulder at the twins, but they were far enough away that he wasn't sure whether or not they were truly following him. However, once he reached Seventh Street and turned the corner and disappeared from their sight, they tied bandanas over the bottom halves of their faces and began to jog in order to catch up with him. He heard the rapid footsteps approaching from behind him and felt a pang of fear. Instinctively, the large man spun around and pulled a ten-inch blade from the holster on his belt-loop under his over-sized shirt and held it out to greet Jasiel and Jose as they rounded the corner. The fat man backed up towards the driver's side of his vehicle, a white GMC Yukon Denali with twenty-four inch rims, and waved the long knife in the air towards his assailants, who had drawn their guns before they turned the corner.

"You motherfuckers get away from me," he panted. "I'll cut you up real good! I'll gut you like a pig," he threatened.

"You ain't doing shit, old-head! Now give up the chain, the bracelet, the watch and the cash," Jasiel barked. Jasiel liked to take the lead in the robberies. He was more aggressive so it worked out well for the twins.

"I'm not giving up shit," the fat man replied. "Come on and get stabbed!"

"Come on, man," Jose calmly replied. "We got guns… you're not gonna win this! Just give up your shit, man."

"Just let me get in my truck and leave," the fat man said as he reached in his pocket and pulled out his keys.

"That's your truck?" Jasiel's voice cracked as he cocked back his gun. Jose looked at his brother, knowing what he was thinking. Jose shook his head "no" at his brother, but Jasiel just ignored him. "Give me your keys, too, or I'ma pop you." They both knew that the fat man was stubborn and wasn't planning on easily giving his jewelry or money up, so why would he surrender his truck? Jose could tell Jasiel was ready to kill the man. Jose wasn't ready to get into the murder game, that's why he had shaken his head "no" at his brother. But Jasiel had changed since he had been shot. He was much quicker to fight, much quicker to shoot, and he talked about murdering people often, especially Will.

"I'm not giving you shit!" the fat man growled. As he turned halfway around in order to unlock his truck door with the keyless entry, Jasiel stepped closer to the man.

"Run that shit, nigga!" Jasiel demanded. "Give me all of it! I'm not gonna tell you again! I'm gonna pop you, dog!"

"Ahhhhh!" The fat man lunged at Jasiel, knife first, and tried to stab him. Jasiel, whose gun was already cocked, jumped to the side and shot the fat man in the side of the head, shooting him right above his ear. The man's body went limp in mid-air, his knife clanged as the metal hit the ground, and there was a loud thud as his massive body fell on the pavement.

"Oh shit! What are you doing, man?" Jose panted, his heart racing.

"Getting this nigga's shit," Jasiel replied, smiling as he hurriedly took the man's watch, chain, rings, and money. Jasiel could not get the man's bracelet off, however, and he struggled with it for a few moments. Jasiel's heart was racing, too, but out of excitement and adrenaline.

"Nigga, hurry the fuck up! Fuck that bracelet, man!" Jose whispered loudly. "We gotta get the fuck outta here, man!"

"You're right," Jasiel replied as he put the stolen items in his pockets.

"Go back to your wheel and meet me at the chop-shop down the Badlands. We gonna sell this motherfucker's truck!"

"Alright bet!" Jose ran back down Seventh Street onto Hunting Park Avenue and jumped into his Impala and sped off toward the Badlands.

Meanwhile, Jasiel grabbed the fat man's keys off the ground, hopped into the Yukon and pulled off. As he pulled off, however, he ran over the man's legs, crushing the bones in the dead man's limp body.

"Oh well, whatcha gonna do?" Jasiel thought to himself as he sped off, hoping the police weren't on their way to the scene. Jose arrived at the chop-shop about three minutes before Jasiel did and was anxious the entire time he waited for Jasiel to arrive. Jose was deeply relieved when he saw his brother pull up behind him. Jasiel had called the owner, Tito, while on his way and the shop owner said he would arrive shortly. Five minutes after Jasiel had arrived, Tito pulled up to his chop-shop. Of course, Tito operated a front business there, too – a legitimate collision repair shop.

"So, what you twins got for me?" the short, stocky, middle-aged Puerto-Rican man asked as he smoked a cigar. Jasiel put his arm around Tito and walked him to the Yukon.

"Isn't this wheel tough, Tito? I just came up on this shit. It has the keys and everything man," Jasiel bragged. "What can you give me for it?"

"Yeah, it is nice, man," Tito concurred. "What you want for it?"

"Twenty-five-hundred dollars," Jasiel intentionally started the bidding high.

"Naw. Now you know I only give twelve-hundred for trucks, Jasiel," Tito sternly replied.

"Two-thousand then," Jasiel countered. "The rims are worth more than that!"

"I can give you fifteen-hundred cash right now – final offer," Tito stated firmly.

"Alright man, but I feel like you're robbing me," Jasiel laughed.

"Me? Rob you? You're the stick-up artist!" Both men laughed.

"Hey, what's up with Jose? Why's he staying in the car and not saying nothing?"

"We smoked some wet earlier and maybe it didn't agree with him," Jasiel answered. They had smoked before they went to the bar, but Jasiel knew that wasn't the real reason why Jose was acting strangely. Jose was acting that way because his twin brother had just shot a man in the head right in front of his face. "Alright, Tito, thanks man," Jasiel said as he counted the money and put it in his pocket. "Talk to you later."

Jasiel got into the car with his brother, and Jose pulled off slowly and headed home. Jasiel noticed his brother moping. He hadn't even turned the CD player on.

"What's wrong with you, man?" Jasiel barked. "Why you acting like a bitch?"

"I'm not acting like a bitch, man! You just shot that man in the head like it was nothing! Now you're a killer! I didn't wanna be no killer," Jose whined.

"Well, you still ain't a killer," Jasiel snapped. "I'm the one who blew his head off! Besides, that motherfucker was trying to stab me – you saw it! If you weren't so shook you would have been shooting at him, too! You're supposed to have my back!"

"My fault man," Jose apologized. "He caught me off guard. But on some real shit… I ain't built for no bodies, man. I ain't tryna go to jail for life!"

"Stop talking like a bitch, Jose! Ain't nobody going to jail motherfucker! Matter-of-fact, pull over to that dumpster so I can toss this ratchet."

Jose pulled over to a dumpster on Cumberland Street and Jasiel quickly got out of the car, looked around to make sure nobody was watching, and then threw his gun into the dumpster. He then quickly got back into the vehicle and they pulled off.

"So, how's it feel to be a killer?" Jose asked with genuine interest.

"Same as the first time," Jasiel grinned slyly in the darkness.

"The first time? What first time?" Jose asked in shock.

"Oh, that's right! I never told you!" Jasiel pretended that the fact that he had never told his brother about the first murder he had committed had slipped his mind. "Remember when that motherfucker shot me in the stomach? Well, a couple months later, after I was all healed up, I went back to the park with my gun cocked, crept up on that nigga and shot him four times in his back. He was gasping for air and shit and coughing up blood when I turned him over and emptied his pockets. He had like twenty dime bags of coke on him and three-hundred dollars."

"That's fucked up, man... why didn't you tell me about that?"

"'Cause I knew you would talk shit and act like a pussy like you are now! Plus I know you 'ain't built for no bodies' like you said a minute ago, so I went by myself."

"Damn, bro..." Jose exclaimed, "I can't believe you've killed two people!"

"So far," Jasiel chuckled.

"Damn, kid... you sound crazy," Jose sighed.

"I just haven't given a fuck since Mom died," Jasiel explained. "And after I got shot I had to get that motherfucker, na'mean? I ain't crazy, though. I'm just a street-nigga. Plus, it comes with the territory. When you robbing for long enough, you're gonna have to merck somebody eventually! Even you'll have to do it one day – you'll see..."

"Naw, not me," Jose protested.

"Well, whatever," Jasiel replied nonchalantly as he pulled out the cash he had taken from the fat man's pockets. "Yo, dog, there's eight-hundred dollars here! Plus, we got fifteen-hundred from Tito for the truck and we'll get something nice for the jewelry! We came up man!"

"Yeah, we did, but you caught a body behind that shit," Jose replied, downtrodden.

"Whatever, man! That's how I get down! And you better get down like that, too, before you get mercked out here! Anyway – enough talking about this shit. Put that Peedi Crakk CD on!"

Meanwhile, Will was walking home from the bus stop towards Hunting Park Avenue. He saw the flashing lights from the police squad-cars and decided to stash his gun in some bushes and continue walking. Will hadn't completed crossing over Hunting Park Avenue when a police squad-car sped up next to him and two officers jumped out and ran towards him.

"Up against the wall," they commanded as the one officer slammed Will face-first against the brick wall. Will barely had enough time to put his hands up to prevent his face from colliding with the wall.

"What the fuck, yo? What did I do?" Will protested.

"Spread 'em," the officer barked as he kicked the inside of Will's feet and began to frisk him. "Anything in your pockets that will stick me or cut me?"

"Naw, man! What is this about?"

"There was a homicide a couple blocks away about forty-five minutes ago. Where were you? Where are you coming from, son?" the officer asked abruptly.

"I'm coming from my girl's crib over in Nicetown. I just got off the bus," Will replied truthfully.

"Is that so?" The officers looked at Will's driver's license. "Kinda young to be out at two-thirty in the morning, aren't you? You have a lot of money on you for a seventeen-year-old, too!"

"My mother gave it to me to go pay the electric bill tomorrow while she's at work," Will lied. "And she doesn't mind me being out late as long as I'm with my girl."

"Yeah, I'm sure," the officer snapped. "Well, get in the car… we're going to see your alleged girlfriend to see if your story adds up. If not, you're coming with us to the station!"

Will reluctantly went with the officers. He was uneasy but he wasn't worried, however, because he had been with Stacy the entire time and he knew she would vouch for him. Besides, he hadn't killed anybody! A few minutes later, they pulled up to Stacy's place and the officer banged on her door. After a minute, Stacy answered the door only to be greeted by her boyfriend with a police officer on either side of him. Her expression was that of pure fear.

"W-what's going on?" Stacy stuttered as she tried to catch her breath.

"Sorry to bother you so late at night, honey," the one officer replied. "But is this your boyfriend?"

"Yes, he is, officer! What's this about?" Stacy asked.

"There was a murder a little while ago…"

"Well, Will couldn't have done it! He just left here twenty minutes ago," Stacy cut the officer off.

"Are you sure about that, Miss?" the officer asked skeptically.

"Yes, for sure! I swear," Stacy put her right hand in the air.

"Okay, thanks, Miss. That'll do for now. Have a good night," the officer replied. The officers walked Will outside and back down to the squad car.

"Told y'all," Will replied with an attitude. "Can I go now?"

"No! We're taking your ass home," the officers replied, both smirking.

"Get in the car!"

They arrived at Will's house and the officers banged on the door before Will even had a chance to take his keys out of his pocket.

"What the fuck, dog? You're gonna wake up my mother," Will snapped.

"That's the idea," the officer grinned. A few minutes later Will's mother, an attractive, light-skinned, middle-aged woman, came to the door wearing a robe and slippers and curlers in her hair. She was still half asleep but when she realized that her son had two police officers with him, she quickly woke up.

"William Bonner! What is the meaning of this?" Misses Bonner, Will's mother, screamed.

"Mom, it was a mistake!"

"You come home with two cops and you tell me it was a mistake?"

"Ma'am, please let me explain," the officer who had knocked on the door began. "There was a murder on Seventh and Hunting Park about an hour ago and we saw your son walking, so we stopped him for questioning, but everything's fine now. We just wanted to make sure he made it home safely."

"So he's not a suspect or anything, right?" Misses Bonner asked.

"No, ma'am," the officer reassured Will's mother. "But for his safety and your peace of mind, you might want to make sure you don't let him stay out so late."

"I understand, Officer. Thank you and good night."

"Good night, ma'am," the two police officers replied.

"Will, get your ass in this house," Misses Bonner commanded as Will watched the officers walk to the squad-car and drive away. Will gave them the middle finger and then strolled into the house behind his mother.

"What you doing getting brought home by the cops at almost three-o-clock in the morning, waking me up on my last night off before I gotta go back to work? And you better be glad they didn't catch you with nothing, boy!"

"I'm too slick for that, Ma," Will laughed.

"Don't ever think you're too slick, little nigga! Those cops are real slick! They'll have you hemmed up real good! What are they doing grabbing you up for a murder anyway?" Misses Bonner asked.

"I don't know, ma. It was some bullshi…" Will caught himself before he cursed in front of his mother. Misses Bonner gave her son a stern look. She could curse as much as she wanted but, out of respect, she did not want her children cursing in front of her. "Anyway, I was with Stacy the whole time and she vouched for me."

"Well, I'm glad to hear that. She's a nice girl! I'm glad you're dealing with a Black girl again. There's nothing wrong with the Puerto-Rican girls – they're pretty and all that. I just say, what's wrong with dealing with your own kind?" Misses Bonner ranted.

"Yeah okay, Ma," Will dismissed his mother's comments.

"But anyway, boy," Misses Bonner continued, "this whole situation with the cops brings me back to what I keep telling you. You need to get out of the streets and focus on playing basketball. I appreciate all the bills you pay. Lord knows I don't know how I would do it without you, but what if those cops had caught you with some drugs on you? Then you would be in jail! You need to focus on this basketball – you're good at it! You can go to college. Me and your brother will be fine."

"Come on, ma, I'm not tryna hear that! You and Carl will not be fine if I go away and I'm not bringing any money in. You don't hardly make any money at the nursing home, and I don't want you working two jobs like you used to before I started hustling – especially with your diabetes. Just chill, ma, I got this. I'm tryna go to the NBA and get this real money or stay in these streets and make even more money than I have been making! I'm tryna skip the whole college thing."

"Just think about it baby," Misses Bonner pleaded. "I don't want anything bad to happen to you."

"Don't worry about me, ma. I'm good." Will kissed his mother on the forehead.

"What happened?" Carl, Will's younger brother, asked as he came downstairs and into the kitchen where Will and his mother had been conversing.

"Don't worry about it, C," Will replied. "Everything's good."

"I'm going back to bed then," Carl responded.

"Me too," Misses Bonner yawned. "Think about what I said, though, Will."

"Okay, ma, I'll think about it." Will said this just to appease his mother, however. He viewed college as a waste of time. If he didn't go straight to the NBA, he'd rather be making money in the streets. And there was no way he was going to stop hustling at this point. It was going too well for him. Besides, he had goals – get a stash spot, get a car, get an apartment. Maybe he would even convince Tiny to front him a kilogram of cocaine after he got his stash-spot. Then he would *really* get paid. Yeah, everything would fall into place. He didn't need college. Sometimes Will felt like he didn't even need or want to play basketball anymore – he just wanted to sell coke.

CHAPTER 3

Later that morning, Will woke up angry with himself because he overslept. He didn't wake up until ten-o'clock and he wanted to be up before a lot of people in the neighborhood were out and about so that he could discreetly retrieve his gun. He took a quick shower, got dressed, skipped breakfast, and ran over to the bushes in the park where he had stashed his gun.

"Oh shit! It's not here!" Will instantly grew paranoid. He was suspicious that someone had been watching him the night before when he had thrown his gun into the bushes. He tore through the greenery to make sure he hadn't missed it and looked around wildly to make sure nobody was watching him too closely, but the gun was gone. "Damn!" Will walked away angry and disappointed. Still, he was happy that he didn't have the gun when the police had grabbed him. He took out his cell phone and called his friend, Pop.

"Yo, Pop! What up, my nigga?" Will greeted his friend over the phone. "You up?"

"Yeah, my nigga, I just got dressed. You tryna hit the block now?" Pop asked. "You sound like you in the streets already."

"Yeah, I got a problem... I'll holler at you when I get there." A few minutes later, Will arrived at Pop's house. Will told Pop about what had transpired the previous night and just moments earlier. "So, I need to get with your cousin out in Germantown so I can cop another burner, na'mean? I want a forty or a forty-five this time, though. That twenty-five was too small for me!"

"I got you, dog," Pop replied. "I'll hit him up now." Pop reached for his cell phone and dialed his older cousin, Cannon's, number.

"Yo, what up, my young-boy?" Cannon's deep voice answered the line. Cannon was a thirty-year-old parolee who had done five years in state prison for a gun charge, along with possession with intent to distribute marijuana. He had a lot of tattoos, made his living selling guns, and was known around the hood as an "O.G." or "Original Gangsta."

"What's up, O.G.? What's good with you?"

"Ain't shit, cuz... what's the deal?" Cannon asked, getting straight to the point.

"My homey needs one of those bitches you got," Pop began. "He needs either a forty-year-old bitch or a forty-five-year-old bitch. You got one lying around?"

"Yeah man, I got a pretty-ass, forty-five-year-old bitch here right now," Cannon replied.

"Oh, that's what's up! How much is she going for?" Pop asked.

"Four beans," Cannon replied coolly.

"Alright bet. I'll let him know. Can we come through in like a half?"

"Yeah, that's cool."

"Alright. Peace, Cannon," Pop hung up and turned to Will. "He has a forty-five caliber jawn for four-hundred dollars. He said we can come through now."

"Alright bet," Will replied happily. "Let me run back to my crib and get the bread for the burner and for a taxi."

"You feel like running ball?" Pop asked.

"Yeah, I guess so," Will replied nonchalantly. "We can't be out there too long, though, 'cause we need to get this money! I'll change into basketball gear. I'll be back in five minutes." Will walked down the block, changed his clothes, went into his safe and took four-hundred and thirty dollars out of it and placed it in his book bag before going back to Pop's house. When he came back up the block, Pop was waiting on his stoop.

"So I guess you're ready, huh, Pop?"

"Yeah, man," Pop replied as he walked down the steps, bouncing his basketball. "Let's walk to the Ave so we can catch a cab." The two teenagers walked to Hunting Park Avenue and waited about five minutes before successfully hailing a taxi. Within about ten minutes they had reached Cannon's apartment in the Germantown section of Philadelphia on Wayne Avenue near Queen Lane. They rang his doorbell, but the buzzer that would automatically open the front door of the apartment building was broken, so Cannon, who was expecting them, came to the door and let them in. He probably would have come to the door anyway just to make sure it was Will and Pop. He had a dozen guns and a pound of marijuana in the apartment, so he couldn't afford to take any unnecessary chances.

"What's good, my young-boys?" Cannon shook both Will and Pop's hands as he let them in, looked out the doorway and shut it, before walking them to his first-floor apartment.

"Ain't shit, Cannon. I came to get that joint from you and run some ball if you're up to it," Will replied as they walked into Cannon's apartment.

"Yeah, nigga... I see y'all got your ball gear on. I'll run ball with y'all. Ay, yo, Will, don't think 'cause you an all-star I won't bust your ass on the court!" Cannon chuckled.

"You ain't got nothing for me, old-head," Will laughed.

"My cousin's been through here," Cannon continued, "but I ain't seen your ass since you bought that twenty-five from me last year when I first came home. What... you need a new joint 'cause you had to pop a nigga?"

"Not exactly," Will explained. "I had to stash the jawn last night before the cops ran up on me and when I went back to get it this morning, it was gone."

"Ain't that fucked up?" Pop chimed in.

"Yeah, it is! Well, look at this pretty chrome four-five I've got for you," Cannon replied as he brandished the firearm. "This shit will blow a nigga's head clean off!"

"That's cool," Will replied coolly as he exchanged the money for the gun. "I mean, I'll do what I gotta do to protect myself, but I'm just tryna get money, na'mean?"

"I feel you," Pop replied. "But I have a feeling about them Rican niggas over on Marshall Street – Tiny's nephews."

"Who? Jasiel and Jose?" Will replied. "What about them?"

"You know they're stick-up kids!" Pop exclaimed.

"Yeah, of course I know," Will stated sarcastically. "*Everybody* knows that shit! But they would never try to rob us. We're Tiny's customers... that would be a conflict of interest!"

"Man, I swear, they act like they don't give a fuck by the way they stare at us when they drive by us on the block," Pop continued.

"Look, y'all young-boys got any problems you just let me know," Cannon interjected. "Fuck these niggas' lives, man. I'll merck them niggas for y'all!"

"That might be a good idea, Will," Pop began.

"Good looking out, Cannon, but I'm not worried about them niggas," Will protested. "Besides, the block is already hot enough. There was just a murder a couple blocks away last night. Too many killings makes it hard to get money, you know?"

"You're right," Pop replied, defeated. "I just want them niggas out the way so we don't have to worry about them tryna rob us!"

"Like I said, fuck them niggas' lives, man," Cannon roared with his deep voice. "Just say the word and I'll be in Hunting Park spraying shit up!"

"Uh... good looking out, Cannon," Will hesitated. "Anyway, y'all ready to run some ball?" Will placed the gun in his backpack and headed for the front door of the apartment.

"Yeah, I'm ready," Pop replied. The two teenagers turned to Cannon.

"Yeah, I guess we can blow this tree when we get back," Cannon chuckled as he got up slowly. He had been lounging around his apartment all morning and was already wearing basketball shorts, a t-shirt and sneakers. The three men piled into Cannon's black Ford Mustang Convertible, put the top down and made the short trip down Wayne Avenue to Happy Hollow Playground to play basketball. When they arrived, there were five men, all in their early-twenties, playing basketball.

"How about a four-on-four game when y'all done?" Pop asked as they approached the men. The men agreed. Less than ten minutes later, they began to play a pick-up game: Pop, Will, Cannon and another man on one team against the four other men.

Everything was going smoothly at first because Will wasn't really showcasing his mastery of the sport. But after a while, he couldn't help but show off. He was crossing people over, making them fall, and scoring a lot of points. Then he started dunking on people, blocking shots - not only blocking the shots, but throwing the ball across the court when he blocked the shots. The men were supposed to play up to twenty-one points, by ones. When the score reached eighteen to six, with Will's team winning, things boiled over – the opposing team was tired of losing, and they were tired of Will embarrassing them. As Will dribbled down the lane to dunk again, a brown-skinned man with protruding eyeballs who was about six-feet, three-inches tall – the same height as Will, but who weighed about forty pounds more than Will – ran up, stuck his arm straight out and clotheslined Will, causing him to fall flat on his back and knocking the wind out of him. Will laid there for a moment then sat up on his elbows, confused, and glared at the brown-skinned man. The man stood over Will menacingly. Cannon and Pop ran up to them while yelling.

"What the fuck was that?" Will said hoarsely as he rubbed his throat and got up.

"Yea, nigga!" Cannon said gruffly. "Don't get fucked up out here!"

"I'm tired of this nigga showing off!" the brown-skinned man huffed. "Maybe that will calm you down!"

"Fuck you, nigga!" Will screamed as he stepped into the man's face.

"I'm tired of it, too," another man interjected. Will turned around to see who had chimed in.

"Nigga, I'm on *your* team!" Will exclaimed with surprise. "Y'all just some hating-ass niggas, man!"

"And you just a bitch-ass young-boy," said the brown-skinned man who had knocked Will down. They were still standing face-to-face. The man stared Will down, trying to intimidate him, but Will was not easily intimidated, even though the man was much brawnier than he was.

"Oh, so I'm a bitch-ass young-boy, huh?" Will chuckled as he turned his back to the brown-skinned man with the protruding eyes. Then, without warning, Will cocked-back and swung as hard as he could, turning back around and hitting the man square in the nose. The man saw only black as he fell backwards and into unconsciousness, cracking the back of his head on the pavement. Instantly, the other four men charged at Will. The biggest one was about six-feet, seven-inches tall, and he jumped on Will and began to pummel him while the other men kicked and stomped him. Pop balled his fists and immediately turned to Cannon.

"Fuck this fighting shit... I did enough of that in prison!" Cannon exclaimed. "Pop, come wait in the car." Cannon ran to his car at the curb, while Pop followed him.

"What you 'bout to do?" Pop asked.

"Just get in the back! Hurry up, nigga!" Cannon commanded. Pop obeyed as Cannon reached under the driver's seat for his revolver and ran back to the basketball court.

The four men were so preoccupied with trying to get the best of Will that they hadn't noticed Cannon approaching. They didn't feel his presence until it was too late. Cannon leveled his revolver and fired high enough to make sure that he didn't hit Will.

Pop!

Once the first shot rang out the three men who could run, ran. The fourth man had been hit in the lower back and was lying on the ground, unable to move. Cannon didn't stop with that. He pointed the revolver at the running men and emptied the gun in their direction...

Pop! Pop! Pop! Pop! Pop!

He hit two more men, one in the hamstring and another twice in the back. Cannon laughed like a madman as he watched them fall. He paused for a moment before helping Will up.

"Come on, nigga, we out!" Both men ran to Cannon's Mustang and jumped in. Pop looked at his older cousin with admiration for having the courage to shoot in broad daylight like that. Cannon made a U-turn on

Wayne Avenue, sped down Manheim to Wissahickon, then onto the expressway. "Y'all niggas gotta take a ride with me."

"I'm sore as shit," Will complained. "I could use that weed right now! Where we going?"

"Down Penn's Landing… I gotta throw this revolver in the river," Cannon replied.

"Yo, good looking out, Cannon," Will started, "but we could've fought them niggas man! You didn't have to pop them!"

"Nigga, look… fuck these niggas' lives, man! I did enough fighting and stabbing Upstate," Cannon replied matter-of-factly. "Besides, I'm a shooter! That's why they call me 'Cannon!'" The three of them laughed as they drove down I-76. Cannon had slowed down since they were far enough away from the scene of the crime now and he didn't want to risk getting pulled over for speeding because all three of them were armed.

They arrived at Penn's Landing and found parking on Delaware Avenue. Cannon hopped out of the car and walked to the end of Penn's Landing. Fortunately for him, nobody was really there yet since it was still early in the day. Cannon looked around, and when the few people who were there seemed like they weren't paying attention, he pulled out the revolver and threw it as far out into the water as he could. He walked back to the car and got in.

"Mission accomplished," Cannon smiled.

"That's what's up," Pop replied.

"Now let's get back and get that tree," Will sighed.

Back on Marshall Street, there was a knock on Jasiel and Jose's front door. Jasiel quickly jumped up from the sofa where he had been playing video games, turned off the television, grabbed his nine-millimeter handgun and crept towards the front door. Although he was very pleased with the money he and his brother had made from the robbery, he had been paranoid all night that either the police or somebody associated with the man they had robbed and killed would be looking for them. He hadn't slept yet. Jose hadn't slept either, due to a troubled conscience. They had gone out early in the day and sold the gold rings, watch and necklace to a pawn shop for another thousand dollars; so, altogether, they had made a profit of three-thousand and three-hundred dollars from this robbery alone. They had picked the perfect victim in Jasiel's opinion.

By the time Jasiel had reached the front door, Jose had stumbled downstairs and asked who was at the door. Jasiel motioned for Jose to be quiet and placed the barrel of his gun against the inside of the front door as he looked out through the peep hole.

"Oh! It's just Uncle Tiny," Jasiel exclaimed with a sigh of relief as he unlocked the door.

"T-T-That's what's up… l-l-let him in," Jose stuttered.

"What the fuck do you think I'm doing, you high motherfucker? You stuck like a motherfucker, dog… you need to go sit down," Jasiel barked impatiently as he opened the door for his uncle. The weight of the night's events had taken a toll on Jose's conscience and he couldn't deal with the guilt while he was sober, so he had been smoking wet for hours. He had reached the point where he was "stuck" – he could barely walk, barely talk and he could barely function at all because he was so high. He took his brother's advice and shuffled over to the sofa and collapsed onto it, passing out.

"What up, Unc?" Jasiel greeted his uncle as Tiny walked past him without a word. Tiny had a very stern expression on his face and Jasiel immediately knew that something was wrong.

"*Mira*," Tiny began in Spanish as he sat down in a chair positioned across from the sofa. "I need to talk to y'all about something real important! What's wrong with this motherfucker, Jose?"

"Aw man… this nigga's been smoking wet all morning like a dumbass," Jasiel replied. "He wasn't pacing himself and he just passed out right before you came in."

"That's that bullshit," Tiny replied. "Well, I need to talk to both of y'all now so this motherfucker needs to wake the fuck up! Wake him up."

"Jose! Jose! Jose!" Jasiel screamed as he shook his unconscious brother by the shoulders as he lay on the sofa. Jose didn't wake up, however.

"Man, he's knocked the fuck out. That wet got him!"

"I'll wake him up," Tiny stated resolutely as his muscular, five-foot, five-inch frame walked over to the sofa. He bent over Jose, lifted a vascular arm and slapped him viciously in the face four times. "Get the fuck up, Jose!"

"W-What the f-f-fuck?" Jose blurted out as he sat up and opened his eyes. His cheek and jaw ached tremendously. Jasiel just stared in shock, not knowing how to react.

"Drink some water, Jose, and sober the fuck up," Tiny commanded.

"I need to talk to y'all now!"

Their uncle was obviously upset about something and the twins were growing nervous. Jasiel felt badly for Jose that he had been viciously slapped in the face like that, especially while he was sleeping. The side of his face was all red. Jasiel hastily walked to the kitchen, retrieved two bottles of water for his brother, and asked his uncle if he wanted anything. Tiny refused. It was obvious Tiny was in a bad mood and was growing more and more impatient by the minute, so Jasiel rushed back to the living room, gave his brother the bottles of water and sat down.

"So what's up, Uncle Tiny? What's wrong?" Jasiel asked concerned.

"I think I need some ice for my face," Jose blurted out.

"Ay yo, shut the fuck up, Jose!" Tiny barked. "What's wrong is my homey, Chris Martinez, got robbed and murdered on Seventh Street last night! Motherfucking low-lives shot him *and* ran him over and everything! Shit happens in the streets, but motherfuckers always gotta take shit too far!"

"Sorry to hear that, Unc, that's drawing! I don't think I ever met him though," Jasiel replied with mock sympathy. Jose turned white with fear, realizing they had killed their uncle's friend. He stared at Jasiel, but remained silent. Jasiel noticed Jose staring at him from his peripheral vision, but never returned his brother's glare.

"You might not have ever met him formally, but you would know him if you saw him," Tiny continued. "He bought a lot of coke from me and he was always in my bar on Hunting Park. Matter-of-fact, he was in there last night before he got killed! I know y'all saw him. He was wearing a yellow Polo shirt, a lot of gold and diamond rings with a diamond watch - tall, heavyset dude. He's hard to miss. Actually, you left the bar right after he did! So what did y'all motherfuckers do when y'all left my bar last night?"

"We came home and had a couple jawns over here," Jasiel lied. "Ain't that right, Jose?"

"Uh, yeah… yup," Jose reluctantly replied. Jasiel stared angrily at his brother for his hesitation, then caught himself and regained his composure.

"You good, Jose?" Tiny asked suspiciously.

"Yeah, Unc… I'm just still fucked up!"

"You lying-ass stick-up kids!" Tiny roared as he stood up and pointed at the twins. "I know y'all followed Chris outta the bar to rob him! I saw y'all looking at him when he was leaving, and y'all rushed outta there when I was talking to y'all motherfuckers to catch up with him! You killed my friend… you demon, low-life motherfuckers!"

"Naw, Uncle Tiny! We didn't do it!" Jasiel protested.

"You lying-ass motherfucker!" Tiny screamed, foaming at the mouth as he ran over to Jasiel and gripped him by the collar of his shirt. "I know you did it! You didn't have to kill him, you fucking sociopath motherfuckers! I swear… if you weren't my sister's kids I would kill you myself for this shit!"

Both Jasiel and Jose were somewhat intimidated at this point. They knew what they had done and they knew their uncle was a killer. Jasiel tried to release himself from his uncle's vice-like grip, but he was too short (short stature ran in their family), and he was nowhere near as strong as his uncle. He had to think of a way to calm his uncle down. Jose just looked on in fear, wondering what Tiny would do to them if he didn't snap out of this fit of rage.

"I swear on my mother's grave we didn't do it, Uncle Tiny," the words rolled off of Jasiel's tongue. He lied as if it were a reflex. When Jose heard his brother's outlandish statement, he almost choked on his water. However, his uncle's face softened and he released his grip.

"You swear on my sister's grave?" Tiny asked softly.

"Yes, *Tio*, I swear on Mom's grave," Jasiel replied resolutely. Jose stared at his brother in disbelief as Tiny stepped away from Jasiel.

"Okay, well then, I believe you. I know you wouldn't lie when it comes to that! Sorry nephew," Tiny hugged Jasiel. "I'ma get outta here now. I gotta handle business. Plus I gotta get some guys out here to find out what happened to Chris. Sorry about slapping the shit outta you, Jose… get some ice for your face, nephew."

Jose sat on the sofa, staring in disbelief as Jasiel walked Tiny to the door. Jasiel watched as Tiny entered his Lincoln Navigator truck and pulled off, then closed and locked the door.

"Shit! That was close!" Jasiel exclaimed as he sat on the sofa next to Jose.

"Yo, what the fuck?" Jose exclaimed angrily. "How are you gonna swear on Mom's grave to a lie, knowing we did that shit?"

"Yo, I did what I had to do, Jose," Jasiel explained. "I didn't wanna do it, but I had to get him off of me! Besides, you don't want beef with Uncle Tiny, do you?"

"Naw," Jose replied, downtrodden.

"Okay, then! I did what I had to do. You saw how that nigga was snapping, talking about killing us and shit!"

"Yeah, I feel you," Jose lied. He really wasn't "feeling" his brother right now, though. How could his brother be okay after murdering people? How could his brother just swear on their mother's grave to a lie? He was actually wondering if his uncle was right; was Jasiel a sociopath?

CHAPTER 4

Cannon took a different route back to his apartment so they didn't have to drive by the scene of the shooting and risk being spotted by one of the victims or the police. Cannon put the convertible top back up on his Mustang so the three of them wouldn't be so easy to spot. There were police cameras along Wayne Avenue, and he hoped they hadn't taken any pictures of them as they had driven away from the scene of the shooting. When Cannon, Will and Pop arrived near Cannon's apartment, he decided to circle the block to make sure the police weren't waiting for him at his apartment, then he parked on Queen Lane instead of parking directly in front of his building on Wayne Avenue.

"Man, that was some crazy shit!" Will exclaimed as he limped into the apartment behind Cannon and Pop. "I've never been that close to niggas getting shot before!"

"Yeah, neither have I," Pop admitted. "I wonder if any of them niggas died..."

"I doubt it," Cannon replied nonchalantly. "I only hit them in the back and legs and shit! They're gonna have a hard time walking though! Ha-ha!"

"True! Yo, Cannon, you still got some of that sour-diesel we smoked last time?" Pop asked.

"Yeah I got more than enough of that shit," Cannon affirmed. "I'm about to roll a fat L too!" Cannon opened his top drawer and searched for about a minute before cursing aloud. "Oh shit!"

"What's the deal, my nigga?" Will asked.

"I thought I had a box of the Game™ cigars in here, but I don't have any left! I must smoke more than I realized," Cannon laughed. "Run with me across the street to go get some."

Cannon grabbed his keys, while Will left his backpack and Pop left his gun in the apartment. The three men walked to the corner store on Wayne Avenue. A police car drove by them as they crossed the street and they paid it no mind, as police cars were always driving up and down Wayne

Avenue. However, they didn't notice the young man in the back of the squad-car who pointed at them, and that the vehicle had made a U-turn as they walked into the corner store. The thin, brown-skinned, curly-haired young man, the only one of the three men who hadn't been shot while running away from Cannon, stayed in the squad car while the police rushed inside the corner store. He had come back to the basketball court ten minutes later, after calling the police, and was the only one of the five men who had agreed to testify. As they had driven by Cannon, Will and Pop, the young man, named Devin, had pointed out the "light-skinned, bald-headed, stocky one with the tattoos," as the shooter, and the police had made a U-turn in order to apprehend him.

"Put your hands up!" the police screamed as Cannon dropped his keys and his money on the counter and placed his hands in the air. Actually, everybody in the store placed their hands in the air at first, until one of the officers grabbed Cannon and slammed him on the floor.

"Are those your keys?" the second officer asked.

"Naw, they're my cousin's keys," Cannon lied. "I was holding them for him since he don't have pockets in his shorts. Get your keys cuz!" Pop quickly grabbed the keys and the five-dollar bill from the counter.

"Oh, so you were playing basketball today?" the officer sneered as he handcuffed Cannon and hoisted him off the floor.

"No, sir!"

"Yeah... we'll see about that," the officer snapped and he dragged Cannon outside. Will and Pop followed behind them.

"Hey, Devin!" The officer knocked on the back window of the squad car to get Devin's attention. At that moment another squad car pulled up behind the police vehicle that was already there. "Is this the shooter?"

"Why are you using my name, man?" Devin sighed while looking down. He tried to hide his face so that Cannon, Will and Pop could not see him and identify him, but the feat was nearly impossible, for it was broad daylight in the summertime. "Yeah, that's him," Devin reluctantly replied. He wondered if he had made a wise choice in becoming a snitch and why the police had him identify the shooter in this manner. "Maybe the cops really don't care about Black people's lives," Devin thought to himself, because this was certainly not how they did things on the police shows he watched on television!

"You don't have any identification on you... what's your name, shooter?" the officer asked Cannon.

"I didn't shoot nobody," Cannon replied nonchalantly.

"Well I got a witness saying you did, so you're coming with us," the officer replied smugly. "What's your name anyway? And don't give me any fake bullshit 'cause we'll find out when we run your prints. You look like you have a record!"

"Man... what's that supposed to mean?" Cannon rebuffed. "Anyway, my name is Malik Davidson," Cannon answered truthfully.

"Well, get your ass in this squad car," the officer commanded as he walked Cannon to the second car and shoved him into the back seat.

"I'll meet you at the District with the witness," the officer said to the other officer who was driving the second squad car. Will and Pop glared at Devin, who kept staring at the floor of the car. Their hatred was evident, and they both were hatching the same plot to deal with him in their minds without any verbal communication. They would, however, discuss it soon enough. Within a few seconds, though, both cars had pulled off, and both Devin and Cannon were no longer in their sights.

"Damn, that's fucked up! I can't believe my cousin got bagged, dog," Pop exclaimed as they walked back to Cannon's apartment to retrieve their things.

"Yeah I know, right?" Will replied, demoralized. "That nigga had my back, and now he's getting locked up! I wish there was something we could do."

"Well, I know why he had me take the keys," Pop stated. "He wants us to get the guns and anything else outta his crib before they get a search warrant for that jawn!"

"Yeah I figured we had to do that! You know how many guns he has?"

"Naw," Pop admitted as they walked into the building and towards Cannon's apartment. "He showed me a few the last time I was here. I know some of the spots where he keeps them though." Pop perused the numerous keys on Cannon's key ring until he found the apartment key and unlocked the door. They walked in and locked the door behind them. Will followed Pop as he began walking around the apartment searching for guns. There was a sawed-off shotgun under the mattress, along with a nine-millimeter handgun. There was a forty-caliber handgun under his pillow. There was twenty-two caliber pistol propped behind the toilet. There were also two small twenty-five-caliber handguns in his entertainment center drawer and another shotgun under his sofa cushions. Then there were five different handguns in a duffle bag in Cannon's closet in his living room. While Pop was looking in the living room closet he also found a bonus – a pound of sour-diesel: exotic marijuana.

"Damn, nigga! Smell this shit!" Pop exclaimed and opened the lid of the large plastic storage bowl and held it up to Will's nose.

"Damn, dog! That shit is potent as hell!"

"I know," Pop said excitedly. "I smelled it before I saw it! Now, when he calls me and tells me which jail he's at and we go see him, we can ask him if he wants us to sell this shit so he can pay for a good lawyer. There's a big suitcase in here so we can take all these guns out and the tree and put it in the trunk."

The teenagers carefully placed the twelve guns in the suitcase, then they placed the marijuana in large sandwich bags and placed those in the suitcase too. Then they grabbed their belongings, and Pop rolled the heavy suitcase out the front door as Will followed. Pop locked the bottom and top locks and they rolled the heavy suitcase full of guns and weed, in broad daylight, to Cannon's Mustang. The large suitcase barely fit in the small trunk. After managing to carefully cram the luggage in the trunk, the teenagers entered the car and Pop drove back to Hunting Park and stashed the guns and marijuana at Pop's house. After they had both taken showers and changed, Pop drove to the corner so they could sell the rest of the ounce of cocaine they had bought and bagged up. They had been receiving phone calls while they were in Germantown and told their customers they would be back in a couple of hours. Within ten minutes of arriving on the corner, they had a steady stream of customers.

"I like chilling in the car doing this shit," Will said as he threw the bag of ice that he had been holding to his swollen eye out the window. "It's more incognito and all that!"

"Yeah, man, especially with these tinted windows," Pop agreed. "I need a wheel, though, man!"

"That's why you need to stack your paper my nigga," Will replied thoughtlessly, then noticed Pop's grimace at his comment. "I mean, I know it's hard with all your mom's bills though," Will tried to redeem himself. "You can borrow my car when I cop one, though."

"Good looking out," Pop thanked his friend. "What you thinking about grabbing?"

"Well, I've looked in the paper and seen some used Caddie DTSs at some of those dealers on the Boulevard that wouldn't have a problem taking all cash, for like thirteen. They were only a few years old with low-mileage," Will continued.

"You got thirteen-thousand dollars, nigga?" Pop asked, intrigued.

"Naw, man... that's my goal," Will lied. He felt uneasy, especially due to the jealous look on Pop's face when he asked the question. It was stupid of him to mention the "all-cash" option, but he trusted Pop. They had grown up together and did business together. But Will also knew that when people aren't doing as well as you are financially, it can make them do shady things. "So what are we gonna do about this snitch nigga? What's his name... Kevin?" Will changed the subject quickly.

"Naw, I'm pretty sure the dumb-ass cop said 'Devin,'" Pop replied, taking the bait because it was something that had been weighing on his mind and that they needed to discuss. "I can't believe they brought this nigga around us without the detectives – no confidential line-up, no one-way glass, no nothing. They put that nigga's life on the line for real!"

"I know," Will agreed. "Did you see how shook that nigga was? He was shitting himself in the back of that car!"

"He should be scared, though," Pop started before his phone began ringing. "Yo! Yeah, we here. Same corner, we just in a black Mustang.

Yeah, I'm looking at you right now – come through!" A few seconds later, the man Pop had just spoken to on the phone had walked over to the car.

"Oh, I see you getting money now, Pop," the tall, slim Puerto-Rican man said jovially.

"I'm just tryna survive out here like everybody else, na'mean?" Pop replied casually. "What you need, old-head?"

"Let me get five, rich-kid," the man laughed as he discreetly handed Pop fifty dollars, and Pop even more discreetly slipped five dime-bags of coke into the man's palm. "Thanks!" Pop and Will watched as the man walked down the street to his old, beat-up pickup truck and pulled off.

"Yo, Pop. Why your customers be some nut-ass niggas, man?" Will laughed. "My customers are some cool-ass O.G.s, but your customers are some nut-ass, drawing motherfuckers! Ha-ha!"

"I know, right? He was loud as shit," Pop agreed. "But don't shit on my customers... they pay just like yours! But anyway, that bitch-ass-nigga Devin needs to be shook 'cause I'ma merck his ass!"

"Word? I was thinking that's what needs to be done," Will confessed. "I just never even shot nobody before. I'm kinda nervous about that shit – aren't you?"

"Yeah, but if Cannon can pop three niggas in broad daylight, then we can ride around Germantown looking for this nigga, Devin, and find a good time to murder him, right? He's snitching on Cannon... you know Cannon would do it for us," Pop reasoned.

"You're right. Let's see what he says when he calls you though, alright? Let's not rush this shit!"

"We won't rush it, but we won't take forever either," Pop replied aggressively. "Remember, he did that shit 'cause you were getting jumped!"

Will really didn't appreciate how Pop was talking to him, but he figured he would let it slide. He didn't want to argue and he figured Pop was stressed because his older cousin, with whom he was very close, had just been imprisoned hours earlier. It was a Friday night and the two teenagers just sat in the car, listening to DJ Cosmic Kev's "Come-Up Show" on the Power 99 radio station, as they served their customers until about one-o-clock in the morning. They didn't say much to each other until they noticed a silver Pontiac Bonneville pull up across the street and sit idle for about fifteen minutes.

"Yo, Pop! You see that Bonnie parked over there?" Will tapped Pop on the arm and motioned towards the parked car with a sense of urgency.

"Yeah... I see it," Pop replied as he pulled out his gun. Will did the same. "It's been there like ten, fifteen minutes! Wait... isn't that Jasiel's whip?"

"I think you're right!" Will gasped. "And I see two people sittin' in there so that's probably Jasiel and Jose! You think they're gonna try to run up on us and rob us?"

"You never know; that's why I pulled my burner out," Pop replied solemnly. "And I guess that's why you grabbed yours, too! At least we'll be ready for them."

"I don't need any more drama today," Will sighed as he cocked back his forty-five.

Meanwhile, in the Bonneville, Jasiel and Jose were having their own discussion. Actually, they were having a debate.

"Since when did them motherfuckers get a drop-top Mustang?" Jasiel steamed.

"Well, they didn't seem to have it yesterday," Jose explained. "They were out there on foot when we drove by them yesterday, right?"

"Yeah, they were," Jasiel stated angrily. "And today that Black motherfucker has a new, drop-top Mustang with twenty-inch rims on it? I want those rims for my Bonnie!"

"No, Jasiel," Jose protested. "Uncle Tiny doesn't want us to rob them, remember? We can't go against him! Besides, we just robbed and killed his friend last night and made over three-thousand dollars; we don't need to rob anybody for at least a few weeks till the heat dies down."

"First of all," Jasiel began, "it's never enough money! Second, *we* didn't kill Uncle Tiny's friend – *I* did! Maybe I should make you go over there and blow Will's head off so you can earn your stripes," Jasiel smirked.

"You're sick, man," Jose yelled at his twin. "You're really fucking sick! You think killing people is funny or a game or something?"

"It *is* fun! You should play sometime," Jasiel laughed.

"You're crazy… I love you, bro, but you're crazy," Jose sighed.

"Whatever, man," Jasiel dismissed his brother's comment. "Let's get out and go fuck with these young-boys!"

"What do you mean? You mean just go talk to them, right?" Jose asked incredulously. The two young men exited the Bonneville and slowly walked across the street, in plain sight, towards the Mustang with smiles on their faces.

"What the fuck?" Will exclaimed. "Why are they coming over here, smiling and shit?"

"I don't know… should I blast at them and pull off?" Pop asked.

"Naw, be cool man. They don't have their burners out or nothing and they're smiling, but I don't trust them. Keep your gat in your hand though," Will instructed as he rolled down his window half-way.

"What's up, fellas?" Jasiel greeted the teenagers as he and Jose walked up to the passenger's side window where Will was seated.

"What up?" the teenagers said in unison.

"We just came to see how y'all were doing," Jasiel continued with a large, forced smile.

"Why have you been watching us for the past fifteen minutes?" Pop asked aggressively. "You got a crush on Will or something?"

"Oh, you got jokes?" Jasiel chuckled. "Naw, but I do like this car. It's real nice... I might get one just like it, or take this one from you sometime."

At that comment, and at the same time, both Pop and Will raised their guns high enough for Jasiel and Jose to see. Jose's eyes grew large and he backed up a few steps. Jasiel stood his ground and his phony smile disappeared.

"Guns... I see," Jasiel commented. "We got those – a lot of them! And we can take everything you have whenever we want to!"

"Not if I take your life first," Will threatened. Jasiel and Will's eyes met and they glared at each other with pure hatred.

"Oh, don't take my brother so seriously," Jose interjected. "He's just fucking with y'all. We just came over here to mess with y'all. We wouldn't rob you – we know you do business with our Uncle Tiny. Ain't that right, Jasiel?"

"Yeah, that's right," Jasiel reluctantly agreed as his expression slowly softened and he forced another smile. "I was just fucking with you. It's stick-up kid humor... you gotta get used to it!"

"Yeah, whatever," Pop said as he put the Mustang in gear and sped off.

"Where you going?" Will asked.

"I'm just getting the fuck away from them!"

Two days later, on Monday morning, Pop received a phone call from Cannon. He was being held at Curran-Fromhold Correctional Facility, or CFCF, on State Road in Northeast Philadelphia. The police hadn't let him make any phone calls while he was in the local District lockup. He had a video-bail hearing and was transported the next night to CFCF.

"Yo, cuz, what up?" Cannon greeted Pop.

"It's good to hear from you, cousin! How you holding up?" Pop asked, concerned.

"I'm good. You know I'm a soldier! But fuck all that – I don't have a lot of time on this jack. You know why I wanted you to take my keys, right?" Cannon asked.

"Yeah, Cannon," Pop confirmed. "I got all that outta there – everything, right after you got booked."

"That's what's up! Good looking out, 'cause I'm on parole and as soon as they got my address when they processed me, I know they were gonna run up in my shit!"

"You know I got your back, cuz," Pop replied. "What you want me to do with them bitches and that P?"

"Yo, my nigga, listen… my bail is five-hundred stacks at ten percent, so fifty stacks! I don't think we can raise that even with them bitches and that P. I got a public defender. I'm facing two attempted murder charges for the niggas who I allegedly shot in the back and an assault with a deadly weapon for the nigga who got shot in the leg. I don't know how much time I'm facing yet but I know it's a lot, plus I had five years left when I was paroled and this is a parole violation if I'm convicted. You can off a couple of them bitches to put money on my books. You can take that P and put it in the air or do whatever with it, but if you flip it, I'ma need some of that bread."

"Damn, cuz… that's crazy," Pop replied sadly. "Good looking out though. I'll handle business for you."

"I ain't sweating it though. I think that nigga who snitched on me is the only witness. He only has three chances to come to court and then they throw out the case."

"I really don't think he'll show up, cousin… na'mean?" Pop assured Cannon.

"Yeah, I hope not," Cannon chuckled.

"One minute left," an automated female voice broke into the phone call.

"Alright, my young-boy," Cannon continued. "Listen, you can drive my shit, but don't crash my shit, don't even scratch my shit! Keep oil and gas in my shit! And please keep money on my books in here!"

"Alright, Cannon! We're gonna come see you soon…"

-Click-

Just like that, the last minute was over and the call was disconnected. Shortly thereafter, Pop's cell phone rang.

"Yo, Pop, Rick said we can come through to his spot. He grabbed that O for us from Tiny already," Will informed his business partner and friend. "You ready?"

"Yeah, I'm ready," Pop confirmed. "Meet me outside at the Mustang. I'll drive. I need to holler at you about some deep shit."

"Alright, cool," Will replied. Within minutes, both teenagers were outside on Ninth Street standing by Cannon's Mustang. They both got into the car, which Pop had taken a liking to, and Pop began driving towards Rick's spot on Sixth Street and Butler Street. They talked as they rode along.

"Yo, Will," Pop said. "Cannon called me today."

"Oh word? How's he doing?" Will asked.

"He's maintaining, but it's not looking good," Pop continued. "His bail is five-hundred stacks!"

"Goddamn! Five-hundred-thousand dollars?"

"He's facing two counts of attempted murder," Pop went on, "and one count of assault with a deadly weapon. He's facing mad time."

"What does the lawyer say?" Will asked.

"I don't know," Pop admitted. "Cannon said he has a public defender. He didn't even mention tryna get him a high-powered lawyer or nothing. He just wants me to sell some of these burners and put money on his commissary. He said we can either smoke or sell that pound of sour-diesel."

"That's love," Will smiled. "That sour-diesel goes for like three-fifty or four-hundred an ounce. We can make some bread off that jawn! But uh… what are we gonna do about Cannon's case?"

"Cannon said that if that snitch-nigga, Devin, doesn't show up to court three times then the case gets thrown out. So you know what we gotta do, right?" Pop looked his friend squarely in the eyes as they pulled up to Rick's spot. "Are you ready to go on a mission to kill this nigga for Cannon?"

"I ain't never done it before, but yeah," Will agreed. "I owe it to Cannon. I'm down."

The two teenagers sat in the car for ten more minutes before going into the house, devising a plan on how they would find, setup and kill the man who could possibly testify against Cannon and place him in prison for decades. They knew what they had to do and they were prepared to do it. At the tender age of seventeen, they were prepared to become killers.

CHAPTER 5

"Hey, sexy!" Will had answered his cell phone in an upbeat manner when he saw the call from his girlfriend, Stacy, come through. Stacy, who had grown accustomed to being unable to reach Will while he was handling his business, was shocked that he had answered his phone the first time she had called him, and that he sounded so excited to hear from her.

"Hey, baby," she replied happily. "What you up to?" She asked because she assumed there was no way Will would have answered the phone so quickly if he had been working.

"At Rick's spot, working. We'll be done in about a half, though. Then Pop's gonna drop me off at your spot," Will informed his girlfriend.

"Really?" Stacy squealed with excitement. "I can't wait to see you Will! Wait, Pop has a car?"

"I'll explain when I see you. Is your mother home?"

"Yeah... unfortunately," Stacy complained. "She didn't get home till like five-thirty in the morning. She came in all high, acting like a damn nut, waking me up and shit. She's chilling, watching TV now, though."

"Damn, I'm sorry to hear that she was tripping like that, ma," Will replied sympathetically. "Well, I'll be over there soon. I'll make you feel better," Will said slyly.

"Okay, baby, sounds good. See you soon. Bye." Stacy hung up. About twenty minutes later, at about two-thirty in the afternoon, Will and Pop finished bagging up yet another ounce of cocaine they had purchased from Tiny, via Rick. After meeting up, they had spent all morning and the early afternoon bagging up. As usual, they were happy to be finished.

"Maybe we should pay Stacy to bag up for us," Pop suggested as they walked out of Rick's, backpacks in tow, and hopped into the shiny, black Mustang. "I'm tired of bagging up! It takes forever to bag this powder!"

"You're right, it does… but I don't want Stacy involved in the business on a regular basis, na'mean?" Will protested. "She's already gonna get involved with this Devin shit if I can convince her to help us."

"Nigga, that girl is so in love with you, she'll do anything you ask her to do," Pop continued as he drove to Ninth Street. "She'll definitely do it if you dick her down right before you ask! Ha-ha! She'll probably even merck the nigga Devin for us and bag up the coke for free!"

"Fuck that, nigga!" Will snapped angrily as Pop parallel parked on Ninth Street. "Why you tryna exploit my girl? Why don't you use one of your bitches that you be fucking with?"

"Stop being all sensitive, motherfucker," Pop retorted. "I ain't talking about using none of the girls I fuck with because I don't really trust none of them. I'm not as close with none of them as you are with Stacy. We both know you can trust Stacy. I don't want one of these other bitches stealing the work or snorting it when we ain't watching them!"

"Yeah, Pop, I understand. But I don't want Stacy around the drugs man," Will explained. "Her mom's a smoker; she already has to deal with enough. As long as I can get her to setup Devin I'll be happy with that. Let me put this coke in the crib… I'll be right back."

"Yeah, I'll wait for you," Pop replied. "I'ma hit the block while you're with Stacy." Pop turned on his Meek Mill CD and listened to it as he waited for Will to return. He had made himself at home in Cannon's Mustang over the past several days. He had brought a case of CDs into the car, bought some air fresheners and bought a custom steering wheel cover.

"I better not get too accustomed to this, though," Pop thought to himself. He thought about Cannon and who he would sell the first gun to so that he could put money on his cousin's commissary. Just then, Will entered the passenger's side of the Mustang.

"Yo, I was thinking while I was in there," Will began, "what about that Puerto Rican jawn, CeCe, that you been messing with off and on for the past couple years?"

"Yeah, what about her?" Pop asked as he pulled away from the curb and headed for Stacy's house. "She's real cool, and finer than a motherfucker, but you know I can't commit to one jawn!"

"Naw, not that," Will replied. "I meant since you've known her so long, would you trust her to bag up for us? We could pay her a bean every time."

"Oh yeah," Pop exclaimed. "I don't know why I didn't think about CeCe for that. She's Tiny's niece so she wouldn't rip us off. That's a good idea, Will!"

"Yeah, I have those sometimes," Will replied sarcastically. "Anyway, just tell her she can get a trustworthy friend to help her, we'll pay them a hundred dollars each time, it'll take like four hours and we'll need them every two days, maybe more often, so they'll be making like four-hundred a week each. They should be cool with that."

"Yeah, she definitely should be," Pop concurred. "I saw her a few weeks ago, right after she graduated, and she said she was looking for a job but they all paid minimum wage, so she wasn't really with that shit. I'll hit her up now." They had just arrived at Stacy's building and she was sitting on the stoop waiting for her man to arrive.

"Hey, baby," she said excitedly as she ran over to meet Will and hugged and kissed him. "This jawn is nice, Pop! Getting money I see!"

"Something like that," Pop grinned, not letting on that the car wasn't his. He had always had a secret crush on Stacy, and he thought Will was foolish for cheating on her. He grew somewhat jealous every time he saw them embrace or kiss. "I would be faithful to Stacy if I had her," Pop thought to himself as he watched them. "Remember what we talked about, Will," Pop called out through the open driver's side window as he pulled off. Will nodded and walked into the house, which was subdivided into small apartments, with his arm around Stacy.

"What was Pop talking about?" Stacy inquired.

"I'll talk to you about it later, sexy," Will replied evasively.

As they walked through the front door and into the living room of the small, two-bedroom apartment, they saw Miss Lee, Stacy's mother. She was sitting on the dilapidated sofa, watching television, actually yelling at the television. When the woman saw the teenaged couple enter the apartment, she rolled her eyes. Miss Lee was a ghost of her former self. She used to be a beautiful woman sixteen years prior. But when Stacy's father abandoned her shortly before Stacy's second birthday, Miss Lee turned to smoking crack. The years of abusing the hard drug had destroyed her looks – she only had a few teeth left in her mouth, her lips were dry and chapped, her hair was short and thin, as was her frame because she had lost her voluptuous body long ago. Her skin was dry and cracked. That's not to mention what the drug had done to her mind. You would have never known, without her telling you, that she had been the prom queen and that the picture on the mantle was a picture of Miss Lee herself when she was eighteen, because it looked just like Stacy.

"What's up, coke-boy?" Miss Lee addressed Will sarcastically. "You got anything for me?"

"No, ma'am," Will replied respectfully.

"What about some money? I need some money!" Miss Lee yelled belligerently.

"I have no problem helping y'all out, Miss Lee, but I hope you don't mind if I give the money to Stacy," Will replied.

"Oh, you think I'm gonna go get fucked up with it?"

"Mommy," Stacy interjected. "Please stop… Will's just tryna help us out!"

"I raised this girl before you came along, coke-boy!" Miss Lee screamed. "I got money and food stamps! You don't have to give me shit! You just wanna give it to Stacy 'cause she sucks your dick!"

"Mommy! Please don't be like that," Stacy sobbed.

"Fuck y'all kids! I'm outta here!" With that Miss Lee stormed out of the apartment and slammed the door behind her. Will was dumb-founded. Stacy was crying.

"I'm sorry, Stace," Will put his arms around his girlfriend, hugging her. "I didn't mean to upset your mother…"

"It wasn't your fault baby. She is always arguing, looking for an excuse to leave and get high," Stacy whimpered. "But at least we're alone now," she smiled.

"Hell yeah," Will grinned slyly as he locked the front door. "Let's go to your room so I can give you some sexual healing!"

Stacy led the way to her bedroom. Will took the lead in undressing Stacy. He wiped the tears from her face before she lifted up her arms so he could remove her small t-shirt. He then unbuttoned Stacy's short shorts, they dropped down to her feet and she kicked them off. He gripped her soft behind as his tongue caressed her neck and she shivered. Will let his hands slide up Stacy's spine to her bra and he unhooked her bra-strap. Stacy took off her own bra and Will caressed one nipple, then the other, as they stood there, before licking and sucking them gently. Stacy moaned in sheer delight as her knees grew weak and she sat down. As she sat down, Will took off his chain and placed it on Stacy's nightstand, then climbed on the bed on top of his girlfriend. She removed his shirt and unbuttoned his pants, but he had something else planned.

Will kissed and licked Stacy's breasts, then moved to her stomach, her pelvis, then lower. He teased her at first, kissing and licking her inner thighs, before removing her panties and slowly licking her private parts. Stacy moaned and whined as she rotated her pelvis in a circular motion.

After several minutes, her legs began to tremble and she screamed aloud as she reached her climax. Will didn't waste any time however – he pulled his pants and boxers off and plunged his manhood deep into his girlfriend. In and out Will went as Stacy moaned and groaned, her eyes rolling into the back of her head as she dug her nails into his back as she climaxed again. Finally, Will was finished as well. It was a hot day in early July, and although the small air conditioner in Stacy's window was on high, Will and Stacy were both sweating profusely from their sexual activity.

"Damn, baby! You put your thing down!" Stacy panted. "That was new! Where'd you learn how to do that shit?"

"I just figured I'd try it," Will admitted as he caught his breath. He sat up, reached in his pants pocket and pulled out a pre-rolled blunt. "Did you enjoy it?"

"I loved it, baby," Stacy exclaimed. "I think I'm addicted! Ha-ha!"

"Yeah, that's cool, but we're gonna save that for special occasions, ma," Will stated matter-of-factly. "You smoking?"

"Yeah, I'll smoke with you," Stacy replied as Will lit the blunt, took a few drags and passed it to her. "This shit is strong as hell, baby," Stacy coughed. "What kind of weed is this?"

"It's sour-diesel," Will informed her as they lay in bed smoking.

"But, baby… I gotta talk to you about something."

"What's that, love?" Stacy asked as she took another puff and passed the blunt back to Will.

"Well, you met Pop's cousin Cannon from Germantown before, right?"

"Yeah, I met that crazy old-head," Stacy chuckled.

"Well, that's Cannon's wheel that Pop's driving," Will began.

"Cannon's letting Pop borrow it?" Stacy asked.

"Kinda," Will responded. "See, the other day, the three of us were running ball and these five niggas jumped me. I knocked one of them out, but Cannon shot three of them. Long-story-short – he got locked up. He's letting Pop hold his car while he's booked down the F."

"That's fucked up," Stacy replied. "I heard CFCF is rough. So, that's what you wanted to talk to me about?"

"Well, not just that," Will hesitated as he inhaled some more marijuana. "I gotta ask you a favor baby."

"You can ask me for anything after what you just did to me!" Stacy laughed.

"Ha! That's what I like to hear," Will chuckled. "But for real – this shit is serious, ma. There's a witness to the shootings that got Cannon locked up. Me and Pop have a plan. We're gonna ride around Germantown for the next few days, tryna find this nigga. His name is Devin. Then we're gonna follow him and find out where he hangs out and shit. After we do that, I need you to go to wherever that nigga hangs out, introduce yourself to that nigga, get him to drop his guard and get him to come to a place I tell you. Make him think he's gonna get some… don't kiss him or nothing, just tell him you wanna go somewhere to be alone and you know the perfect spot. Then, me and Pop will be waiting in the cut and we'll take care of him."

"Y-You're gonna kill somebody Will?" Stacy asked in horror.

"We gotta do it, baby," Will informed his girlfriend. "Cannon saved my ass out there and now he's facing two attempted murder charges and an assault with a deadly weapon charge. He's probably gonna go away for decades if he's found guilty. You're the only person I can trust to help me with this baby. I'll pay you a thousand dollars…"

"It's not about the money, Will," Stacy replied solemnly. "I just don't know if I can be an accessory to murder, you know? I love you and I would do anything for you…"

"Then do this for me, ma. Please…" Will hesitated. His mind worked to think of a way to get Stacy to comply. "When I get my place, I was thinking you could move in with me!"

"Really, baby?" Stacy asked with anticipation.

"Definitely," Will replied. "I just need to know that you're one-hundred- percent down for me. If you do this for me I'll know.

"Well…" Stacy hesitated. "If you really need me and I'm the only person y'all can trust, then I'll do it. But only because I love you with my whole heart baby!"

"Thanks so much, Stace. I love you, too," Will kissed her on her forehead. "But make sure you never, ever tell anyone about this, you understand, baby?"

"I won't, baby," Stacy looked up at Will. "Just let me know when you're ready for me to do it. But honestly, I'm stressed now! Let's finish this tree!"

Back on Ninth Street, in the Mustang, Pop was serving customers and had decided to call CeCe in order to make the business proposition.

"Hello?" CeCe answered the phone after a few rings.

"What's up, sexy?" Pop replied. "I miss you."

"Pop, you stay on some bullshit," CeCe replied. Pop could hear the smile in her voice. "How you go three weeks without seeing me or calling me and then call talking about how you miss a bitch?"

"'Cause I do," Pop replied matter-of-factly. "I wanna see you. Besides, you ain't called me either, ma! The phone works both ways!"

"Well, you know how I love to wear my stilettos, so I can't chase no nigga!" CeCe teased. "Besides, you know Tiny doesn't like us seeing each other. He don't want me messing with no drug-dealing coke-boy!" CeCe failed to mention that although Tiny would do business with Black people and was friends with Black people, he didn't want his niece dating a Black person.

"Chill, ma, you talking all reckless on the phone," Pop warned. "I don't sell drugs," Pop lied in case the phone was tapped. "But anyway, can I see you today? I'll pick you up and take you out to eat…"

"Sounds good to me," CeCe replied. "Wait, you got a car?"

"Now I do…"

"Ooh… what you got?" CeCe asked excitedly.

"You'll see when I come scoop you…"

"Okay, give me an hour to get ready," CeCe instructed. "Can we go to the Applebee's on the Boulevard, papi?"

"Yeah, ma, whatever you wanna do," Pop replied. "I got you. See you in an hour."

While he had been on the block, Pop's mind had also been working on trying to figure out who he could sell his first gun to so that he could put money on his cousin's commissary account at the county jail. As he hung up the phone with CeCe, it dawned on him that he could ask Rick if he needed to buy any extra guns to help protect his stash-house.

"Yo, my man," Pop's husky voice said into the phone after Rick answered. "Can I come back to the spot and holler at you right quick?"

"Yeah, that's cool," Rick replied. "See you in a minute. Peace."

Pop pulled up to Rick's house and exited the Mustang, activated the alarm and knocked on the door. Rick, who was waiting in the living room, came to the door, looked through the peep hole and then opened the door, but didn't immediately let Pop in; he just stood in the door way and looked up and down the street. His gun was on his waist and was already cocked.

"So what's up, young-boy? You tryna cop some more weight already?" Rick asked, looking Pop up and down, suspiciously.

"Naw, man," Pop objected. "I got guns for sale. I wanted to see if you wanted to cop." Rick's demeanor changed and he became more relaxed after he heard the proposition.

"Oh, yeah?" Rick replied coolly. "I can always use another ratchet. What you got?"

"What you need? I got all types of handguns and a couple shotties, too."

"I'll take a shotgun," Rick said. "How much?"

"Two-fifty... I'll give you the jawn that's not sawed off," Pop informed Rick. "It's a twelve-gauge, pistol-grip... beautiful joint!"

"Yeah, I need that in my life," Rick chuckled. "Good looking out, young-boy!"

"No problem, old-head. I'ma go grab it for you. I'll be back in a minute."

Pop walked back to the Mustang and drove back home to Ninth Street. He went into his house, greeted his mother, went into his room and his closet and got Cannon's suitcase full of guns. He sifted through the dozen guns and grabbed the twelve-gauge, pistol-grip shotgun that had not been sawed off. He placed it in a large duffle bag, carried it out to the trunk of the car and drove back over to Rick's spot. They exchanged money for the shotgun, and then Pop went back home to shower and change before his date with CeCe.

CeCe was a lightly brown-skinned Puerto-Rican girl, who was thin but shapely. She was eighteen years old and had just graduated from high school that summer. She had long, curly, black hair which flowed halfway down her back. Pop watched CeCe longingly as she walked down her front steps on Sixth Street and towards the Mustang. He had been waiting in front of her house for about ten minutes, after he had called her and told her he was outside, before she had come out.

"Ooh *papi*," CeCe said excitedly as she climbed in the passenger's side of the Mustang. "This shit is beautiful!"

"Thanks, ma." Pop had decided that he was just going to let people think the Mustang was his, and then deal with the details whenever Cannon was released from jail and he would had to return his car. "You ready to go, sexy?"

"Yeah, I'm ready for some Applebee's," CeCe replied.

"So you tryna make some money, CeCe?" Pop asked as he drove onto Roosevelt Boulevard, holding CeCe's hand with his right hand and holding the steering wheel with his left. "Did you find a job yet?"

"Naw," CeCe admitted, frustrated. "All these jobs that I'm qualified for don't pay shit! I'm about to try to get into modeling!"

"Yeah, you could definitely do that with your bad-ass," Pop agreed. "But how about you come work for me and Will? I got a way you can make like sixteen-hundred a month, working about four or five hours every couple days."

"How you figure I can do that?" CeCe's curiosity was piqued.

"Bagging up our ounces of coke for us," Pop informed her. "We'll need you to do it every two days and it takes like four hours every time if you have two people doing it. So you can get a girl you really trust who ain't gonna burn me and Will. We'll pay y'all a hundred dollars each time you bag up for us. Are you down?"

"Yeah, I'm down," CeCe replied earnestly. "I know the perfect girl to help me, too – my girl, Veronica."

"That's what' up," Pop was happy that CeCe accepted his offer. "Y'all can start in two days."

They arrived at Applebee's, entered the restaurant and enjoyed their meal. They talked and laughed. Pop thought about the fact that he enjoyed CeCe's company a lot, and that maybe he should talk to her about being a real couple. "A couple? Naw," he reconsidered to himself. "She's beautiful and the pussy is good, but there are too many broads out here. A nigga can't tie himself down!"

"Thanks for dinner, *papi*," CeCe told Pop as they exited the restaurant hand-in-hand. "What you wanna do now?"

"You know exactly what I wanna do to you, mami," Pop said as he groped CeCe in the parking lot. "You know, three weeks is too long for me to wait!"

"Don't make it so long then next time, Pop," CeCe scolded him.

"You gonna take me somewhere nice?"

"How about the Days Inn down the Boulevard?"

"That works for me, daddy," CeCe replied as she kissed Pop.

Pop wondered what CeCe saw in him, although he would never admit it. Yeah, he was in good shape, and he dressed well, but he knew he wasn't the best looking guy. CeCe was beautiful – definitely a dime-piece.

"Oh well," Pop thought to himself as he made his way down Roosevelt Boulevard to the hotel, "I'm just gonna take her to the hotel and enjoy tearing that ass up!"

CHAPTER 6

Pop and Will hustled all day Sunday until the entire ounce of cocaine was sold. Will asked Pop to drop him off at Stacy's and, after Pop did that, Pop called CeCe and met up with her. Both of the girls were pleased to see the young men in their lives two days in a row; they felt spoiled. Pop, who already had difficulty saving money, took CeCe to the hotel again. They ordered pizza and sodas and had them delivered to their room. They watched television, smoked some of Cannon's sour-diesel and had sex. Down in Nicetown, Stacy's mother wasn't home, so Will and Stacy had the apartment to themselves, as usual. They had Chinese food delivered and, just as Pop and CeCe were doing in some hotel room in another section of the city, Will and Stacy had sex, smoked some of Cannon's sour-diesel and had more sex.

The following morning, Will and Pop both decided to wake up early so they could arrive at the jail by nine in the morning for visiting hours. They wanted to see Cannon, put money in his commissary account, and discuss business. Pop had already been loading money onto his phone account so Cannon could call him, but since he had sold the shotgun to Rick, he had extra money to help Cannon out so he wouldn't have to get a job while he was in jail and earn meager wages for his commissary. They had brought their official-looking fake Pennsylvania IDs with them because they were too young to visit an inmate at the jail. However, they decided to leave their guns at home – they didn't even want to have them in the car when they arrived at the jail.

When they arrived at the jail and found parking, it was nine-thirty in the morning. They had been held up in traffic while trying to get there. They went into the main entrance and Pop handled the business of depositing the cash that he had for Cannon into Cannon's commissary account. They proceeded into the line for visitors and then they had to wait for Cannon, or Malik Davidson, to be brought down from his cellblock to the visitation room. When Will and Pop finally arrived in the visitation room, Cannon was already seated, waiting for them.

"My young-boys," Cannon greeted them, grinning. His head, usually shaved bald, was dark with hair, and his beard was thicker than it had been and unkempt after almost a week of no maintenance. "Thanks for coming through!"

"Of course, Cannon," Will said coolly.

"You already know, cuz," Pop excitedly replied. "We had to come see you, nigga! I took care of that commissary situation for you, so you can buy shit now."

"Good looking out, my nigga," Cannon thanked Pop. "You know the food here is trash! You getting rid of some of my bitches for me?" Cannon asked, referring to the sale of his firearms.

"I got rid of one of them already... sold a pump for two-fifty," Pop informed Cannon proudly.

"That's what's up... try to get three-fifty next time," Cannon instructed.

Pop frowned, disappointed that his cousin wasn't more pleased with the price he had received from the sale of the shotgun. "What about that sour; are you moving it?"

"Not yet. We wanted to see how good it was, so we blew some," Will interjected. "We'll start moving it soon though."

"Alright, that's cool," Cannon replied casually before his tone grew more serious. "Look y'all... I hooked y'all up with that sour, and that shit's expensive. That's a whole P – that's like four-stacks, so get out there and move that and we can split it. I need y'all to keep my commissary fat, na'mean? My first court date isn't for three months. I'ma be locked up for a little while."

"We got you, cuz," Pop reassured his cousin.

"Now the most important thing, though," Cannon continued, "is this nigga gonna show up to court?"

"Hell naw! We can't tell you the details, but we covering that, too," Pop replied assuredly.

"So you took care of it already?" Cannon asked skeptically.

"The plan is in motion," Will cut in as he sensed Pop's hesitation. "He's not gonna be a threat to you for long, Cannon."

"Alright, that's what's up," Cannon breathed a sigh of relief. "Good looking out y'all."

"No problem," the teenagers said in unison.

"How you holding up in here, man?" Pop asked.

"Man, for real, I'm just tryna workout; you know, pushups, dips, crunches and pull-ups on the top tier steps. Somebody left this book by Donald Goines that I never heard of in my hut, so I'm reading that jawn too. I love his books; you know I read a lot of his shit when I did those five years Upstate. If I don't keep myself busy I'ma merck one of these bitch-ass niggas or one of these nut-ass C.O.s!"

"Aw man, don't do that!" Will exclaimed. "You already got enough charges my nigga!" The three of them laughed.

"Davidson – time's up!" Cannon turned around and glared at the correctional officer who had cut their visit short after overhearing Cannon's comment about "nut-ass C.O.s."

"Alright, y'all," Cannon said and got up and left. The two teenagers watched as Cannon walked through a doorway and disappeared. They left the jail, walked to the Mustang and got in. They drove away from the jail, both in a melancholy mood. They were both happy to see Cannon, but it was hard to see him in jail.

"It's hard to see my cousin in the county, man," Pop said dejectedly as he drove. "Plus that visit was too short!"

"Damn right, it was," Will agreed. "So I guess he's gonna be in there at least three months. That's fucked up, but he can do that time standing on his hands since he's done five joints before!"

"Yeah, you're right," Pop concurred. "That nigga is hard as shit. He'll be good."

"I know you're gonna hate to give him back his car by the time you've had this jawn for three months, though," Will laughed. "I see you already customized this shit!"

"Yeah," Pop admitted. "I love this jawn – it's husky as shit. But yo... why don't you hit up Rick?"

"I already did before I came through to go see Cannon," Will replied. "He said he would have the onion ready for us by eleven, so we should be back right on time."

"That's what's up, but did he say it's cool for the girls to bag up there?" Pop asked. "You know he acts scary about having new motherfuckers at the spot."

"Yeah, he said it was cool since they're Tiny's people," Will informed Pop. "But yo, we need to get our own spot when your birthday comes around, my nigga. On second thought, I can probably use my fake ID to get one now if we're just renting a room. What you think?"

"It doesn't hurt to try," Pop hesitated. "I can put up money for the room right now, but I ain't built to put furniture in it and all that right now."

"You ain't gonna do it by yourself, my nigga," Will replied. "We're gonna split everything. I just wanna get a sofa or even just a futon, a table, a TV, a TV stand and a nice-sized safe. We probably only have to spend like five or six hundred each, plus about two-hundred each for the room for the first month."

"Um... yeah," Pop stuttered. "I ain't built for all that furniture shit, dog. I can pay my half of the rent and probably buy the safe, but I can't afford all the furniture shit."

"Damn, nigga – what the fuck you be doing with your money where you don't even have eight-hundred for the stash-spot?" Will asked in shock.

"I got bills, motherfucker, plus my half of the re-up! Mind your fucking business!" Pop snapped angrily.

"I got mad bills too, my nigga," Will replied. "I'm not tryna be all up in your shit, but you're supposed to be stacking bread for the business! We're selling an ounce of coke every other day, getting money to be some young coke-boys. I know you ain't just blowing it!"

"Look, Will, get the fuck outta my business," Pop retorted. "Do I ask you what you got?"

"You don't have to 'cause you know I got my shit together," Will snapped. "And actually, you did ask the other night when I was talking about buying a wheel!"

"Well maybe that's 'cause I was wondering how you have thirteen stacks lying around!"

"Fuck that shit! I got more...," Will caught himself before he finished his sentence, but he had already said too much. In his anger, he had revealed to his friend that he had more than he had initially admitted to having saved up. Pop was his closest friend, and Will hoped this knowledge wouldn't breed jealousy and envy inside his friend's heart. Will had only been trying to play it safe by keeping the information from his friend and business partner.

"That's what's up," Pop replied coolly, keeping his eyes on the road ahead. "I wish I did too."

"It ain't about nothing, my nigga," Will tried to smooth things over. "How about you just give me your half of the rent if I'm able to get the room with my fake ID, and I'll buy the furniture?"

"That's cool for now, but I'll pay you back," Pop replied.

"I just got an even better idea," Will suggested. "How about you just supply a couple guns from Cannon's collection for the spot and put money on his commissary when you can?"

"That'll work," Pop agreed.

Inside the Mustang, the tension was thick and the two young men finished the ride without speaking. They listened to the A.$.A.P. Rocky CD in silence as Pop drove. Pop pulled up to CeCe's house on Sixth Street, called her, and informed her that they were outside, ready to take her and her friend to "work." Within thirty seconds, CeCe and her friend, Veronica, were out the front door and heading for the Mustang. Will and Pop both exited the vehicle and tilted their seats forward so the females could enter the backseat. As Veronica approached the passenger's side, Will couldn't take his eyes off of her.

"What's up, y'all?" Pop greeted the girls tensely, still upset from his argument with Will. "How y'all doing?"

"We're good," the girls said in unison.

"Ready to work!" CeCe added. "This is my girl, Veronica, or Ronnie, I was telling you about, Pop. She's good people!"

"That's what's up," Pop replied as he drove to Rick's spot. "It's nice to meet you, Veronica. I'm Pop and this is my business partner, Will."

"Nice to meet you, Pop. Nice to meet you, Will," Veronica said as she reached from the back seat and gently placed her hand on Will's shoulder.

"Good to meet you too, ma," Will turned around in his seat. "Do you prefer Veronica or Ronnie?"

"You can call me either or," Veronica replied with a smile.

"Can I call you 'beautiful?'" Will asked slyly, flirting with Veronica. Veronica was a beautiful, young, Puerto Rican woman. She had just turned twenty-one years old, and she had long straight, reddish-brown hair. She was a lighter-skinned Puerto Rican woman, with light green eyes. She was built nicely, too, as Will had noticed while he was staring at her as she got in the car. She had a very small waist with full breasts and he had noticed her round behind as she had stepped into the back of the Mustang.

"Oh boy... you're silly," Veronica chuckled. "Thanks for the compliment!

You can call me that if you want!"

"Oh no he *can't*," CeCe interjected. "She has a man – you know, Jasiel? He would probably snap if he saw her in the car with y'all, so you better chill out, Will."

"CeCe, you know I ain't worried about that motherfucker," Will replied casually. "Sorry, I know he's your cousin or cousin-in-law, but he ain't got nothing for me! That's your man though, Veronica?"

"We've been seeing each other for about a month," Veronica answered honestly.

"Well, we'll just have to change that," Will said with a smirk.

"Well, leave me out of it," CeCe rebuffed.

"Yeah, my nigga, leave me out of it, too," Pop cut in. "You know this is about business. Besides, we don't need no extra beef with Jasiel and Jose!"

"Don't tell me you bitching up!" Will exclaimed, surprised at Pop's comments. Pop turned and glared angrily at Will for so long that the car swerved and almost hit oncoming traffic on Sixth Street. "Nigga, watch where you're going! Don't be mad at me 'cause you worried about them niggas and I'm not!"

"Whatever, nigga," Pop replied and continued to drive. They arrived at Rick's spot a short time later and the older man let the four young people in without a problem since he was expecting them.

Will and Pop stayed with the girls and instructed them on how to use the scale and bag up the cocaine into dimes. They decided to watch over the girls the entire time, figuring it wasn't a waste of time doing so because they were protecting their investment; especially since they didn't know Veronica. She could be a threat – especially since she was dating their enemy, Jasiel.

The girls learned the process of bagging up fairly quickly. Rick's setup was perfect for it. He had a glass-top dining room table in the living room of the two bedroom house, which made it easy to see and separate the cocaine with the razor blades. He had central air conditioning in the house so that there was no need for fans or window units which would blow the product around and result in losses. Each girl had a scale, a razor blade, a playing card, a spoon, well over one-hundred bags and a half-ounce of cocaine on their side of the table. After the girls separated a small line of product with a razor, they would place a playing card which was folded in half onto the scale and hit the "tare" button, which weighed the playing card. Then they proceeded to scoop the cocaine up with a baby's feeding spoon and place the powder into the crease of the playing card. The scale would then register the weight of the cocaine only, (which is why they weighed the card first and hit the "tare" button"). They added or removed product until the scale registered .1 gram. Then they would carefully funnel the contents of the playing card into an open, tiny, zipper-top cocaine bag.

The cocaine was already "stepped-on," or cut, so they didn't cut it any further.

"Y'all are doing a great job," Will commended the girls. "We really appreciate this shit!"

"Yeah, for real," Pop concurred.

"No problem, *papi*," CeCe paused and looked up at Pop. She pursed her lips for Pop to give her a kiss. He walked over, placed his arm on CeCe's shoulder and kissed her. "Thanks, daddy," CeCe exhaled. "Now back to work! I'm tryna get paid!"

The girls were focused on the job at hand. They were working intensely and quickly. First, Will and Pop had demonstrated how the process worked and then let CeCe and Veronica take over. Once they had bagged up the first couple dozen bags, they picked up the pace.

"Y'all going fast as shit!" Will exclaimed. "Y'all wanna take a break and blow some of this sour-diesel with us and listen to some music?"

"Naw, I'm not tryna bag up high," Veronica declined. "That'll slow me down. But I'll listen to some music though!"

"Yeah, same here," CeCe chimed in.

"Yo, my nigga," Will turned to Pop. "Can you grab the CD case out the wheel please?"

"Yeah, I got you." Pop ran outside and returned within thirty seconds with a large CD case. "What y'all wanna listen to? I got mad shit in here – A.$.A.P Rocky, Meek, Peedi Crakk, Styles, Joey Jihad, Jakk Frost, Cassidy, Gillie, Rick Ross, N.O.R.E...."

"Ooh, let's listen to that Peedi Crakk, 'Crakk Files Volume 4' jawn you let me hear the other night," CeCe blurted out excitedly. "That jawn is hot!"

"Yeah it is, but that's all Jasiel listens to," Veronica complained. "You got any R&B?"

"Hell naw," Pop exclaimed. "I'm a motherfucking coke-boy, ma! I don't listen to that soft shit!"

"Well, excuse me for asking," Veronica replied with a slight attitude.

"Nigga, stop fronting! You know you got that Drake shit in there," Will teased Pop.

"Yeah, whatever, nigga," Pop replied as he placed the Peedi Crakk CD into the CD player and turned the volume up. Will and Pop sat down and began smoking a blunt, when Rick came downstairs from one of the bedrooms.

"Hey, yo," Rick yelled. "Turn that fucking music down!" Pop complied immediately but wondered why Rick was so angry.

"What's the deal, old-head?" Pop asked after turning the music down to a reasonable level.

"This is a fucking stash-house," Rick said in a low voice. "Yeah, I spend a lot of time here, but I don't live in this motherfucker. So you wanna turn the music loud as shit, have the neighbors complain and then the cops come through here in ten minutes and we all get booked 'cause of the drugs and guns we got in here? You gotta be smart, young-boy!"

"Damn, I ain't even think of that! My bad, Rick," Pop apologized. With that, Rick went back upstairs and continued to watch television in the bedroom while he bagged up several ounces of his own cocaine. Within three hours of beginning, both CeCe and Veronica had finished bagging up their halves of the ounce.

"We're done," the girls said proudly in unison.

"Damn, ma!" Pop exclaimed as he exhaled some marijuana. "Y'all beasted through that shit!" Pop and Will walked over to the table and examined their work.

"Looks good," Will shook his head in approval. "To tell the truth, we never even finished that fast. We should've put you on the team a long time ago," Will said while staring into Veronica's eyes, trying to see if she had caught the double-meaning of his last statement. She grinned bashfully.

"Well, we were trying to finish quick," Veronica replied. "We're trying to go get our nails done!"

"Well, then, you go get your nails and your toes done on us," Will replied as he pulled out a wad of cash and counted out three-hundred dollars.

He handed each girl one-hundred and fifty dollars. "Y'all get an extra fifty for doing such a good job!"

"Yeah, I'll drop you off at the nail shop," Pop interjected as he stared at Will, puzzled. "Let's be out."

Will and Pop called upstairs to Rick and told him that they were about to leave as they each put half of the pile of dime-bags into their backpacks. Rick came downstairs and locked the door behind them when they left.

The girls chattered with excitement during the ride back to Hunting Park Avenue to the nail salon. They had never made so much money in such a short period of time and, even though they worked for both Will and Pop, they weren't sure which one was really in charge. Pop had the new Mustang, but Will seemed to have all the cash. Veronica was already developing a crush on Will, but she decided not to reveal this fact to CeCe because she knew that CeCe would not approve and would probably tell Jasiel. Veronica knew she was wrong for feeling attracted to Will, but she was so drawn to the tall, slim but vascular, well maintained, good-looking, Black young man. He was well-dressed, had a lot of money and he had game, too. She could tell he liked her, but he was cool about it. The only turn-off was that he was so much younger than she was. If she was going to deal with him romantically, she was going to have to keep it a secret, due to Jasiel and CeCe and due to the age difference.

After arriving at the nail salon, Pop and Will exited the Mustang so the girls could exit the backseat. Pop and CeCe hugged and kissed and said their goodbyes.

"Alright, Veronica," Will hesitated as he reached out his hand. "It was nice meeting you and chilling with you."

"You too, Will," Veronica smiled as she took Will's hand and held it for a while. The beautiful young woman just stood there, gazing up at Will until CeCe called her.

"Ronnie! Let's go before Jasiel rides by and sees you," CeCe commanded.

"Bye, Will. See you in two days," Veronica frowned as she slowly released his hand and walked away. Will and Pop got back into the car.

"Damn, CeCe's cool and all that, but she's cock-blocking like crazy," Will complained.

"How you let that girl get your nose wide open like that?" Pop scolded Will.

"What you mean?" Will asked.

"You showing off, giving them more money than we agreed on, trying to look like a boss and shit," Pop complained. "Now they're gonna expect that shit!"

"You're right," Will agreed. "They are gonna expect it, but they're only gonna get it if they work as fast as they did today! It was supposed to be motivation."

"Oh okay, I got you," Pop finally understood. "But I can tell you got a crush on Veronica. She *is* tough, but you really shouldn't be worried about Veronica when you already got Stacy holding you down. Plus you got mad groupie bitches. You're gonna get caught up, nigga!"

"I'll be good," Will replied confidently as they pulled up to the corner where they normally sold their product. No sooner had they arrived than both of their phones started ringing,

"Yeah, I'm here," Will answered his phone. "Come through."

"Yeah, I'll be available all day," Pop confirmed with a customer. "I can drive to you now if you need me to, but I prefer you come to the block. Alright, peace."

"Yo," Pop turned to Will. "We need to make a trip out Germantown later and start looking for this nigga, Devin."

"Say no more, my nigga," Will agreed. "I'm about to hit up Stacy to see if she can ride with us," Will stated as he pulled out his cell phone and began to dial Stacy's number.

"Hey, baby," Stacy answered the phone.

"What's up, sexy?"

"Nothing... just watching TV while my mother is sleeping," Stacy replied.

"Remember what I talked to you about before?" Will began. "Well, I need you to take a ride with us today."

"You ready for me to do that already?" Stacy asked reluctantly.

"Naw, just preliminary shit," Will informed Stacy. "We're going to look for him and we want you to know what he looks like when we find him."

"Ugh... ok," Stacy groaned.

"I'll be over there in a few hours, sexy... thanks. I love you!"

"I love you, too, Will. That's the only reason why I'm doing this shit," Stacy admitted.

"I know, ma, you're the best!" Will hung up and turned to Pop. "She's down!"

CHAPTER 7

After selling cocaine out of Cannon's Mustang for several hours, Will and Pop decided it was time to take a trip to Germantown and search for the snitch, Devin. It was five-o'clock in the evening, and they decided they would pick Stacy up, drive around for a while looking for Devin and then drop her off at her house and get back to the block. Both Will and Pop had burned the image of the informant's face into their memory. How could they forget him? They had played basketball with him for about a half-hour, prior to the shooting, and then he had been so bold as to identify Cannon as the shooter and he had done so right in front of their faces. They were determined to make him pay for snitching.

"Hey, sexy, we're outside," Will said into the telephone, informing his still reluctant girlfriend that they had arrived. He waited outside the car for her so that she could get into the backseat. "What's up, baby?" Will hugged Stacy tight and kissed her on the mouth when she finally reached the vehicle.

"Hey, baby," Stacy whimpered. "Hey, Pop," she greeted Pop in an equally whiny voice. She was not happy to be involved in this plot at all, but she loved her man and, as Pop had predicted, she would do anything for him.

"What's up, Stacy?" Pop greeted her. "What's wrong?"

"She's shook about doing this shit," Will answered for his girlfriend.

"I just don't wanna go to jail," Stacy whined.

"Shit! Neither do we," Pop chuckled.

"Baby, trust me," Will turned around in the passenger seat and faced Stacy, looking her in the eye. "I wouldn't put you in harm's way. That's why we're gonna do this shit right, so none of us have to worry about a thing, and our nigga, Cannon, can get the fuck up outta jail!"

"Okay, baby," Stacy sighed, "I trust you..."

"Damn right, you should," Will stated firmly. "I always look out for my baby!" Pop rolled his eyes as he drove. Will noticed it but didn't say anything about it.

The first stop on their list of places to check for Devin was the Happy Hollow Playground on Wayne Avenue where they had played basketball and where the shooting had occurred. They pulled up to the curb across the street from the playground and surveyed the players on the basketball court. Devin was not among them. They drove to the basketball courts by the housing projects at the corner of Queen Lane and Pulaski Avenue, but they were deserted. They drove up and down the different streets in Germantown – Hansberry, Midvale, Abbottsford, Greene, Chelten, Coulter, Wyneva, Schoolhouse Lane and Germantown Avenue, to name a few. They drove around for an hour and a half, until Pop needed more gas in the Mustang.

"Well, it looks like we ain't finding this nigga tonight," Will said out the window to Pop as he pumped his gas.

"Yeah, I don't think so," Pop agreed. "I mean, we can keep looking, but we're losing money by not being out on the block."

"Plus, we're wasting my girl's time," Will acknowledged.

"I'm just happy to spend time with you, baby," Stacy grinned.

"Thanks, that's what's up, ma," Will replied. "But we're gonna get you home now."

Pop got back into the Mustang after he finished pumping the gas and pulled off. They arrived at Stacy's building about five minutes later.

"Are you coming in, baby?" Stacy asked Will, hoping he would answer in the affirmative.

"Naw, I'm sorry, ma. I gotta get back out and make this money," Will explained. "But it's not even seven-o'clock yet. I'll be over later if that's cool."

"Of course that's cool, baby," Stacy confirmed before getting out, kissing Will and going into her building.

"Damn, man," Pop sighed. "I was really hoping we would spot that nigga tonight!"

"Yeah, me too," Will replied. "Maybe we should go out in the early afternoon tomorrow and see if we can find him."

They were unaware, however, that while they were driving down Pulaski Avenue, past the projects and the other houses, they had just missed Devin. He had just opened the front door to his parents' house and was about to exit in order to walk to the corner store, when he noticed the black, convertible Mustang with shiny, chrome rims and dark, tinted windows cruise by slowly. Devin immediately recognized the Mustang as the same car from the basketball court and was paralyzed with fear. He stood frozen in the doorway of his home with the door half-open. He imagined the shooter had made bail and was looking for him, to get rid of him before his trial date. Finally, Devin mustered enough strength to slam the door shut, although he was quivering, breathing heavily and sweating profusely out of fear. What he didn't know was that the three teenagers in the Mustang hadn't even noticed him.

"So, since you're my nigga I wanted to let you know I'm gonna go try to get a car tomorrow morning," Will informed Pop as they sat in the Mustang waiting for customers to arrive.

"That's what's up," Pop replied, disinterested. "Thanks for telling me."

"Yeah, I was looking online," Will continued excitedly. "I saw this jawn at one of those dealerships on the Boulevard – a husky-ass, pearl-white Caddy DTS. That jawn is ill from the pictures I seen online! You wanna come with me?"

"Will, if you need a ride, you can just ask me for one," Pop replied coldly.

"Nigga, since when do I have a problem taking the bus?" Will snapped. "I wanted you to go since you're my nigga! Why you being a dickhead?"

"I'm not being a dickhead," Pop replied coolly. "I'm just saying that if you need a ride, you can ask me!"

"Alright, nigga! Whatever! Fuck it," Will replied impatiently. "I'll take the fucking bus since you're being cocky. You really been feeling yourself since you got Cannon's wheel!"

"What you tryna say, Will?"

"I ain't *tryna* say shit," Will retorted. "I'm *saying* it! You've been acting cocky as shit for no damn reason ever since you been riding around in this jawn and it ain't even yours! You fronting like it's your wheel, acting like you got bread, knowing you ain't hardly got no money saved! Step your game up my nigga!"

"Fuck you, Will!" Pop screamed. "You think because you got all this bread stacked that you better than a nigga? You think 'cause you buying a Caddy you a fucking kingpin?"

"Naw, my nigga," Will recanted. "I don't think none of that shit. I'm just saying I think both of our egos have been getting in the way lately for different reasons, and it's causing us to argue. I don't want no beef with you my nigga, so my fault," Will apologized.

"Alright, that's cool," Pop replied coolly. Will looked at him, waiting for an apology or, at least, more of a reaction.

"That's why I asked you if you wanted to be down after I had been hustling for a while," Will continued. "'Cause you're my nigga and I want us to be getting money together! I wanna be driving nice cars together, fucking bad bitches together, rocking the hottest gear together. We've known each other all our lives – that's how it should be!"

"Well, we already fuck the baddest bitches and have the hottest gear," Pop chuckled, his demeanor finally more relaxed. "But I'ma have to give my cousin his car back when he gets out of jail, and I ain't doing a good job of saving money!"

"Well, I was thinking about the car situation and the money situation," Will started. "And if we can start moving two ounces every couple days, we could double our bread. We just moved that last onion in a day – I was thinking we could work both sides of the park and try to get some new customers. Then you could start stacking some bread and save money for a wheel, or at least a down-payment, depending on what you trying to get…"

"That might work," Pop nodded in agreement. "I definitely need more bread. But I only have my half of another ounce – I can't cop a whole onion on my own, especially since we're about to rent a room for the stash-spot."

"It's cool," Will sighed, not understanding how his friend could be so broke. "I'll cop the other ounce and we can just take your half out of your part of the profit at first. Does that work for you? You should still make profits from the first jawn." Will was trying every possible way to make the business side of things work out between him and Pop. He wanted Pop to be happy in the situation so that Pop wouldn't have any reason to complain. Will sensed that Pop was growing jealous of him, and that was not a good thing in a friendship, in the streets, or in the drug business.

"Yeah, I guess that will work," Pop agreed, and they shook hands to confirm the deal. Business was steady that night, and by the time eleven-thirty had arrived, they had sold all of their product. The fact that they had done so in one day alone had solidified their resolve to follow through with Will's plan to buy two ounces of cocaine from that point on. As soon as their last three dime-bags were sold, Will pulled out his cell phone and began to dial.

"Yo, what up, old-head?" he addressed Rick without using his name. "You know who it is…"

"Yeah, yeah," Rick replied. "What up, young-boy? What you need?"

"I need two circles. We gonna be there by noon tomorrow," Will informed Rick.

"Damn! Already?" Rick exclaimed. "Alright, young-buck. See you then. Peace!"

After Will hung up with Rick, Pop called CeCe to let her know that he and Will would be around at about eleven-forty-five in the morning to pick her up, along with Veronica, for more "work." He explained to her that it was twice as much work so they would be paid twice as much, as long as they worked just as diligently as they had that morning.

"Okay, daddy," CeCe replied. "We definitely will! See you tomorrow." CeCe ended the call with Pop and called Veronica. "Ooh girl… we're gonna be paid!" CeCe said excitedly as Veronica answered the phone.

"Oh yeah?" Veronica replied casually as she discreetly turned down the volume on her phone. "What you mean, girl?"

"Pop just called and said that they got twice as much work and they need us tomorrow," CeCe spoke rapidly. "He said we'll get paid twice as much as long as we work just as hard as we did this morning! Isn't that good news?"

"That's what's up," Veronica replied coolly. "What time do you want me to come over tomorrow and check out your new outfits?"

"Huh… what?" CeCe stuttered, confused. "What the hell are you talking about girl? Are you high?"

"What am I doing, you asked?" Veronica responded, ignoring CeCe's questions. "I'm just sitting here next to Jasiel, chilling at his crib watching a movie."

"Oh, I got you girl," CeCe realized that Veronica did not want Jasiel to know what they had been discussing. "Okay, well, be here by eleven-thirty in the morning. See you then."

"Okay, I can't wait! Bye, girl," Veronica hung up.

"Who the fuck was that?" Jasiel demanded to know. Veronica turned her head away and rolled her eyes before answering.

"It was CeCe," Veronica replied. "She wants me to come look at some new clothes she boosted. She went to Franklin Mills today after we got our nails done," Veronica lied.

"It better have been CeCe and not some nigga," Jasiel snapped while glaring at Veronica jealously.

"Now, Jasiel, you know I don't talk to nobody but my family and my girlfriends," Veronica stated matter-of-factly. "Chill the fuck out!"

"Let me see your phone," Jasiel commanded.

"Nigga, are you serious?" Veronica asked in shock.

"I'm dead-serious," Jasiel got up and stood menacingly over Veronica with his hands balled into fists and a crazed look in his eyes. "Don't make me fuck you up!"

Veronica, who had never seen this side of Jasiel, instantly grew afraid and timidly handed him her phone. He looked through her call log and saw that CeCe was the last person to call her.

"Good," Jasiel stated coldly as he tossed Veronica's phone on the sofa next to her. He plopped down on the sofa next to her and put his arm around her. "Now, *dame un beso mami!*" Jasiel commanded Veronica to give him a kiss.

"For real, Jasiel? After all that? I'm really not in the mood," Veronica declined.

"Bitch," Jasiel barked as he smacked Veronica in the face, then grabbed her by her cheeks and shoved his tongue into her mouth. Veronica whimpered. Then Jasiel unbuttoned his jeans, placed his gun on the opposite side of him, and pulled his pants halfway down as he grabbed the back of Veronica's head and forced it down into his lap.

"Please no, Jasiel," Veronica sobbed. "Please, don't make me do it like this! I'll do it… but not like this!"

"Bitch, you'll do it how I say you'll do it!" Jasiel roared as he grabbed his gun and placed the barrel against Veronica's hairline. She sobbed and hyperventilated to the point where she couldn't even perform the forced oral sex because she could barely breathe. "Bitch, you're pitiful! Get off me," Jasiel said in disgust, yanking Veronica's head up out of his lap by her hair. Veronica lay on the sofa, curled up in the fetal position, sobbing. "I want you out of here!"

Veronica tried to compose herself and then rose from the sofa and left. Having no car, she walked towards her home, to Sixth Street and Lycoming Street, which was right down the block and around the corner from where CeCe lived on Sixth Street. She wanted to go to CeCe's house and tell her what had transpired, but she didn't know how CeCe would respond. Veronica figured she would just suffer in silence. "At least nothing actually happened," she reasoned. "He just slapped me and put a gun to my head – it could have been worse!" She was definitely not going to call Jasiel anymore. This had been their first sexual encounter with each other and he had tried to rape her. "That motherfucker is crazy," she said aloud to herself as she walked briskly home. "I'm lucky to be alive!" Little did she know that Jose had overheard the entire encounter from upstairs. He was now convinced that his twin brother was a sociopath, but he was too afraid of him to intervene, even if it meant an innocent young woman was almost raped in their living room.

The next morning Will rose early, took a shower, shaped up his moustache and goatee, and got dressed. He ate breakfast while talking to his mother. He was in a great mood. He was finally going to get his own car! A few minutes before he finished eating his breakfast, there was a knock at the front door. Will's mother answered the door.

"Hi, Misses Bonner," Pop greeted Will's mother. "How are you?"

"I'm doing fine, Darryl, and you?" Misses Bonner greeted Pop using his given name.

"I'm fine, thanks. Is Will home?"

"Yeah, he's just finishing up breakfast," Misses Bonner opened the door all the way and stood aside so Pop could enter. "Come on in!"

"Thanks, Misses Bonner," Pop walked through the living room to the kitchen and greeted Will, who was surprised to see him.

"What's up, my nigga?" Will shook Pop's hand. "What you doing up so early? We don't have to be to Rick's until twelve."

"I came to take you to get your whip," Pop replied. "I don't want my nigga riding the bus up there. Besides… I wanna be the first one to see it!"

"Oh, that's what up! Good looking out, cuz," Will thanked Pop.

"You ready to roll out?"

"I'm ready when you are, dog…"

"Let's go then!" Will exclaimed eagerly. He grabbed his backpack, which he was guarding with his life. It was full of bills wrapped in rubber bands – fifteen-thousand dollars' worth of ones, fives and tens, with some twenties mixed in.

When they arrived at the dealership Will had found online, he immediately saw the vehicle he wanted. A shiny, pearl-white 2006 Cadillac DTS. It already had the Cadillac chrome, twenty-inch rims on it, leather interior, wood-grain steering wheel, navigation system and all the bells and whistles. Will was in love with the car. Even Pop had to admit the vehicle was beautiful. Will entered the dealership immediately and asked about the car.

"How's your credit, son?" the salesman asked him.

"I don't need credit," Will replied bluntly. The salesman smirked and looked at the secretary.

"That car is listed for fourteen-five, son," the salesman replied smugly.

"I know what it's listed for," Will replied matter-of-factly. "And if you give it to me for fourteen, with all the taxes and tags included, I'll pay cash right now," Will informed the salesman, unzipping the backpack halfway and revealing the rolls of cash.

"Uh… okay," the salesman stuttered and smiled. "That's great, sir! Let me get my manager!" The salesman scurried off into a back office and returned with his manager after explaining the situation to him.

"Yes, we can make that deal for you today, sir," the manager began. "If you could just bear with us while we count the money and break it down into two different transactions. We have to report any cash transactions over ten-thousand dollars to the IRS, but I'm sure you don't want that…"

Will and Pop sat down in the waiting room and drank sodas while they waited the forty-five minutes it took for the manager and salesman to count the money twice and draw up the paperwork for the car.

"Thank you so much for your patience, Mister Bonner," the salesman said as he returned with Will's legitimate driver's license and the vehicle paperwork, along with the keys. "We're all done here. Thank you so much for your patronage. And if you have any friends or colleagues who you can refer to us, here are some of my business cards. I'll take care of them, too!"

"Thanks, man," Will shook the salesman's hand, grabbed his belongings and walked to the car smiling. He was proud of his accomplishment and happy that he had saved money on this purchase. "You ready, Pop?"

"Yeah, let's go pick up the girls, my nigga," Pop replied.

"Young kids," the manager shook his head and turned to the salesman as the teenagers drove out of the used car lot. "That kid was seventeen years old! You *know* he's gotta be a drug dealer!"

"Yeah, but at least I got a good commission," the salesman laughed.

Both the Mustang and the Cadillac arrived on Sixth Street at CeCe's home thirty minutes earlier than expected. Pop exited the Mustang and walked up to Will's Cadillac.

"This shit is nice, my nigga," Pop complimented his friend sincerely.

"Thanks, my nigga," Will beamed with pride.

"But anyway, I'ma call CeCe to see if the girls are ready. Yo, what's up, ma? Y'all ready?" Pop asked CeCe when she answered her phone. "Yeah, I know we're early but we finished handling our other shit sooner than we thought so we just came through. We're outside. Alright, peace." Pop hung up. "She said she'll be out in a couple minutes to chill with us until Veronica gets here. She said she told Veronica to be here by eleven-thirty."

"Alright bet," Will replied. "I can't wait for that jawn, Veronica, to see my ride!"

"You crazy, nigga," Pop remarked. "What about Stacy?"

"Yeah, yeah, of course," Will stuttered. "Stacy's my baby. But Veronica is my new target!"

Just then, CeCe walked out of her front door, down the stoop and towards the cars, which were park-ed directly in front of her house.

"What's up, baby?" she greeted Pop as she hugged and kissed him. "Damn, Will! You got a Caddy though, nigga? Y'all niggas balling out here in North Philly! Can I get in for a minute?"

"Sure, as long as Pop doesn't mind," Will commented.

"Do you mind, baby?" CeCe asked. "Baby, are you okay?" Pop, who didn't realize his face had been frowned up, was slow to respond.

"Yeah, whatever," Pop hesitated. "Just don't make your home in it!"

CeCe entered the passenger's side of the Cadillac and asked Will about all the electronic features. She rubbed the leather seats and touched the wood-grain on the dashboard and the door. When she noticed Pop staring enviously, she decided to exit the vehicle in a hurry. Shortly thereafter, Veronica came walking up Sixth Street from Lycoming Street. Will noticed her through the windshield of his car and brushed his hair, placed a new piece of mint-flavored gum in his mouth and hopped out of his car, leaning up against it, waiting for Veronica to approach the three of them.

"Hey y'all," Veronica greeted everybody. "Damn, Will, is this yours?" Veronica asked in shock, pointing to the Cadillac.

"Yeah, that's mine," Will replied proudly. "I grabbed it this morning. You like it?"

"Yeah, I love it!"

"You wanna ride with me to the spot?" Will offered.

"Yeah, I would like that," Veronica accepted.

"I don't think that's a good idea, Ronnie," CeCe interjected. "We're still in the hood... what if Jasiel..."

"Girl, please," Veronica cut CeCe off. "I'm done with your cousin! After me and you got off the phone last night, that crazy nigga was calling me all types of bitches, made me give him my phone to check my call log, and then smacked me in the face! Look at my cheek!" She revealed her bruised left cheek. She decided to keep the rest of the horrible details of the night to herself, however.

"That nigga hit you?" CeCe gasped. "I can't believe that nigga!"

"Believe it!" Veronica snapped.

"I'm sorry, girl…"

"Yeah well, it's over now," Veronica replied. "I'm done with him."

"Damn, ma, I'm sorry to hear that nigga did that to you," Will replied, rubbing Veronica's shoulder. "You wanna hop in so we can talk on the way to the spot?"

Veronica rode with Will, while CeCe rode with Pop to Rick's spot that morning. Will decided this would be the best time for him to make his move on Veronica.

"So I hope this isn't bad timing, ma," Will started, "but like I told you yesterday, I think you're beautiful and I wanna get to know you better. What you think about that?"

"I would like that," Veronica replied. "But as cute as you are, I know you have a girlfriend…"

"Well, thanks for the compliment," Will grinned. "I'm seeing a girl from my school," he admitted. "But it's not that serious," he lied.

"Uh… well, I really don't wanna be a side-jawn," Veronica confessed. "I wanna be your one-and-only, you know?"

"Well, as cool as you seem and as beautiful as you are, I don't think that will be too difficult," Will said slyly. Veronica smiled bashfully. "Here's my number…"

The two exchanged phone numbers as Will and Pop both arrived at Rick's spot.

"Let's keep this between us though," Veronica suggested. "I'm done with Jasiel, but he's so crazy and jealous that I'm afraid what he'll do if he finds out."

"Ma, I told y'all yesterday I ain't worried about that nigga!"

"I know you're not... but I am," Veronica replied. "Please just keep it quiet for me?"

Veronica had no idea at that moment just how worried she needed to be about Jasiel. She also didn't know at the time that even though she thought she was through with Jasiel – he wasn't through with her.

CHAPTER 8

Almost a week had passed and Will and Pop were consistently selling an ounce of coke per day. The teenagers were pleased because they were making more money than ever before, Rick was proud of his protégé, Will, and Tiny was happy as well because it meant more business for him. Will and Pop had also told their customers that they were now selling sour-diesel and requested that they ask their friends if they smoked it and to buy from them if so. They even handed out free jars to some of their customers to see if that would attract business, and it worked.

"Man, we really got this shit popping off!" Pop said excitedly one night when they met up before going out to sell. "The extra ounce was your best idea, my nigga! Good looking out on copping it since I didn't have the bread. I got it now, though," Pop proclaimed as he smiled and pulled out a wad of cash.

"I'm glad to see you with all that bread, my nigga," Will smiled. "Just don't be flashing it around like that when we get outside!"

"Aw shit, Will, you know I'm smarter than that," Pop chuckled, putting his money back into his pocket as they walked out his front door. "Let's hustle together on the same side of the park tonight like we used to. I need to holler at you about something. We can just go to the old spot in my wheel tonight if you don't mind."

"Yeah, that's cool," Will agreed. "The fiends will just call me and I'll tell them to come over. I just hope we don't draw too much attention with all them motherfuckers coming to the wheel all night!"

The teenagers parked on the corner of Ninth Street and Lycoming Street, and shortly thereafter their customers, who they hadn't sold to earlier in the day, and some who they had sold to, started to come around. When there was a gap between customers, Pop began to discuss what he needed to speak to Will about.

"Yo, Will," Pop began. "Cannon called me today."

"Oh word? How's he doing?"

"He's stressed about the Devin situation," Pop replied. "He just kept saying, 'That's not handled yet? I can't believe that's not handled yet! I need y'all to handle that for me!'"

"First of all, we gotta find the nigga first!" Will exclaimed. "Why is Cannon tripping? We have time! Second, I don't know why he's talking about it over a recorded, jail telephone line!"

"Naw, he didn't say what 'that' was," Pop protested. "And he's tripping because he doesn't want us to wait until it's too late! I told him we're doing everything we can. He's just gotta trust us. I told him we're handling it. But yo, we gotta find that nigga, Devin, soon!"

"Yeah, I feel you, dog," Will responded coolly. "How about we grab Stacy tomorrow night and go look for the nigga?"

"What about in the afternoon?" Pop suggested. "The girls only been taking like five hours to bag up both ounces, so if we pick them up at eight in the morning, they can be done by one or one-thirty. We can go look for Devin after that."

"The girls ain't gonna be ready that early," Will objected. "Besides, I found an ad online for this room in Nicetown on Twenty-First and Venango and I wanna look at it tomorrow. If it goes well, we can have our own spot by tomorrow; we'll just have to cop the furniture when we get a chance. You down?"

"Yeah, I'm down," Pop affirmed. "We can do that early and then go get the girls. I been stacking the past week so I have my half of the furniture and the rent," Pop mentioned eagerly.

"That's what's up!"

Just then, one of their older associates from the neighborhood, a Black man in his late twenties named Tommy, drove up alongside the black Mustang in a white Buick Le Sabre and rolled down his window.

"What up, y'all?" Tommy called out as Pop rolled down the driver's side window. "I figured I could find y'all out here."

"What's the deal, Tommy?" Pop greeted the man.

"What's good, my nigga?" Will asked.

"Yo, the nigga, Eduardo, sold me a twenty jar of that sour-diesel – told me I could get it from y'all," Tommy said quietly.

"He wasn't lying to you," Pop chuckled.

"I sell sour with my nigga, Jay, down Southwest," Tommy continued. "We been going to his connect in Harlem to get it, but that drive is too much, plus that shit you had was that kill! How much you selling ounces for?"

"They're going for three-seventy-five," Will replied. "No sticks, no seeds, no stems. We take all that bullshit out."

"Alright, that's what's up," Tommy said eagerly. "When can I get two ounces of that?"

"When will you have the bread?" Pop asked.

"Shit! I'll go meet up with Jay and have the bread together in an hour. We sell like two ounces a day out the crib in Southwest, so if this is gonna be the same good shit you're gonna give me, then we'll be doing some big shit together," Tommy informed the young hustlers. "I'll be back," Tommy said before pulling off.

"This is good shit!" Pop exclaimed as the young men smiled at each other and pounded their fists together.

"Yeah, it is," Will concurred. "But remember, we gotta put half of this sour-diesel money away to put on Cannon's commissary."

"Yeah, of course I remember," Pop said gruffly. "He's *my* cousin! But anyway… I was thinking – I'ma ask Cannon who his connect is for the sour-diesel. We're gonna need it if shit pops off the way Tommy says it will!"

"True," Will agreed. "I hope it does!"

Meanwhile, at Devin's parents' house on Pulaski Street in Germantown, Devin's younger brother, Darren, was trying to figure out what was wrong with his brother. Devin was twenty-five years old. Darren was twenty-three, and they both lived with their parents. Devin had lived with a girlfriend for two years but when they broke up, he moved back home and decided to go to college. Now, at twenty-five years of age, his schedule consisted of working part-time at a sneaker store, going to community college part-time, playing pick-up games of basketball often and playing video games. On the other hand, Darren was a marijuana dealer who worked part-time as a bartender. He made a decent amount of money, but he also spent it all.

For the past week and a half, Darren had been trying to figure out why his older brother wouldn't leave the house. He hadn't gone to work, he hadn't gone to school, they hadn't played basketball together and, as a matter of fact, his brother seemed to be depressed. He stayed in his room all the time with the door closed and barely came out to take a shower, from what Darren had noticed. On this particular night and time, while Will and Pop were discussing selling sour diesel and killing Devin, Darren was knocking on Devin's bedroom door.

"Come in," Devin called out lazily. He lay in bed staring at the television. He didn't even look up to see who had entered his room.

"Yo, Devin, I need to talk to you, bro," Darren said urgently as he closed the bedroom door behind him. "Come on nigga, get up," he tapped his brother's feet.

"Why, what's up?" Devin asked, unconcerned, as he lifted his feet and sat up on his bed, leaning against the wall and staring at the ceiling.

"I know something's wrong with you, man," Darren began. "Talk to me about it…"

"Nothing's wrong," Devin sighed.

"Well, I was tryna be nice, but to tell you the truth, you've been acting like a bitch this past week and a half!" Darren snapped. "You've been moping around and shit, you haven't left the crib and you're barely taking showers – what the fuck is wrong with you?"

"I'm scared, Darren," Devin admitted and started to get choked up. "I'm really scared!"

"Scared about what, Devin? What you got to be afraid of?

"Remember when I told you Tracey and them got shot on the basketball courts and I was there?" Devin began.

"Yeah, and I said we should go look for the nigga who did that," Darren blurted out.

"What I didn't tell you was that I volunteered to identify the shooter and got him locked up," Devin confessed.

"You snitched on him?" Darren asked in shock. "I know you don't have a gangster bone in your body, but damn, dog! I told you we could go look for the nigga!"

"But let me explain," Devin continued. "I didn't tell you about it until that night. By the time I told you about it he was already locked up! It was weird the way the cops did it, though. After the ambulances took everybody away and the cops got my statement, they had me get in the car with them and drive around the hood looking for the nigga who did it. After about a half-hour, I saw the shooter and pointed him out. They followed him into the corner store and gripped him up and brought him outside. I was still in the back of the squad-car. Then they asked me, right in front of him and his homeys, if he did it! I thought they were gonna take us to the district and do a line-up and all that, but they didn't make me do that till afterward. I can't believe they let him see me! They even called me 'Devin' right in front of the guy and his homeys!"

"That's fucked up," Darren gasped. "You should file a complaint."

"What's that gonna do at this point?" Devin made a valid point. "But that's not the worst part! Last week I was coming out the crib and I saw the nigga's car ride past. The same exact twenty-twelve, convertible Mustang - a black jawn with dark-ass tints and twenties on it! I couldn't see inside but I know if I could, it would've been him – Malik Davidson; he told the cops that's what his name was. I think he made bail and he's looking for me now! He was staring at me like he wanted to murder me right then and there when I pointed him out. He's kind of intimidating, Darren; diesel, bald-head nigga with a beard and a lot of tattoos!"

"Stop acting like a bitch, Devin," Darren smirked. "Ain't nobody gonna hurt my brother! You know I got your back! Now you need to get your ass out of this funky-ass mood and get out the crib. It's too late tonight, but you're going to the Crab House with me tomorrow, nigga!"

The next morning, Will woke up at eight-o'clock and got ready for the day. When he finished, he called the number he had found online for the room-for-rent in Nicetown. The man he spoke to told him they could meet there in an hour. So, Will decided to walk down the block to Pop's house and see if he was going to be ready soon.

"Hi, Will," Miss Davidson, Pop's mother, greeted him as she opened the front door and let him in. "Darryl is still in the shower. You can take a seat."

"Thank you, Miss Davidson," Will answered politely as he sat down on the sofa.

"Would you like anything to drink, Will?" Miss Davidson asked.

"No, thank you, ma'am."

"That's a nice Cadillac you have parked on the block," Miss Davidson continued. "And my son is driving my nephew's new car around…"

"I'm sorry, but I don't know what you're saying, ma'am," Will hesitated.

"You boys and your drugs!" Miss Davidson shook her head. "My advice is to stick with the basketball, Will. At least you've got talent there! You can probably get a scholarship to college."

"Thank you, ma'am," Will replied.

An awkward silence followed. Miss Davidson went about her business around the house and Will just sat in silence on the sofa and waited for Pop, who came downstairs about fifteen minutes later.

"You ready, homey?" Will asked.

"Yeah, no doubt," Pop replied. The two teenagers walked outside.

"Yo, Pop, your mom was all up in my shit about hustling, dog," Will sighed. "She was like, 'stick with basketball; go to college; why you got a Cadillac?'"

"Yeah, she be coming at me about hustling, too," Pop replied. "She never tells me to go to college though – probably 'cause she knows we can't afford it!"

Within the hour, Will drove himself and Pop to the property with the room-for-rent at Twenty-First Street and Venango Street in Nicetown. When he pulled up in his Cadillac, all the young hustlers standing on the corner stared enviously at Will and his car. Even though the Cadillac wasn't brand new, it was still very luxurious. All Will felt the need to do was get the windows tinted, which he planned on doing at his earliest opportunity.

The maintenance man of the property was waiting on the stoop of the house, which was a three-story row-home. He stared at Will and Pop when they pulled up, wondering if they were the future tenants who had called about the room.

"Hey, sir, I talked to you on the phone about a room-for-rent," Will called out to the maintenance man as he walked up the first set of steps, leading up to the stoop.

"Hey, buddy! Your name was James, right?" the maintenance man said as he reached out to shake Will's hand. Will had told the man that his name was James because he was using a fake driver's license and Social Security Number under the name 'James Wright' just in case the place was ever raided by the police while he wasn't there, there would be no connection to him and Pop. "I'm Ernie!"

"Nice to meet you, Ernie," Will replied. "This is my friend Johnnie… you'll probably see him around here with me sometimes."

"That's fine! Do what you do; I don't judge," Ernie replied, winking at the two and smiling.

"Naw, man! Not like that," Pop objected. "Never mind!"

"So, everything looks good. Where do I sign?" Will asked after seeing the medium-sized room.

"Here's the month-to-month lease," Ernie replied. "I just need your driver's license and Social Security card for a minute. Rent for the medium-sized room is four-fifty per month."

"Here's two months in advance," Will said as he handed the documents over, along with nine-hundred dollars cash to cover the first two month's rent.

"Oh, thanks," Ernie smiled. "I'll write you out a receipt! Here's your keys – one for the front door and one for your room."

Will and Pop left the house. It was only nine-fifteen in the morning and they weren't meeting the girls until eleven-thirty, so they decided to go to the store and buy some furniture for the room. Will's uncle had a pickup truck, so they drove to his house and borrowed the truck. After leaving Will's uncle's house, they made their way to Wal-Mart on Adams Avenue and Roosevelt Boulevard and bought a futon, a thirty-two-inch television, a television stand, a window air conditioner and a safe, and put them in the back of the truck. Next they went to a furniture store on the way back to their new room and bought a round, glass-top dining room table, similar to what Rick had, and secured that in the back of the pickup truck as well. By the time they had purchased everything and moved the boxes and furnishings into the room and then returned the pickup truck to Will's uncle, it was time to pick up the girls.

"What's up, ladies?" the teenagers greeted CeCe and Veronica as they hopped into the back seat of Will's Cadillac.

"Not too much," Veronica replied.

"We're ready to get this paper!" CeCe answered eagerly.

"That's cool," Will started. "Look girls, we don't want you to say anything to Rick yet... we wanna tell him; but we got our own stash-spot and y'all gonna be working out of there probably starting in two days. We just gotta get it set up first."

"Okay, okay! Y'all moving up in the world, I see!" Veronica grinned.

"That's what's up, baby! Congratulations!" CeCe congratulated Pop as she rubbed his shoulders from the backseat. "Naw, we won't say anything to Rick."

"Yeah, we don't even know him like that," Veronica agreed. Just then, Veronica's phone rang. She looked at it to see who was calling – it was Jasiel. He had been calling her repeatedly ever since the horrible incident had occurred, and she had been ignoring every one of his calls. Little did she know how angry this was making Jasiel. "Oh my God! Jasiel will not stop calling me!" Veronica complained.

"I can put a bullet in his head and make him stop," Will muttered under his breath.

"Hey, that's my cousin!" CeCe objected. "It's through marriage, but still!"

Five hours later, after the girls had bagged up the cocaine, Will dropped them off at CeCe's house. As they were the only ones home, they went into CeCe's room, closed and locked the door, listened to music, danced and smoked some weed that Pop had given CeCe.

After about an hour, there was a loud, persistent banging on the front door. CeCe rushed to the bathroom and flushed the rest of the weed down the toilet thinking it might be the police at the door. She sprayed some air freshener and then answered the door.

"Where the fuck is she at?" Jasiel stormed in, looking around the living room. CeCe just stared at him, confused. "That bitch, Ronnie!" Jasiel barked. "I know she's here! She better be here! She's not at home!"

"Yeah, Jasiel… she's upstairs," CeCe admitted. "But why she gotta be a bitch though? And why did you smack her?"

"None of your fucking business! Mind your goddamn business, Cyndal, okay?" Jasiel roared, using his cousin's government name.

Upstairs, Veronica was quaking in fear. She heard the whole conversation and had a flashback of that night in Jasiel's living room. She thought about hiding in CeCe's closet, or under her bed, but then felt the idea was childish. Besides, what would Jasiel possibly do to her in front of his cousin?

Veronica exited CeCe's bedroom and slowly walked down the stairs into the living room. As soon as Jasiel caught sight of Veronica out of the corner of his eye, he rushed over to the young woman, who was several inches taller than he was, and gripped her by her throat.

"Don't you ever ignore my calls, bitch!" Jasiel growled. Veronica's eyes watered as Jasiel pressed down on her throat with a vice-like grip. She fell backwards onto the stairs, but Jasiel remained on top of her. "Don't treat me like I'm some fucking sucker, bitch!"

CeCe rushed over to the stairs and attempted to remove Jasiel's hand from Veronica's throat, but to no avail. Then she began to punch and kick Jasiel in his back, desperately trying to get him off of her friend.

"Get off of her!" CeCe screamed. "You're crazy! What's wrong with you? Get off of her!"

Jasiel finally released his grip. Veronica rubbed her throat in pain as she coughed and gasped for air, while still lying on the steps.

"You don't leave me – I leave you!" Jasiel screamed, pointing his finger in Veronica's face. "We're not over until I say we're over!" Then he stormed out of the front door, slamming it shut. The girls looked at each other in horror as they heard the tires of Jasiel's car squeal as he sped off.

That night, in Germantown, Devin and Darren were preparing themselves to go out and finally have some fun.

"You ready, nigga?" Darren asked as he knocked on Devin's bedroom door.

"Yeah, I'm ready, but I really think I should stay home," Devin groaned.

"I told you I got your back, big brother! Ain't nobody gonna do shit to you while I'm around," Darren assured his brother.

"Shit, how does that sound?" Devin chuckled. "A younger brother protecting his older brother? I guess it is what it is…"

"Yeah man, it is what it is," Darren agreed. "We all know you ain't no thug! Let's just go out, have some drinks and meet some bitches!"

Meanwhile, in Nicetown, Pop and Will picked up Stacy in the Mustang to go search for Devin. This night they rode around until eleven-thirty, not only driving around the Greater Germantown Area, but also around parts of Mount Airy, too. Up and down the blocks they went, but with no success in finding Devin. They were headed home, down Germantown Avenue, to make a right onto Chelten Avenue, when Devin and Darren walked out of the Crab House.

"Oh shit!" Devin exclaimed as he jumped behind his brother in an attempt to hide. "That's the Mustang right there!"

"You want me to bust at that nigga?" Darren asked, reaching for the gun on his waist.

"Naw, man," Devin grabbed his brother's arm and pulled it down. "Not with all these cops out here! But now you see why I'm shook?"

"Don't worry, nigga, I got you!" Darren said, attempting to reassure his frightened brother.

Once Pop and Will dropped Stacy off and went back to Ninth Street, unaware that they had just missed Devin and had almost been shot at while they were in Germantown, they started hustling again. Will's mind was going a mile-per-minute. He was frustrated that they couldn't find Devin. He thought they definitely would have seen him around Germantown by now. They had gone looking for him several times already, and spent hours doing so. Then it dawned on him.

"This nigga's avoiding us, Pop," Will blurted out.

"Huh? Who?" Pop asked, not understanding who Will was referring to.

"Devin... he probably knows the Mustang from the day of the shooting," Will continued. "I wouldn't be surprised if this nigga has seen us riding around and has been fleeing us."

"True, that might be a possibility," Pop agreed.

"So, tomorrow morning I'ma get the Caddy tinted, and tomorrow night we'll take my car when we go hunting..."

CHAPTER 9

At ten-o'clock the next morning, true to his word, Will went to an automobile accessory shop on Broad Street and had fifteen-percent tints installed on the windows of the Cadillac. The tints were dark and he hoped he wouldn't be harassed by the police for their darkness, especially since he sold drugs out of his car and carried a gun. But it was a risk he would have to take, especially since he and Pop needed to find Devin.

After Will had the Cadillac's windows tinted, he called Tommy to obtain the phone number for Tommy's friend, Mitch, who installed stash-boxes in cars and trucks. Will figured he needed one now that he had a nice-looking vehicle, a "cop-magnet." He went to Mitch's house in West Philadelphia and, for one-thousand dollars, Mitch installed a compartment in Will's vehicle in which he could hide a fair amount of drugs and one handgun.

By the time Will had finished having the modifications made to his car it was one-o'clock in the afternoon. As Will entered his vehicle, he reached into his pocket and pulled out his phone to call Pop. When he looked at his phone, he saw that he had inadvertently left it on silent from when he was sleeping and had missed several calls – a few from customers, two from Pop and one from Veronica. Will cursed under his breath for his negligence. All of the phone calls were important to him – especially those from his customers. He figured Pop was calling about business as well. Will and Veronica had spoken on the telephone several times already since they had exchanged phone numbers, although she had confessed to Will that she had started dating Jasiel again out of fear of what Jasiel might do if she continued to avoid him. Will had offered to confront Jasiel and "handle him for her," but Veronica decided against it. In any event, when Will saw that he had so many missed phone calls, he decided to return Pop's calls first.

"What up, Will?" Pop answered. "I called you a couple times to see where you're at with it. I'm on the block now."

"Yeah, my fault I missed your calls, my nigga," Will apologized. "My phone was on silent. I had to get the windows tinted on the wheel and get a stash-box put in."

"Oh okay, that's what's up," Pop responded. "I wanna get a stashbox but I can't start chopping up Cannon's wheel like that. I gotta wait till I get my own. He probably has one in here, but I don't know where. Oh... by the way, some of your customers came through the block so I served them while I was out here."

"Good looking out," Will thanked Pop. "Ay, yo... I'm tryna get the stash-spot together today before I get out on the block. Are you gonna come with me and put this furniture together when I get back to the hood? I'm on my way back from West Philly now."

"I would, but I gotta go see Cannon," Pop reminded Will. "I gotta find out about the connect and put money on his books. I'll get with you when I get back, though, so we can go find that snitch nigga!"

"Alright, cool," Will said and hung up. Next, he called the customers back who had tried to reach him while he had been out that morning, but they all told him that they had received their product from Pop. After completing the phone calls to his customers, Will finally called Veronica back.

"Hello, *papi*," Veronica answered, using her sexiest voice.

"What's up, sexy?" Will replied, turned on by Veronica's greeting.

"My fault I missed your call. What you up to?"

"Nothing, just thinking about you, *papi*!" In actuality, Veronica was waiting for Jasiel to pick her up and take her to the movies, even though she didn't want to have anything to do with him. Will had been on her mind, though, which is why she had called him, hoping to reach him before Jasiel arrived. "What you up to?"

"Shit! You know just what to say," Will smiled. "I'm on my way back from out West. I was handling some shit. I'm about to go get the spot ready for when we cop tomorrow so y'all can work out of the new spot."

"I can't wait to see it!" Veronica exclaimed, excitedly.

"Well, I can't wait to see you, ma," Will replied. "I was thinking we could chill later on tonight. I got some shit to handle in the evening, but maybe around eleven I can pick you up and bring you over to Ninth Street."

"I can't wait to see you either, Will," Veronica responded. "Yeah, eleven works. But I think I'll walk, though. I don't want that crazy-ass Jasiel to see you picking me up! He would probably wile out!"

Twenty minutes later, as Will was pulling up to the building in Nicetown, Pop was parking at the jail. He had his fake identification ready in order to visit his older cousin and he had the cash on hand to add to Cannon's commissary account like he promised he would. After being searched, depositing the money and waiting in line for what seemed like an eternity, Pop was finally able to see Cannon.

"What up, Pop?" Cannon greeted his cousin with a smile. "What's good with you, my nigga?"

"Ain't too much, man," Pop replied. "Out here grinding, man. I got bread stacked for you. I put some on your books today."

"Good looking out," Cannon thanked Pop. "You get rid of any more of those bitches yet?" Cannon asked, referring to the guns.

"Only two of them," Pop replied, referring to the two that he was paying for himself for the stash-spot. "I'm tryna find people to grab them, without getting caught; and I'm not tryna sell them to my customers for obvious reasons. But that sour is moving. Matter-of-fact – I need your connect..."

"Word?" Cannon asked, surprised. "It's moving like that?"

"We hooked up with some Southwest niggas and they do their thing," Pop explained. "They about to start copping QPs instead of circles," Pop proclaimed proudly.

"Okay, little cousin!" Cannon chuckled. "I see you're doing your thing out here! The connect is an African old-head, Jeremiah, at Front and Rising Sun. He uses the pay phone there at the 7-Eleven. Tell him you're my cousin."

"Alright, bet! Good looking out, Cannon!"

"So what's up with the other boy from Germantown?" Cannon asked, obviously worried. "Do I still need to stress about that?"

"Naw, you don't need to stress about it, cousin," Pop assured Cannon. "We have a new plan. We're going out tonight to look for the nigga."

"Well, I hope you actually find 'something' this time," Cannon snapped under his breath. "Seems like y'all been doing a lot of looking without finding shit!"

"We will, cuz, we will! Trust me," Pop tried to reassure his older cousin.

"Yeah… I trust you, but I'll feel better when it's done!"

"It'll get done, Cannon. I promise." Pop hesitated before asking Cannon a question. "What about your connect for the bitches? Where do you get them from? I'ma need to get more when I run out…"

"Nigga, what… you tryna put me outta business?" Cannon whispered fiercely. "You ain't even off them jawns yet! Just be happy I gave you the sour connect and stop being greedy! I should be out this motherfucker soon if you handle your business!"

"You're right," Pop replied as he looked at the floor, embarrassed. "But I would never try to steal your connects, Cannon! I'm just tryna help you out, dog. You feel me?"

"Davidson – time's up!" Cannon got up and walked away without answering Pop. Pop left CFCF in a bad mood, hoping his cousin didn't think that he would try to do anything sneaky and also hoping his cousin didn't have any ill-will towards him.

It was after three-o'clock in the afternoon by the time Pop arrived at the room he and Will had rented to use as a stash-spot in Nicetown. Will had borrowed his uncle's tools and had assembled the table, chairs and TV stand, but decided to wait for Pop before he assembled the futon.

"Yo, can you give me a hand with this jawn?" Will asked Pop, pointing to the large futon that was sitting in the middle of the floor.

"Yeah, no problem. You already did everything else," Pop replied as they began to use their knives to open the large box. "I'm looking at this TV and wondering why we didn't get a DVD player…"

"Yeah," Will agreed. "I thought about that after I put the TV stand together! I'ma grab one soon, though, or just bring my Xbox 360 over so we can play games, watch movies or listen to music while the girls are bagging up. How did the visit with Cannon go?"

"Oh, it was alright, I guess," Pop replied, dejected.

"If it was alright, then why are you looking all miserable?"

"Because it didn't end well. I asked him about his gun connect and he got pissed at me, then the visit was over. He was acting like I was tryna jerk him for all his business. He gave me the sour connect, though – some African nigga who hangs out in Feltonville by the 7-Eleven on Rising Sun. Cannon told me to go holler at him when we need to."

"That's what's up! We got the sour-diesel connect," Will replied happily. "Especially since Tommy and Jay are about to start copping quarter-pounds. When I got Tommy's homey's number from him earlier, Tommy was saying he might have some more business for us too!"

"That *is* good," Pop agreed. "I'm definitely happy about that! I just don't want my cousin thinking I'm shiesty. He was also complaining about how we didn't find Devin yet. I don't want him to think I'm not looking out for him while he's sitting in jail."

"Why would he think that?" Will objected. "You're keeping his commissary as fat as the jail will let you. You visit him every week. Why wouldn't he trust you? I know you're not shiesty, and Cannon knows it, too. He just getting impatient 'cause he's sitting up in that cell thinking Devin might show up to court and wishing he could merck him himself! But we'll get him soon. Don't worry. I know your cousin trusts you. I trust you with my life and this is what we're dealing with – Cannon's life. Y'all are family, so he *has* to trust you! If he didn't, he wouldn't have given you his keys to his crib, the guns, the weed and his car, na'mean?"

"I guess you're right," Pop sighed. "Thanks for the pep-talk, my nigga!"

"No problem, my nigga! Now let's put this futon together so we can pick up Stacy and go find this snitch-nigga, Devin!"

Will called Stacy and let her know he and Pop would be over after they were finished assembling the futon so they could go to Germantown and search for the snitch. Stacy was still reluctant to do the job, but after going with them on several occasions and not finding the guy, she had actually started to feel hopeful that they would never find who they were looking for. Maybe then she wouldn't have to be involved in the murder plot after all.

Within an hour, the two teenagers pulled up to Stacy's building. Will called Stacy on her cell phone and she came outside. As Will and Pop had discussed the previous night, they were taking Will's newly-tinted vehicle, just in case Devin had spotted the Mustang around Germantown and remembered it from the day of the shooting at the basketball court. Both Will and Pop hoped changing vehicles would make a difference, but this remained to be seen.

"Hey, baby. Hey, Pop," Stacy greeted the young men as she climbed into the back seat of the Cadillac.

"What's up, sexy?" Will greeted his girlfriend. The words seemed strange to him, as he had just used the very same phrase when addressing Veronica on the phone a couple of hours prior. Was he perhaps developing a conscience? "You look good as hell, baby."

"You know I always wanna impress you, Will," Stacy said with a large smile.

"And you definitely do that, Stace," Will confirmed, "But you're gonna have to impress this snitch-nigga when we find him and put you on his top!"

"Damn, Will! Do you have to say it like that?" Stacy whined.

"Sorry, baby, but it is what it is," Will replied matter-of-factly. "We need you for this."

"But you make it sound so harsh," Stacy complained.

"What Will means," Pop intervened, "is that you're the only one that we can trust to do this for us, Stacy, and we really appreciate it. You just have to be really nice to the guy so that he wants to go out with you after you meet him the first time – then we can handle our business."

"Oh, okay," Stacy said, feeling a bit more calm. "I still don't like the whole idea, but I know you're doing it for Cannon and I'll do anything for my man, so it's cool."

"Thanks, baby," Will said, and the three made their way to Germantown. They rode around for a little over an hour before Will and Pop were both overcome with frustration.

"Where the fuck is this nigga, man?" Pop exclaimed.

"Why you asking me, nigga?" Will snapped back. "How am I supposed to know? We drove all over Germantown and shit – up and down every block looking for this nigga!"

"Guys, don't fight," Stacy chimed in. "It's nobody's fault. Maybe we should take a break. I'm hungry anyway. There's a Burger King right there – can we stop, baby?"

Will turned into the parking lot of the Burger King on Chelten Avenue. As his car idled in the long drive-through line and he was about to ask Stacy what she wanted to order, he looked to his left and noticed a man sitting by the window inside of the restaurant. Will frantically tapped Pop, who was looking out of the passenger's side window, steaming mad, on the arm.

"Look, Pop, look!" Will excitedly pointed out of his dark, driver's side window, toward the restaurant. "You see that brown-skinned, curly-haired nigga sitting down?"

"Oh, shit!" Pop's eyes grew large with recognition. The two teenagers pounded fists in excitement as they watched the man take a bite out of his hamburger.

"What?" Stacy asked curiously as she looked in the direction Will was pointing.

"That's the nigga we've been looking for," the two boys answered in unison. Will cut his wheel to the right and pulled out of the line for the drive-through window and parked on the opposite side of the parking lot so the back of his car was facing the window of the building.

"Okay, baby," Will instructed Stacy. "You gotta get in there and talk to him before he finishes eating. What you gotta do is go in there, act like he caught your eye, *before you order your food*, because it might take too long to get it line first, start a conversation with him and exchange numbers with him. Can you handle that, ma?"

"Uh... um...," Stacy stuttered. "I guess..."

"Baby, come on... I really need you to do this for me," Will pleaded. "I love you, baby. This is gonna help us out so much!"

"Oh... okay!" Stacy exited the car, cursing herself for wanting something to eat in the first place. She figured if she hadn't asked to get some food, the three of them would have driven around for another hour or two and then gone home.

Stacy purposely strutted into the Burger King hoping the young man, Devin, would notice her when she walked in. He had just taken a bite of his hamburger and looked up at Stacy and stared for a moment before looking back down. Stacy fixed her gaze on Devin as she approached the line for service then, as she was halfway to the line, Devin looked back up at her and stared back. She smiled at him and he smiled back. The voluptuous teenager changed her course and began to walk in Devin's direction, at which point Devin sat up straight in his seat and awaited her arrival.

"Hey, you," Stacy greeted the thin, brown-skinned, curly-haired stranger. "I'm Stacy... what's your name?"

"I'm Devin. How are you doing, Stacy?" Devin replied. "You wanna sit down?"

"Well, I was about to get my food, but you are so cute, I *had* to introduce myself," Stacy almost choked on her words. She didn't feel right talking to anybody other than Will in that manner.

"Well, you're beautiful, sis," Devin replied. "I'm glad you came over! I know I'm not supposed to ask a woman how old she is, but how old are you?"

"Twenty-one," Stacy lied, as she was still a teenager going into her senior-year in high-school. "How old are you?"

"Oh me? I'm twenty-five," Devin informed her. "So, I was wondering if I could call you…"

"You sure can, Devin," Stacy replied as she saved her phone number in his cell phone. "You can call me now so I have your number, too."

After Stacy saved Devin's number into her phone, they said their goodbyes and she entered the line to order her food. Devin finished eating while Stacy was still in line and he waved to her again as he was leaving. Stacy was so upset with herself for being involved in this plot. They had only spoken for a few moments but Devin seemed like a nice enough person. Here she was, involved in a plot to have him killed. She voiced her thoughts and concerns to Will and Pop when she got back into Will's Cadillac.

"Baby, he's a snitch," Will reminded Stacy.

"And he's snitching on my cousin," Pop added. "My cousin could go to prison for decades because of this dude's rat-ass."

"But…"

"And he did it right in front of our faces," Will interrupted before Stacy could continue. "He knew what could happen!"

"You shouldn't feel sorry for him, Stacy," Pop stated calmly. "It is what it is – snitches have to get dealt with in the hood."

"Yeah… I guess y'all are right," Stacy agreed.

"Good," Will said. "So, do me a favor, baby. Call him tonight, talk to him for a while and make him feel comfortable with you. Then set up a date and time when you can go out together and let us know when. You still got that fake ID I got you, right?"

"Yeah."

"Good. Tell him you wanna go to that bar down Second and Cumberland, Three Elements, the jawn I took you to before," Will instructed. "We're gonna be waiting on the side-street, where they rob people sometimes, you know, Palethorp. Matter-of-fact, tell him to park there. Then, at midnight, tell him you wanna go out to his car and get freaky. There's no way he'll turn that down. When you get out there, we'll be there and we'll handle our business. You just gotta text us the information on his car when he picks you up, okay baby?"

"Oh my God," Stacy exclaimed when she heard the plot. "But okay," Stacy reluctantly agreed. "Anything for my baby! Are you coming over tonight after you drop Pop off?"

"Naw, ma, sorry," Will apologized as he pulled up to Stacy's building. "I didn't even get out on the block at all today and we gotta go cop some more tomorrow. I need to be out making this money tonight, baby."

Will wasn't lying. He was going to hustle for a few hours, but he knew that when eleven-o'clock came around, he would be spending time with Veronica.

Will dropped Pop off and went to the corner of Ninth Street and Lycoming Street to hustle. Pop got into Cannon's Mustang and went to the other side of the park on the corner of Old York Road and Lycoming Street. They had picked up some customers from the new corner since they had been posted up over there, and it was proving profitable for them to be on both corners at the same time.

On this night, however, Will had an ulterior motive for wanting to be stationed on the old block on Ninth and Lycoming Streets. Veronica lived on Sixth and Lycoming, so when she came to visit Will that night, he would be closer to where she was coming from and Pop wouldn't see her coming as he would if he had been hustling there. Will had a dilemma, however, because although he would be close to home on the same block, he couldn't take Veronica to his mother's house because his mother liked Stacy so much and would probably tell on him. Maybe he could take her to the stash-spot, but that was around the corner from Stacy so that wasn't a good idea either. He had two options – stay in the car or take Veronica to a hotel if they were going to be intimate. But it was all just wishful thinking at the moment. This was the first time they were hanging out one-on-one.

At eleven-o'clock sharp, Veronica came walking around the corner. Will rolled down his window and called out to her and she quickly ran over to the passenger's side of the car and hopped in. She had had a rough day with Jasiel. He had promised to take Veronica to the movies, but instead he took her back to his house and had unpleasantly rough sex with her. She decided not to share this with Will. She honestly just didn't know what to do. Maybe when they grew closer she would let him save her from Jasiel.

Will had pulled away from the corner so his customers didn't think he was still working and, instead, pulled in front of his house up the street. Will could tell Veronica had something weighing on her mind, but she insisted that she was okay and didn't need to talk about anything. Will and Veronica sat in his car and talked and listened to music for several hours before she decided to kiss Will goodbye and walk home. As she exited the vehicle, Pop drove by and saw her.

"I thought that nigga was supposed to be working, but he's fucking with Veronica," Pop thought to himself as he shook his head in disappointment. "He's fucking up!" Pop said to himself. "That's gonna bring more beef with Jasiel and Jose."

CHAPTER 10

The next morning around eleven-o'clock, Will and Pop picked up CeCe and Veronica from CeCe's house and drove to Rick's spot. When they arrived, they instructed the girls to wait in the Cadillac as they went in and procured the two ounces of cocaine and spoke with Rick.

"What's up, fellas?" Rick greeted Will and Pop at the door. "Come on in! You ain't got the young girls with you today?" Rick asked, as he couldn't see the girls waiting in the car due to the dark tints on the windows.

"Yeah, we do," Pop hesitated as he and Will followed Rick upstairs. "They're in the wheel."

"Oh, okay," Rick replied as he opened his safe. "Why aren't they coming in?"

"That's actually what we wanted to talk to you about." Will watched Rick as he took an eighth of a kilogram (four and a half ounces) of cocaine out of the safe, placed it on the scale and weighed and bagged two ounces for the teenagers.

"What you needed to talk to me about?" Rick asked with a quite stern look on his face as he handed the two ounces to Will and Will handed Rick twenty-two hundred dollars.

"Oh, not much," Will tried to minimize things, hoping the news he was about to share wouldn't upset Rick. "We got our own stash-spot the other day, so we won't need to bag up here anymore. That's why the girls waited in the car. We're about to head over there." Will handed the ounces to Pop so he could put them in his backpack where he had also been keeping his gun.

"Oh, I see," Rick scratched his chin. "I'm happy for y'all that you're getting money like that, but you know the agreement was that Tiny wanted me to make sure you do things right and don't fuck up, right?"

"Yeah, I know," Will acknowledged, "but I've been hustling for almost five years now and if I was gonna fuck up, I would've done it by now, na'mean? I ain't never been booked, I've never been robbed, and when y'all was fronting me the work, before I had money to buy it outright, I never came up short. I'm not gonna fuck up!"

"I see your point," Rick acknowledged. "Well, I'll tell Tiny and see what he says about it…"

"Damn, man," Will sighed. "Why you gotta go and tell Tiny? Why can't we just keep it between the three of us?"

"First of all, because that's my boss," Rick replied sharply. "Second of all, 'cause it ain't just between the three of us – those two young girls in the car know too, and one of them is Tiny's niece! What if she tells him? That would be my ass!"

"She ain't gonna tell him," Pop interjected. "They don't even want him to know they work for us!"

"Yeah, come on Rick," Will pleaded. "Keep it gangster, dog! Don't tell Tiny…"

"Oh… alright, y'all," Rick agreed hesitantly. "But if he finds out, it's gonna be a problem!"

"Good looking out, Rick! We'll get with you in two days for the next two onions!" they said and then left.

The four young people left Rick's stash-house near Sixth and Butler Streets and headed to Will and Pop's spot near the intersection of Twenty-First and Venango Streets. When they arrived, they all exited the vehicle; Pop grabbed his backpack with the ounces of coke while Will went into the trunk and retrieved the duffle bag Pop brought which held the sawed-off shotgun and a forty-caliber handgun for the stash-spot. Pop unlocked the door and led the way as Will and the girls followed him upstairs to the second floor and into the room.

"Oh, this is nice!" CeCe exclaimed as she entered the room and looked around.

"Yeah, it is," Veronica concurred. "Y'all hooked this room up! CeCe, we're fucking with some ballers!" Veronica winked at Will.

"Thanks, y'all," Pop replied, smiling proudly. "It ain't a house, but we did what we could!"

Will pulled the guns out of the duffle bag, carefully placed the forty-caliber handgun under the cushion of the futon, and placed the shotgun in the narrow closet.

"Damn Will! What, you ready for war?" Veronica chuckled.

"Pretty much," Will laughed. "We don't want nobody running up in here tryna take our shit. If they try we'll be ready for them!"

The girls bagged up the product until about four-thirty in the afternoon while Will and Pop smoked and played video games. When they had finished, Will dropped the girls back off at CeCe's house. When Will and Pop were finally alone, Pop decided to bring up what had been weighing on his mind since the previous night.

"Yo, Will, what you doing, dog?" Pop sighed.

"What you mean? I'm going back to Ninth Street to drop you off at your car so we can get out on the block! The customers have been calling all day!"

"Naw man... what you doing fucking with the girl, Ronnie?" Pop clarified. "You been mixing business with pleasure, nigga? I saw her getting out your wheel late last night. You're fucking up!"

"You mix business with pleasure, too," Will replied. "You mess with CeCe, so what's the difference?"

"The difference is, Veronica is Jasiel's girl," Pop snapped. "What if he was the one who drove by instead of me? He probably would've snapped and sprayed up your wheel! We don't need beef with them niggas Jasiel and Jose, man!"

"Listen to you, talking like you shook of them niggas," Will smirked slyly. "How many times do I have to tell y'all that I ain't worried about that nigga? That nigga ain't killing shit!"

"Now, you know I ain't scared of *nobody!*" Pop roared as they pulled up next to the Mustang. "I just don't want any unnecessary beef! I already know it's gonna be us against them one of these days!"

"Fuck it then," Will replied. "If they want beef, they can come get it!"

Pop shook his head as he grabbed his backpack with his gun and drugs inside and exited the passenger's side door. Just then, Jasiel's silver Pontiac Bonneville pulled up next to the pearl-white Cadillac. Pop was still standing in the doorway of the Cadillac and he grew nervous when he saw Jasiel's diabolical smile as he rolled down the driver's side window of the Pontiac. Pop unzipped his backpack and reached into it, gripping the handle of his gun while standing his ground. Will looked up and, as he noticed Jasiel and Jose, grabbed his gun off of his waist and placed it in his lap.

"What's up, Pop? What's up, Will?" Jasiel called out in the heat of the late afternoon. "Nice Caddy, Will!"

"Thanks," Will replied coldly as he gripped his firearm. "What y'all want?"

"Aw, we're just out here looking for a come-up, so we decided to come through your block," Jasiel grinned menacingly.

"For real, nigga? We ain't no come-ups, so you can get the fuck outta here! You really wanna do this in broad daylight?" Pop asked as he looked around to make sure the police weren't within sight and partially lifted his gun from his backpack, revealing the handle.

"Maybe next time, *maricon*," Jasiel peeled off down Ninth Street, laughing wildly, tires squealing.

"You see what I mean?" Pop leaned over into the car and addressed Will. "Imagine if he knew you were fucking his girl!"

"Look, I didn't even fuck – *yet!*" Will laughed at his own comment and put his gun back on his waist. "Don't worry about those niggas, Pop. Let's get on the block and do what we do best; get this money. I'm going to see Stacy later and find out about this nigga, Devin."

"Alright man, but I think you need to take things more seriously…"

Jose was shaking his head as his brother drove around the neighborhood. His mind was racing. He needed to talk to Jasiel.

"Jasiel, why do you keep riding up on Will and Pop, telling them we're trying to rob them?" Jose asked. "They seem like they're always strapped. If you keep doing that, eventually they're going to come looking for us and try to kill us!"

"Jose, stop acting like a *puta*," Jasiel snapped. "You're bitching-up like Ronnie right now! I'm not worried about those motherfuckers doing anything! If they were gonna do anything, they would have done it by now!"

"Speaking of Veronica," Jose took a long pause before continuing. "Uh... speaking of Veronica, a week or two ago, when I was upstairs, I kinda heard how you slapped her and forced her to give you head ..."

"So what?"

"So... Mama didn't raise us that way. Don't you think that's kind of fucked up?" Jose asked his brother. "She was hysterically crying, man."

"Man, fuck that bitch," Jasiel replied coldly. "She thinks just because she looks good that she can do whatever she wants. I'ma put that bitch in her place!"

"I just think it's kinda fucked up, Jasiel," Jose admitted. "You've been doing some messed up shit lately, dog."

"Like what?" Jasiel turned to his brother and stared at him menacingly. "Look – if you don't like anything I do, just let me know, but I'm not changing for shit! I do what I do 'cause I am who I am! If you don't like it, you can stop fucking with me! I really don't give a fuck!"

"Never mind bro, never mind," Jose changed his mind about having this talk with his brother. He was too intimidated. And by the way Jasiel was acting, he didn't even know what Jasiel might do to him.

Later on, at around ten-thirty that night, Will showed up at Stacy's apartment. Her mother had just left to go out and get high, so Will and Stacy decided to have sex as soon as Will arrived. Stacy's phone rang while she and Will were being intimate so she ignored the call. When they were finished they lay in Stacy's bed, breathing heavily.

"That was great," Stacy panted.

"Isn't it always?" Will smiled as he got up, reached into his pocket and pulled out a jar of sour-diesel, along with a cigar and began rolling the weed for him and Stacy to smoke. Stacy put her bra and panties back on, walked over to her dresser and looked at her phone.

"It was that guy, Devin, who called while we were making love," Stacy informed Will. "Let me call him back, baby."

"Damn, ma, why you in a rush to call the nigga back?" Will questioned his girlfriend gruffly as he continued to roll the blunt.

"Nigga, you're the one who got me involved in this whole mess!" Stacy replied sharply. "Don't talk shit about me calling the nigga back! You told me to get his number and you told me to talk to him on the phone! I'd rather talk to him while you're here anyway."

"You're right," Will replied, defeated. "How'd your conversation go last night?"

"It was cool, I guess," Stacy hesitated, being careful of what she said so as not to upset Will. "We talked for an hour."

"An hour?" Will exclaimed as he finished rolling the blunt and lit it. "I didn't tell you to start dating the nigga!"

"What do you want from me, Will? You told me to make him feel comfortable, so I didn't wanna just get off the phone with him when he was talking a lot," Stacy explained.

"I guess that makes sense…" Will exhaled a mouth full of weed and passed the lit blunt to Stacy.

"Anyway," Stacy continued as she took a long drag of the blunt, "I'm pretty sure he's feeling me. He was telling me all this personal shit about himself."

"Well, just make sure you tell him a bunch of lies," Will directed. "If he tells his friends about you, we don't want this shit traced back to us after me and Pop merck the nigga! You can go ahead and call him now. I'll put my phone on silent in case anybody calls while you're on the phone with him. And make sure you tell him you're trying to hook up with him this Friday."

"Okay, baby," Stacy nodded in agreement before dialing Devin's number.

"Hey Stacy, what's up, ma?" Devin answered the phone eagerly when he saw Stacy's name on his caller ID. She didn't like that he had called her "ma." Will called her "ma," and only he was allowed to call her that.

"P-Please don't call me that," Stacy stuttered. "Uh... my ex used to call me that," Stacy lied.

"Uh... no problem. Sorry, Stacy," Devin replied timidly. "So how are you?"

"I'm good," Stacy answered. "I'm tired though... getting ready for bed. I was in the shower when you called," Stacy lied again, "but I wanted to call you back before I got in bed."

"Oh okay, that's cool. I'll let you go..."

"Wait a second," Stacy interrupted Devin. "What you doing Friday night?"

"I'm working and I have class during the day, but nothing that night. Why, what's up?" Devin asked excitedly.

"I was thinking we could go out – I wanna see you again," Stacy replied with a smile in her voice. Will looked at her, nodded and winked. Her smile immediately vanished, due to her guilt.

"Yeah, that would be great," Devin responded eagerly. "You want me to pick you up at your crib?"

"Maybe when we know each other better, Devin," Stacy declined. "But could you pick me up at the corner of Wayne and Manheim at the bus stop?"

"Definitely, Stacy! What time works for you?"

"I was thinking around nine-thirty if that works for you..."

"Sure does!" Devin was excited. He didn't know what they were doing yet, but he didn't care. He was happy to be meeting up with this fine young woman and to take her out.

"Hey, Devin," Stacy said. "What kind of car do you have so I know what to look for when you pick me up?"

"I have a white Buick Riviera."

"Okay. I'll see you then." Stacy then feigned a yawn. "I'm tired. I'm gonna go to sleep now. Bye."

"See you later, Stacy."

The entire time Stacy had been on the phone, Will had been smoking, listening to the conversation Stacy and Devin were having, and thinking. He attempted to pass Stacy the blunt, but she declined. He shrugged his shoulders, continued smoking, and began speaking.

"Hey ma, I've been thinking – when y'all go to that bar you should leave at like eleven-thirty instead of midnight. Tell him you wanna go to the car and get freaky. Actually, don't tell him you wanna get freaky, just make him think that. Then hold out for like a half-hour and then at eleven-fifty-five tell him you need some more to drink to get comfortable. Send him back in the bar for a forty or some wine-coolers or something. That way, the bartenders and all those people will see that he's back in there by himself a half-hour later, in case the detectives ask. I was thinking the detectives might ask the people in the bar if he was in there with anybody, so this way, the people will tell them 'yeah, but he came back in by himself later', na'mean?"

When Stacy heard Will's instructions, she broke into tears. He just looked at her in shock for a while, not knowing what had prompted her to cry, then he placed his arm around her and pulled her close to him.

"Will, baby, I don't know if I can go through with it," Stacy sobbed. "Devin seems nice. He's so excited to go out with me!"

"What, are you catching feelings for the nigga?" Will snapped as he snatched his arm away from Stacy. "Are you excited to go out with him too?"

"No! You got it all wrong," Stacy objected. "I just feel so shady and evil for doing this! And I don't wanna get caught, baby!"

"We won't," Will tried to reassure her. "And you're not shady or evil. You're helping me and Pop help Cannon. Devin's the shady one – he's the one who snitched."

"Oh... okay baby," Stacy sniffled. "By the way... he drives a white Buick Riviera."

"Okay cool, thanks, ma. Now blow some more of this sour... it will make you feel better!"

That Friday night, Will and Pop were preparing for the events of the evening. They were going to commit murder for the first time and they were both nervous, but they had already decided they were going to go through with it. They had each chosen a gun out of Cannon's stash to use for the job – Will had chosen a revolver and Pop had chosen a forty-five caliber handgun. Will had suggested that Pop bring a revolver along as well, because it wouldn't leave any shell casings on the ground, but Pop had an affinity for this particular nickel-plated gun. They had dressed in all black– plain, black t-shirts, black jeans and black Timberland boots. They also had black bandanas tied loosely around their necks so they could pull them up around their faces to disguise themselves before they killed Devin.

In Nicetown, Stacy was getting dressed for her "date" and, when nine-o'clock came around, she went outside so she could catch the bus from Nicetown to Germantown. At exactly nine-thirty, Devin pulled up to the corner of Wayne Avenue and Manheim Street and picked Stacy up.

"Hey Devin," Stacy forced a smile as she entered the passenger's side of Devin's vehicle. "Thanks for picking me up here!"

"Hey Stacy, no problem," Devin replied. "So where do you wanna go?"

"There's this popping bar called Three Elements, down Second and Cumberland we can go to."

"Damn! You hang out in the Badlands? All the way down there?" Devin hesitated. "Well, anything to please you, Stacy," the infatuated young man conceded.

Devin and Stacy arrived at the bar shortly before ten-o'clock that night. They played a game of pool at first, and then a security guard put the pool table away and the dance floor opened up. The two of them danced for an hour, then found two seats at the bar and Devin ordered them drinks.

"You know, I'm really feeling you, Stacy," Devin began. "I told my brother I met someone. I didn't get a chance to tell him I had a date with you tonight, though, because we've been missing each other the past couple days. I'd like you to meet him though. I think he would like you."

"Excuse me…," Stacy got choked up and rushed to the bathroom so Devin wouldn't see her crying. She came back five minutes later, after a long line had developed for the ladies' room, her eyes red and wet from crying. The guilt of knowing what was about to happen to Devin in less than an hour had been too much for her to bear at the moment. "Sorry Devin, I'm back," Stacy forced a smiled.

"Are you okay, Stacy? It looks like you've been crying…"

"My grandmother died this time of year a few years ago, and it's always hard for me," Stacy lied. Her grandmother was alive and well, living in the Strawberry Mansion section of the city.

"Oh, I'm so sorry to hear that," Devin placed his hand on Stacy's shoulder.

"Well, enough of that! Let me buy you a drink, Devin!"

They sat, drank and talked until Stacy looked at her phone and realized that it was eleven-forty. The time had flown by and she was actually enjoying herself, which made her feel worse about what was about to transpire. But she had a job to do. It was too late to turn back now. She had committed herself to her man, Will, and promised that she would follow through. Besides, Will and Pop would be there by midnight anyway. Devin's fate was already sealed.

"You wanna, um, go out to your car?" Stacy asked Devin as seductively as possible, while rubbing her hand up and down his leg beneath the bar.

"S-S-Sure! We c-c-can do that," Devin stuttered excitedly as the blood rushed to his manhood. He wasn't thinking about anything at that point except for getting physical with the attractive young woman before him, and he quickly got up without finishing his drink and led her out of the side door of the bar.

They walked to the side-block where Stacy had directed Devin to park, Palethorp Street, and entered his vehicle. Devin's Buick Riviera was the only car parked on the block. Devin was anticipating sex, oral sex, kissing – at least something, but Stacy seemed to have cooled off by the time they reached his car. Devin wondered if he had seemed too anxious and had blown his chances with Stacy.

"Can we listen to some music please?" Stacy asked politely.

Devin inserted an old Dru Hill CD into his CD player in an attempt to get Stacy back into the mood. After about fifteen minutes, it seemed to have worked. She rubbed her hand on his leg and kissed him slowly and passionately. Stacy immediately felt guilty for betraying Will, but she felt she owed this act of intimacy to Devin for the horror she was setting him up for.

"Devin," Stacy said, regaining her focus. "I just need a little something else to get me more comfortable, you know? I saw they had wine coolers back at the bar in the fridge for sale. Would you do me a favor and go grab some?"

"No problem, Stacy. I'll be right back."

Devin walked across the street and into the bar. Stacy's timing couldn't have been better because Will and Pop were approaching in the black Mustang from the bottom of the block at that very moment with its headlights turned off. Will got out of the car, ran to the passenger's side of Devin's Buick Riviera, quickly escorted Stacy to Cannon's Mustang and hurried her into the backseat. The three waited in the black Mustang, which was parked directly behind Devin's Buick but was barely visible in the dark without any light shining on it.

Within minutes, Devin happily exited the side door of the bar and walked across the street. He briskly walked up to his car with the wine coolers in hand and, as he opened the door, he noticed that Stacy wasn't inside. At that very terror-filled moment, Devin recognized the black Mustang in the darkness, and for a millisecond feared for Stacy's safety; that is, until the realization that she had set him up had registered in his consciousness. No sooner had Devin turned to view the Mustang than he noticed the two shadowy figures; one short, one taller, dressed in all black and pointing guns at him. Glass shattered as he dropped the wine coolers. Devin froze in fear, too scared to run. Stacy watched in horror as the gunshots rang out – *Pop! Pop! Pop! Pap! Pap! Pap! Pap! Pap! Pop! Pop! Pop!* – eleven shots in total from both guns; and Devin's chest caught every single bullet. His body fell to the ground, quivering, and a pool of blood quickly formed around his body. The informant was dying. With every shallow breath, the life was leaving his body. Within thirty seconds Devin was dead and the three teenagers had fled the scene. Stacy was devastated. Will and Pop were ecstatic. Their mission had been accomplished.

CHAPTER 11

Will and Pop went to CFCF to visit Cannon that following Monday to give him the good news.

"You don't have to worry about nothing anymore, cousin," Pop declared proudly. "It's done."

"For real?" Cannon grinned devilishly. "Y'all handled that already?"

"Yeah, we sure did... the other night," Will answered matter-of-factly.

"That's what's up y'all! Good looking out," Cannon beamed with excitement. "That means I'll be outta here in a few months!"

"No doubt," Pop replied excitedly. "We can't wait to see you back in these streets!"

"I can't wait to be back!" Cannon replied with equal excitement. "You know a nigga gotta get out and get this paper! But yo, I was thinking... I gotta reward y'all for handling business for me like that. I'ma give you the connect for the bitches so you can start moving some on your own, too."

"Good looking out Cannon," Will and Pop replied simultaneously.

"Hey, no problem. Just make sure that I get the bread for the ones you got from my crib, alright?"

"Yeah, no doubt," Pop agreed.

"The connect is an Arab nigga, named Amin, who owns a Dunkin Donuts on the Boulevard. His number is 267-555-2632. He can get you whatever type of joint you need. Tell him you're my people and that I'm booked, but I'ma get at him when I get out. He usually makes you grab a dozen hammers at a time, though, so make sure you got the bread before you hit him up."

"Alright, thanks, cuz," Pop replied as he tried to memorize the phone number until he got to the car and could save it to his phone. "We're gonna get outta here, man. I put more money on your commissary. Hold your head until you get outta this motherfucker. I'll get with you soon. Hit me if you need anything."

Meanwhile, on Pulaski Street in Germantown, Devin's family was devastated when they received the news about his murder; Darren took the news especially hard and blamed himself for his brother's death, especially since he had promised he would "have his back" and that nothing would happen to Devin while he was around.

Devin and Darren's parents, Mister and Misses Silvera, had no idea that their son was a witness to the shootings during the basketball game at the park and that he had been cooperating with the police, so they had no clue what the motive for his murder could be. Due to the police's sloppy work in the beginning, and allowing Cannon, Will and Pop to be present while Devin identified Cannon, the homicide detectives did not reveal to Devin's parents that Devin was the only person willing to testify regarding the shooting, and that this might have been the motive for his murder. Only his brother, Darren, was privy to this knowledge because Devin had confided in him before he was murdered. Darren wanted to kill whoever had murdered his brother, but he had no idea who had done the deed.

A month and a half passed, the summer was over, and Will, Pop and Stacy began their senior year in high school. As usual, Pop did not attend regularly, though he was regularly out in the streets selling drugs. He made sure he attended class often enough to pass, however, because he wanted to graduate.

Will went to school regularly, and had been dating both Stacy and Veronica. His schedule was full. Directly after school he would drive to either Ninth Street and Lycoming Street or Old York Road and Lycoming Street, whichever corner Pop was not posted on, and begin selling cocaine himself. The two teenagers had discontinued selling jars of sour-diesel because they were making so much money selling quarter- pounds of it. They had hooked up with Cannon's connect, the African man named Jeremiah, and purchased a pound for four-thousand dollars. They then sold quarter-pounds to four people: Tommy, Jay and two of Jay's friends for fifteen-hundred dollars a-piece, making a profit of two-thousand dollars on each pound they sold. They did this every week. This was a nice bonus in addition to the profit they were seeing from selling an ounce of cocaine daily. The teenagers put aside five-hundred dollars for Cannon out of the profit from every pound of sour-diesel they sold.

Will's schedule was also busy because after he was finished selling drugs each evening, he would spend some time with either Stacy or Veronica. Will loved Stacy, but his feelings for Veronica had grown over the previous month and a half. After about a month of seeing each other, Will and Veronica had finally had sex for the first time and Will was amazed at how good Veronica was in bed. He figured that might have had something to do with why he liked her so much.

"Ronnie is *the truth* in bed, dog!" Will exclaimed as he and Pop drove to Southwest Philadelphia to meet Jay and his associates one night. "And the head-game is vicious!"

"Oh, word?" Pop asked curiously. "Is she better than Stacy?"

"Well, Stacy is my girl *for real*, so I don't really wanna talk about her like that," Will replied hypocritically. "But on some real shit – yeah, better than Stacy! I'm really feeling Veronica, man. It's not just the sex, though. She's cool as shit, too."

"Yeah, she might be all that and more, but I think you're doing Stacy dirty, man," Pop admitted. "Stacy's a good chick. She doesn't deserve that, man! Plus she would trip if she found out – especially after how she helped us out with that Devin shit."

"I feel you, homey," Will admitted. "But she ain't gonna find out. I'm a smooth operator!" Will laughed.

"Don't be thinking you're too smooth, nigga," Pop cautioned. "That's when nigga's get caught up! Besides, ain't Veronica still messing with Jasiel?"

"Yeah, but only 'cause she's scared of the nigga. She told me he be slapping the shit out of her and choking her and shit! I'm about to merck that nigga!"

"You gonna kill a nigga over a bitch, though?" Pop asked, surprised.

"It ain't just that," Will justified himself. "You see how that motherfucker kept rolling up on us, talking about robbing us and all that? We need to get at Jasiel and Jose before they get at us! It's just like you were saying before…"

"Yeah, but they haven't done that in a while, though, na'mean?" Pop protested. "I think they realized we're not to be fucked with. I wouldn't kill Jasiel over Veronica. What would Stacy say if you got caught? She definitely wouldn't ride out with you during your bid if she found out it was over another female."

"Yeah, I guess you're right," Will agreed.

Pop's reasoning made sense to Will. What Will did not know was that Pop had another reason for not wanting any problems with Jasiel and Jose. About a month prior, unbeknownst to Will, Pop had met up with Amin, Cannon's gun connect, and purchased a dozen guns. His problem, however, was that he didn't have any customers. He had already sold the rest of the weapons from Cannon's original stash, but it had been difficult for him to find customers because he hadn't been in the business of selling guns for long. So, Pop made it his mission to find customers for his new inventory of firearms. He reached out to Rick one day and asked him if he was interested in purchasing any more guns.

"Yeah, I could always use more hammers," Rick replied when Pop showed up at his stash-house. "What you got?"

Pop opened up his large duffle bag, revealing a dozen firearms – mostly handguns and several shotguns.

"That's what's up," Rick exclaimed as he rifled through the inventory and selected a revolver. "How much for this jawn?"

"For you... three-fifty."

"Alright, cool." Rick went upstairs to his safe, counted out three-hundred and fifty dollars, brought it downstairs and handed it to Pop.

"You know anybody else who needs guns, Rick?" Pop asked.

"On some real shit," Rick started, "those crazy-ass stick-up kids, Jasiel and Jose, probably want some. But you need to get their number from Tiny."

"Man... I don't know if I wanna fuck with them," Pop sighed.

"It's all business, right?" Rick asked.

"Yeah, but me and Will kinda got beef with them."

"Well this might be a way to squash the beef!"

"True," Pop conceded.

"Go holler at Tiny at his bar on Hunting Park," Rick instructed. "You might even see Jasiel and Jose in there. They're in there a lot."

So, that's exactly what Pop did. That night, a Thursday, after he knew Will had met up with Veronica after selling cocaine, Pop drove Cannon's Mustang over to Tiny's bar on Hunting Park Avenue. Pop, however, lied to Will and told him that he was going to meet up with a girl, because he knew Will wouldn't approve of Pop attempting to do business with their long-time foes, Jasiel and Jose. Pop brought his false identification with him so he would be admitted into the bar without any problems. He found parking on Hunting Park Avenue, near the bar, left his gun in the car under the seat, left the large duffle bag full of guns in the trunk where it had been all day, and walked to the bar.

When Pop arrived, he was patted down aggressively by the security guard at the door, an experience Jasiel and Jose never had to endure because they were Tiny's nephews. Pop walked in after being searched, ordered a beer and looked around the bar for Tiny.

Tiny owned three bars, but the bar on Hunting Park Avenue held a special place in his heart. It was the first bar he had opened up, and he had an office there where he often conducted business. Tiny sold a large portion of the cocaine that was distributed in the neighborhood, which meant, of course, that he didn't buy his cocaine by the ounce – he bought it in bulk – multiple kilograms at a time. Tiny had a lot of customers and he held meetings with many of them in his office in the back of his bar on Hunting Park Avenue, in a room behind the deejay booth. Tiny also valued this bar because he had many loyal patrons who showed up regularly and had been coming since he had opened it ten years prior. Tiny was very friendly with his loyal customers, both his cocaine customers and his bar patrons, and they showed him loyalty in return.

Tiny had been holding a meeting in his office with one of his more prominent cocaine customers, who was buying a kilogram from him, which is why Pop hadn't been able to locate him. After roughly fifteen minutes, Tiny emerged from the back of the bar with a glass of vodka in his hand.

"My man, Tiny!" Pop greeted the short, Puerto-Rican drug-dealer with a smile as he approached Tiny. "Just the man I've been looking for!"

"What's up, Pop?" Tiny half-hugged Pop. "Why you been looking for me? You and Will tryna graduate to a key?" Tiny asked, wondering if the teenagers wanted to be fronted a kilogram of cocaine.

"Naw, man, I wish! I actually got something I want to offer you," Pop said into Tiny's ear, due to the loud music which drowned out most conversation. "Can you come to my car with me? I wanna show you something."

Tiny, who didn't trust anybody, and rightfully so, due to the line of business he was in, stared at Pop warily, looking him up and down.

"Outside?" Tiny asked skeptically. "I hold all my meetings in the office."

"Yeah, but they patted me down all crazy when I came in," Pop explained, "and I got a duffle bag full'a guns in my trunk. I wanted to see if you wanted to cop some."

"Oh, is that what it is?" Tiny asked, relieved. "Bring them in! I'll wait by the door to make sure the bouncer lets you in with them."

Pop walked back out to the Mustang, opened the trunk and retrieved the tote full of guns. He walked up to the door of the bar and approached the security guard. The large man stared at Pop, and Pop stared back at him.

"He's with me. Let him through," Tiny instructed the bouncer as he walked up behind him and placed a hand on the tall, muscular man's shoulder.

Tiny and Pop walked through the bar and into Tiny's back office. Tiny locked the door and sat down behind his desk. Pop placed the large duffle bag on Tiny's desk and unzipped it, revealing his collection of firearms.

"You got some nice shit in here," Tiny remarked. "They got bodies on them?"

"Not until you kill somebody with them," Pop chuckled. "Naw, but for real, they're all clean."

Tiny retrieved latex gloves out of a box in his drawer, slipped them on, selected several guns from the duffle bag, placed them on his desk and examined them.

"How much for this pistol-grip pump and this Desert Eagle?"

"Well the shotty is three-fifty and the Desert Eagle is eleven-hundred," Pop replied. "But since you're my old-head, I'll give them both to you for thirteen-hundred."

"Alright, good looking out," Tiny thanked Pop, reached into his pocket, pulled out a large wad of cash, counted out thirteen-hundred dollars, and handed it to Pop. Then Tiny took the guns he had purchased and placed them in a gun-safe in his office while Pop placed the other guns on the table back into the duffle bag and zipped it up.

"Nice doing business with you, Tiny," Pop shook Tiny's hand from the opposite side of the desk. "Um... I was wondering if you could talk to the twins, Jasiel and Jose for me, and see if they want any of these hammers?"

"*Ay dios mio*," Tiny sighed. "You wanna sell guns to those crazy boys? I love my nephews, but they're throwed-off!"

"Yeah, I feel you, Tiny, but I need to sell these guns, man," Pop insisted. "And since they're stick-up kids, they're probably looking for some. Besides... Rick told me to ask you to hook me up."

"Well, I guess so... if you insist..."

"Yes, please," Pop pleaded.

"I think I saw them sitting at the bar when we were walking back here," Tiny informed Pop. "You stay back here for a minute – I'll go grab them real quick."

Pop sat in the chair and admired Tiny's opulent office. A large black-leather chair sat behind his hefty cherry-wood desk. Tiny's office also contained two large, expensive-looking gold lamps, several modern paintings which looked expensive as well, and a modern, black-leather sofa along the wall with a large, black gun-safe standing upright next to the sofa. The final touch was an ornate cherry-wood book case, filled from top-to-bottom with everything from law books and encyclopedias to urban fiction novels.

By the time he was finished admiring Tiny's office, Tiny had entered with Jasiel and Jose. When Jasiel saw Pop sitting there, he smirked slyly.

"What's the deal, Uncle Tiny?" Jasiel grinned. "What's this all about?"

"Yeah, Uncle Tiny, what's going on?" Jose asked nervously.

"Well, Pop here wants to do business with you two and I think you should listen to him," Tiny informed his nephews. "Take a seat on the couch."

"Hey Pop, where's your bodyguard, Will?" Jasiel sneered.

"Hey none of that bullshit!" Tiny yelled. "I'm tired of you starting shit with my customers! Now listen to what Pop has to say motherfucker, you understand me?"

"Yeah, Uncle Tiny, I got you," Jasiel reluctantly agreed.

"So first off, I don't want any more beef with y'all," Pop began. "I don't wanna have to worry about that shit. And I think your uncle agrees with me on that. You feel me?"

Jasiel and Jose sat, nodded their heads and continued to listen.

"I have guns for sale and since y'all do what you do, I figured y'all might wanna cop some," Pop continued. "Are you interested?"

"Yeah, no doubt," Jose said excitedly. "We can always use those, right bro?"

"Yeah, we can always use them," Jasiel replied coolly, "but what's the catch? Are the firing-pins broken or something? You tryna set us up to get killed out here?"

"Naw, man! Nothing like that," Pop objected. "I'm just tryna do business and squash the beef between us. If you wanna do business then cool, if not, then, whatever. Just let a nigga know."

"What kind of guns you got?" Jasiel asked, finally letting on that he wanted to do business.

"I can show you better than I can tell you!" Pop waved Jasiel and Jose over to the desk and unzipped the duffle bag, revealing the guns.

"Oh shit, nigga! You got mad guns in here!" Jose exclaimed happily.

"Yeah, we need revolvers though. All the better to pop a nigga with!" Jasiel laughed maniacally. "Can we get two of those?"

"Yeah, no problem… they're three-seventy-five each. You got it on you?"

"Naw, it's at the crib," Jasiel replied. "*Tio*, I got two-fifty on me now… let me borrow five-hundred and I'll bring it back in like fifteen minutes."

"Yeah, I got you," Tiny huffed as he pulled out his wad of cash once again and handed five-hundred dollars to Pop.

"Good looking out, Pop," Jasiel thanked the teenager as he placed the gun in the back of his pants, behind his belt. "Let me get your number in case we need more."

"Alright, bet," Pop replied eagerly, thinking of the potential profits. "It's 215-555-8095. Hit me up anytime you wanna cop."

So, that's how Pop, Jasiel and Jose ended their enmity. And that's how they began their business relationship. Fast-forward more than a month, and Pop had still not revealed what had transpired to his business partner, Will. He knew Will would not approve and that was how he justified not letting Will know what had occurred.

In the meantime, Jasiel and Jose had bills to pay, so they robbed more people. Jasiel became increasingly violent with the robberies, even when their victims were compliant. He would pistol-whip victims and threaten to kill them, while his brother just gripped his own gun and looked on in sheer terror.

One night in mid-September, Jasiel was in a particularly violent mood. Jasiel and Jose had been staking out a crack house on Seventh Street and Pike Street for about ten days, trying to figure out the patterns of the dealers who worked there. They had finally figured out that the best time to rob the crack house was when there seemed to be only one worker inside, which was between three-o'clock and four-o'clock in the morning after several other dealers left.

On that particular night, they were sitting across the street from the crack house, in Jose's tinted Chevrolet Impala, watching the activity and smoking wet. On this night, just like the previous ten nights, when three-o'clock arrived, Jasiel and Jose watched as three young men exited the crack house. The one who remained had followed the three who had left to the front door and out onto the stoop, as he had the other nights, looked up and down the block, waited for his associates to drive away, and then went back into the crack house and closed and locked the door.

"Now this is what we're gonna do," Jasiel instructed. "We're gonna wait behind that truck right there, and when the next customer comes up we're gonna bum-rush the door and run in there and take everything they got in there, na'mean?"

Jasiel and Jose exited the Impala and crept up behind a Ford Expedition that was parked directly in front of the crack house. They waited and watched for about five minutes until they noticed a gaunt, older Black woman with short, thin dreadlocks walking down Seventh Street towards the crack house. She walked up the stoop and towards the front door.

"This is it," Jasiel whispered excitedly. "Come on!"

The two young men quietly ran from behind the car, up the stoop and on either side of the woman so they wouldn't be seen from the door's peephole. They had reached the woman just as she had knocked on the door and she shrieked out of shock and fear. Jasiel pointed his revolver, which he had purchased from Pop, at the older woman's temple and raised his finger to his lips, indicating that she needed to be quiet. Shortly thereafter, the young man inside the crack house opened the front door. Jasiel and Jose pushed the older woman inside forcibly and Jasiel grabbed the young man by the collar of his shirt and viciously hit him in his face with his gun three times, breaking the man's nose and knocking him to the ground. The young man, who had answered the door with a pistol in his hand, immediately dropped his gun, screaming in pain as blood gushed from his nose and his gun slid across the hardwood floor.

"Get that gun, nigga!" Jasiel commanded Jose. The young man scurried across the floor to try to retrieve the pistol before Jose had a chance to grab it. "Move again and I'll blow your damn head off!" Jasiel barked as Jose retrieved the gun from the floor and put it on his waist.

"Where's the money motherfucker?"

"I-I'll tell y-y-y'all," the man stuttered in fear, "j-j-just don't shoot me!"

"Shit man! I just came to get some rock!" the older woman complained as she stomped her foot.

"Shut the fuck up!" Jasiel commanded the woman as he continued to grip her arm so that she couldn't run away.

The beaten and bloodied young man stood slowly to his feet and led Jasiel, Jose and the woman into the kitchen of the house and opened the refrigerator. He pulled out two paper bags full of money and handed it to Jose, as Jasiel's hands were full, holding his gun and the older woman as well.

"That's it right there," the young man informed them. "That's what we made today so far – a little over eighteen-hundred. I just counted it."

Pop! Pop! Pop!

"Thanks," Jasiel said coldly as he pumped three bullets into the young man's face without giving it a second thought. Jose jumped and the older woman screamed a blood-curdling shriek.

"What's your problem, Jose? You always acting like a *puta* – jumping and shit! Yeah, I saw you," Jasiel poked fun at his twin. "You're too soft! Now go ahead and pop this old lady and toughen up!"

"What?" Jose asked in shock.

"Yeah, we don't leave no witnesses so put one in her head and let's get the fuck outta here!"

"Oh no! Please no," the older woman begged. "I just came to get high! I have grandkids!"

"Then you shouldn't be smoking crack," Jasiel chuckled.

"Please no! Oh my God, no!" The older woman began to sob and actually urinated on herself.

"Yo, man, I ain't killing no lady, bro," Jose objected.

"Oh yes, you are!" Jasiel commanded as he raised his gun and pointed it at his brother's head. "You're gonna get your first body tonight, motherfucker! Either you pop her, or I'ma pop you!"

Jose shook his head in disgust and disappointment. His body began to tremble. Jose slowly raised his gun and pointed it at the woman who dropped to her knees and sobbed even more heavily than she had been before.

"Oh, no! Please don't do it," she pleaded. "Please no! Please no, young man!"

Pop!

The single gunshot to her temple from Jose's revolver stopped the woman's begging and sobbing immediately and melted the dreadlocks to the side of her head.

"Good job Jose!"

"Fuck that and fuck you! I'm going to Hell now!"

"Fuck it," Jasiel replied coldly. "She was a crack-head anyway!"

"Fuck you, man! How the fuck are you gonna threaten me like that?" Jose snapped. "You've really lost your mind!"

"Oh... I wasn't really gonna shoot you, bro," Jasiel grinned as they got into the Impala and drove away. "You're my twin brother! I couldn't do that!"

"Oh, word?" Jose asked incredulously.

"Of course! But at least now we know that Pop sold us some decent guns!"

CHAPTER 12

In Germantown, Darren was experiencing a downward spiral without his older brother, Devin, around to keep him grounded. He was growing more depressed each day over his brother's murder. In order to cope with his depression, he smoked marijuana multiple times a day to the point where he was perpetually high. Darren also drank heavily, regardless of whether he was at home, at work bartending, or out at a bar or club socially. He was also growing ever more homicidal and was frustrated with the fact that he didn't know where to begin in the search for his brother's murderer or murderers.

"I need to find that black Mustang," Darren confided in his girlfriend, Jade, on one occasion as they sat on his bed.

"What black Mustang?"

"Oh, that's right… I never told you," Darren remembered. "Well, remember how I told you Devin witnessed a shooting and cooperated with the police? The nigga who did it had a black, convertible Mustang. Devin thought the boy made bail and was out looking for him. I believed him, too, 'cause one night we were coming out the Crab House and we saw the car on the Ave. I think that nigga is the one who killed my brother – he probably followed him to North Philly or something."

"But didn't you tell me the homicide detective said that there had to be two shooters because Devin was shot with two different caliber bullets?" Jade asked.

"Yeah, it was probably that nigga. What did Devin say his name was – Malik Davidson? It was probably that Malik nigga and one of his homeys. I'm so pissed! They didn't have to do my brother like that! But I'll get them, though," Darren reassured himself as he deeply inhaled some marijuana smoke. "I'ma ride through the hood and spray up any black convertible Mustang I find!"

"Just be careful, boo," Jade cautioned. "I don't wanna see you wind up in jail!"

"Thanks, but right now I don't give a fuck. I just need to avenge my brother's death! You want some of this weed?" Darren changed the subject as he held up the blunt and offered it to his girlfriend.

"No thanks! Now, you know I work at the hospital and they do random drug tests," Jade declined.

That night, after Jade left to go to work, Darren decided to smoke another blunt and drink two forty-ounce bottles of malt liquor. He was extremely depressed and angry and he wanted to suppress his emotions. He wasn't thinking clearly when he grabbed his gun and left the house and decided to go searching for the black Mustang. He wasn't walking straight either, for he was extremely intoxicated from the liquor and the marijuana he had consumed. He stumbled to his vehicle, a late-model Pontiac Grand Prix, and attempted to unlock it. He dropped his keys several times before he managed to successfully press the correct button for the keyless entry and unlock his car doors. He stumbled into the car, clumsily placed the key in the ignition, turned the car on and pulled away from the curb. By the time he had reached Wayne Avenue, his vehicle was swerving all over the road. Other drivers were honking their horns at Darren and flashing their vehicle's hi-beams at him, but he was too intoxicated to care. That was, until he almost had a head-on collision with an approaching police cruiser. The squad-car swerved so as not to be hit, turned on his flashing red and blue lights, and made a U-turn in order to pull Darren over.

"Oh shit!" Darren exclaimed. "These motherfuckers ain't catching me!"

Darren strapped on his seatbelt and sped down Wayne Avenue. At first, the adrenaline which surged through his veins seemed to have a sobering effect on him. His vehicle hardly swerved and he was able to avoid the cars that were passing through the intersection as he ran the red light at Wayne Avenue and Chelten Avenue. The police officer immediately blared his sirens and began his pursuit. The officer slowed down when he reached the intersection, but then sped up as he passed over Chelten Avenue. Darren was far ahead of the officer. But about thirty seconds later, as Darren was approaching the intersection of Wayne Avenue and Washington Lane and attempted to turn the corner, he lost control of his Grand Prix and hit a parked car. His head slammed against the steering wheel, cutting his forehead, although not deeply. Darren was dazed for several moments and by the time he regained his wits, the policeman had snatched him out of his vehicle and slammed him to the ground, handcuffing his wrists tightly.

"Man, them shits are too tight!" Darren yelled, complaining about the tight handcuffs.

"Fuck you!" the officer had yelled at Darren, snatching him up from the pavement. "You almost got me killed! On your feet, motherfucker!"

"Oh shit – I gotta..."

Without another word, Darren vomited violently. The police officer cursed at Darren, took Darren's wallet out of his pocket in order to obtain his identification, walked him to the squad-car and threw him into the back seat.

"Can't hold your liquor, huh?" the officer laughed. "You're gonna do great in lock-up!"

Shortly thereafter, two more officers arrived and they began to search Darren's car. Almost immediately they found Darren's gun, which had been tossed around the vehicle during the accident and ended up on the floor in the front of the car.

"Well, well, well! What do we have here?" the first officer approached the rear side window where Darren was sitting. He held up the gun. "This is your nine, right? Do you have a concealed-carry permit, my man?"

"Naw, man... you know I don't have one of those things, man," an intoxicated Darren slurred.

"Well, Mister Silvera, it looks like we're gonna have to add a gun charge to the resisting arrest, driving under the influence, and reckless endangerment charges! You're going to jail for a hot minute, buddy!"

"Shit!" Darren was upset. He was upset that he was going to jail. He was upset that he hadn't saved money for bail or a lawyer while he had been selling marijuana, and he knew his parents didn't have money. He was upset because he knew the whole thing should not have happened in the first place. But he was mostly upset because now that he was going to jail, he would never have the opportunity to find Malik Davidson and exact revenge for Devin's death.

The officer drove Darren to the 14th District building in order to book him. His handcuffs were removed and Darren was shackled to a bench inside of the building. The officers were very aggressive with Darren while fingerprinting him and they spoke down to him, but he was too intoxicated to notice. The officer who had arrested him was still upset that he had to chase him, and he made his displeasure known at every available opportunity.

"What's this one here for?" one particularly nosy female officer who had walked into the building asked the arresting officer.

"DUI, resisting arrest, reckless endangerment and a gun charge," the arresting officer informed her.

"Damn!"

"You know I had to chase this motherfucker from Wayne and Coulter to Wayne and Washington before he crashed into a parked car," the arresting officer complained. "I wanted to whoop his ass!"

"Ha-ha! I feel you!" the female officer laughed. "What's your name, buddy?" she asked as she walked over to Darren. He just stared at her, his eyes watering and glazed over. "You know you're going away for three-to-five, right?" She laughed again. Then, without warning, Darren vomited on the female officer's shoes and on the floor next to her feet. "Aw, shit," she cursed as she stomped away to the bathroom.

"I should make you clean that shit up, Mister Silvera," the arresting officer groaned.

By the time the officer had processed Darren, taking his fingerprints, photographing his tattoos, taking his mug-shots and doing everything else he needed to do, it was about two-o'clock in the morning and Darren was placed in a filthy holding cell for the night. There was already another man in the cell sleeping on the hard, steel bench, so Darren curled into a ball and slept on the floor. He was too drunk to notice the multitude of roaches crawling around which would cause any sober person to refrain from lying on the filthy floor.

"What the fuck?" Darren quickly jumped up from the floor early the next morning and frantically brushed a roach off of his face. The man sleeping on the bench stirred quietly at the ruckus Darren had made.

Darren looked at the man, and then turned in the small, dirty holding cell, looking at the commode full of dried feces, then at the cell bars. At first he could barely recall the events of the previous night, but eventually it all came back to him. "Aw shit! I got booked!" Darren placed his face in his hands and cursed loudly, waking up his cellmate. He then pounded his fist against the hard cement wall.

"Damn, dog! You woke me up," Darren's cellmate complained as he sat up on the bench.

"My fault, man," Darren apologized. "I'm just fucked up right now!"

"Me too! I'm in this motherfucker with you!" Darren's cellmate, a short, fat, light-skinned man replied. "But at least I was sleeping!"

"Yeah man, I'm sorry about that, dog," Darren apologized once more. "I just didn't remember at first that I got locked up until I woke up!"

"Aw, that's salty! You was fucked up on that good shit last night, huh?"

"Yeah, I ran from the cops, then I banged out," Darren explained. "But I'm real mad 'cause I think they found my burner!"

"Oh, that's no good, my nigga," the fat, light-skinned man responded empathetically. "They *allegedly* caught me selling bootleg DVDs on Germantown Ave. But I'ma beat that shit though. I got a good, Jewish lawyer on deck. What you need to do is hire a liar!"

"What?"

"Oh you've never been booked before, huh?" Darren's cellmate asked, smiling.

"Naw…"

"Well, you need to hire a liar, my nigga. Get a good lawyer who will lie his ass off for you. Pay like you weigh, dog. A good lying-ass lawyer is gonna cost that guap," Darren's cellmate explained.

"But I don't have money for an expensive 'liar.' I'ma have to get a public defender," Darren told his cellmate.

"Well, then, my nigga; I hate to say it… but if you're getting a public 'pretender,' it looks like you're going Upstate!"

Later that afternoon, Darren had his bail hearing. His bail was set at fifty-thousand dollars, a fact which caused Darren much distress because he knew his parents did not have the ten percent, or five thousand dollars, needed in order to bail him out. Within an hour of Darren's bail hearing, he was put in a van, along with several other prisoners, and transported to the County Jail.

By the time Darren arrived at Curran-Fromhold Correctional Facility, or CFCF, he was extremely hungry. He hadn't eaten a decent meal in almost a day. There were dozens of men in the processing unit of the jail and they were each given a cheese sandwich and a small carton of juice. This did little to satisfy Darren's hunger or quench his thirst, or that of the other men, for that matter.

Darren waited in the processing unit for about nine hours to be seen. The wait was grueling for him, especially since it was his first time being incarcerated. Finally, after a nine-hour wait, he was processed. After being processed, he was also seen by a nurse and taken to the Quarantine cell block, where he stayed for twenty-four hours.

By the time Darren reached his regular cell block, he was exhausted from the whole ordeal and realized that there was a reason why he had tried so hard to stay out of jail. In jail, the officials classify the prisoners so that they are housed together based on the crime that they are imprisoned for. Because of Darren's gun charge, he was on a cell-block with other inmates who had pending gun-charges, robbery charges, alleged shootings, alleged drug dealers and charges similar to those.

When Darren was brought to his new cell on his regular cellblock and saw his new cellmate, he hesitated for a moment. Darren was not scared of the man in the least. But there was something familiar about him. He was light-skinned with a thick beard, a lot of tattoos, and a husky build. Darren at once remembered that this was exactly how his brother, Devin, had described the shooter in the black mustang – Malik Davidson.

"But there is no way that this could be the same nigga," Darren thought to himself. "There's a thousand niggas in Philly who fit that description!"

Darren immediately brushed the thought aside in his mind. That was, until he heard the correctional officer's next words to his new cell mate.

"Davidson – you got a new cellie! I don't want any problems with this one!"

Cannon had been fighting often with his old cellmates but had calmed down since he found out Devin had been killed, and that he would be released once the witness did not show up to the three required court appearances.

"Davidson? It can't be," Darren thought to himself. "If it is, this is too good to be true," he thought as a smile formed across his face.

"What you smiling about, nigga? You happy to be locked up or something?" Cannon asked as he looked up from reading his Donald Goines novel.

"Naw, man," Darren replied calmly. "I just thought about something my old cellmate told me," Darren lied.

"Oh," Cannon replied, disinterested, and went back to reading.

"What's your name, dog?" Darren asked.

"Cannon," Cannon replied bluntly.

"That's your real name?"

"Might as well be," Cannon answered coldly without looking up from his book.

"Well, I'm Darren. Nice to meet you." Darren reached out his hand to Cannon, who was lying on the bottom bunk in the cell.

"Yeah… I'ma keep reading though," Cannon replied nonchalantly, without looking up from his book or shaking Darren's hand.

The next morning, as was the routine, breakfast was served at five-o'clock. Cannon was accustomed to the early chow time because he had been in jail for almost two months. The announcement was made and the cell doors opened up so that the inmates could make their way into the common area of the cellblock.

"Damn! Why do they wake us up so early in this motherfucker, Cannon?" Darren sighed.

"That's just what they do, man," Cannon replied, his voice deeper than usual because he had just awoken. "You gotta get with the program, dog!"

"That's some bullshit! A nigga needs sleep!"

"Well, you better bring your Black-ass out here if you wanna eat," Cannon advised Darren as he walked out of the cell.

Darren jumped down from the top bunk, quickly put his shoes on, walked out of the cell and followed behind Cannon. They both fell into line. Cannon was directly in front of Darren in the line. Darren had decided that he was going to try to befriend Cannon. He had plans for Cannon – Malik Davidson – the man who had shot up the basketball court. The same man who Darren believed had something to do with Devin's death.

"I wonder what's for breakfast," Darren commented.

"We'll see. Probably some bullshit," Cannon replied while rolling his eyes. Cannon did not have any desire to make new friends, but his cellmate was being very friendly towards him. Cannon wondered if Darren was a homosexual or if he was an informant.

The men got their trays of food and their juice and proceeded to the tables. Devin looked around for a place to sit and noticed an empty seat next to Cannon. He walked over to the table and stood there momentarily before speaking.

"You mind if I sit here?" Darren asked Cannon.

"It's a free country," Cannon replied coolly.

"Except for us niggas!" Darren chuckled as he sat down next to Cannon. Cannon laughed as well.

"Yeah, I guess you're right!" Cannon chuckled.

"So, where you from?" Darren asked.

"The Hollow, you know, Germantown?" Cannon replied. "What about you?"

"Oh, me? The Twelfth District pigs got me! I'm from Southwest," Darren lied. "This must be that nigga my brother was telling me about. Same description and same last name – it *has* to be him!" Darren thought to himself. He didn't want Cannon to know that they were from the same neighborhood. Then he might put two-and-two together and recognize the family resemblance between him and his brother. Darren couldn't risk that.

"That's fucked up," Cannon empathized with Darren, "but somebody got us all, na'mean! I hate the cops!"

After they had finished eating, the vast majority of the men went back to their cells and went back to sleep, including Cannon and Darren. An hour later, Darren woke up to the sound of heavy breathing. He looked down from the top bunk and saw Cannon doing pushups in their cell. His hands were on the floor, while his feet were on his bunk.

"I need to start working out like you, since I'm in here," Darren commented. "I'm skinny as shit! I'm tryna get big like you, Cannon!"

"I wouldn't say I'm big," Cannon replied modestly as he stood up. "I'm stocky with some muscle on me though. What you need to do is these pushups and these dips and these crunches. I do a thousand of each every day since they don't have any weights in this motherfucker anymore."

"That's what's up," Darren said excitedly. "I need to get on that! Yo, Cannon… let me ask you a personal question…"

"What's up?"

"So, I'm in here for a gun charge and resisting arrest," Darren began.

"What you in here for?"

"I'd rather not say," Cannon admitted. "Nothing personal, Darren. I just don't like to tell my personal business like that."

"But isn't that what all cellies do – tell each other why they got locked up?" Darren asked.

"I guess it depends who you talk to," Cannon replied coolly. He paused and thought for a moment before his ego got the better of him. He thought it would make him look good in the setting that he was in, jail, and add to his street credibility if people knew that he had shot three people. He just didn't want to tell the wrong person. "Look, I guess it doesn't matter 'cause you're not even from Germantown. I allegedly shot a few niggas a couple months ago in my hood. I'ma beat the case, though."

"Damn nigga, you a rider, huh?" Darren replied. "That's what's up you think you're gonna beat the case, though. Your lawyer told you that?"

"Naw. I know if the witness doesn't show up to court three times they throw your case out. And I'm pretty sure that nigga ain't gonna show up!" Cannon grinned devilishly.

"What makes you think that?"

"Look, my nigga, I plead the Fifth!" Cannon laughed heartily.

Darren forced a smile, using all the acting skills he could muster in order to hide his true feelings of repulsion and hatred. He told Cannon he was tired and was going back to sleep until lunch time but, in fact, Darren lay in bed crying silently, thinking about Devin and how he had been slaughtered. There was no doubt in his mind at this point – his cellmate was Malik Davidson, the man his brother had warned him about. Darren didn't know how it had been done, but he was certain that Malik, or "Cannon" as he called himself, was involved in his brother's murder in some way. He was also certain that he needed to make him pay.

Darren plotted and planned what he would do and how and when he would do it. He tried to act the same towards Cannon, but it was very difficult for him to do so. Cannon wasn't the friendliest person anyway. Even though he had opened up to Darren, Cannon mostly read, exercised and kept to himself, sometimes playing cards with other inmates in the day room; so it was easier for Darren to seem normal around Cannon. True to his word, Darren had started his own exercise regimen, following the routine Cannon had recommended.

Darren didn't sleep much. He stayed up thinking about how his life would change if he followed through with his plan for revenge. The lack of sleep worked to his advantage, however, because the nighttime was when he intended to put his plan into action.

Four nights after Cannon had revealed to Darren why he was incarcerated, Darren lay wide awake on the top bunk. He waited until he heard the sound of Cannon breathing heavily – the sound of sleep. Then he waited longer. Darren waited until he heard the sound of Cannon snoring lightly. Once he heard Cannon snoring, Darren reached under his thin, County Jail mattress and slowly pulled out a shank he had made. It was made out of a toothbrush, with one end sharpened to a very hard, razor-sharp point. Darren had spent time converting the toothbrush into a weapon over the previous four days while Cannon was absent from their cell and at night while Cannon was in a deep sleep.

After Darren grabbed the shank, he swiftly and nimbly jumped onto the floor from the top bunk. He stood over Cannon for an entire minute, contemplating his actions. The act that he was about to commit would ensure that he would spend most, if not his entire life in prison. His parents would be devastated. Jade would be upset, but she would move on. He knew what he had to do. He owed it to the memory of his older brother, Devin.

Darren ducked down under the top bunk, and with one fluid motion took his left hand and placed it on Cannon's head while jamming the sharpened toothbrush into a vein in the side of Cannon's neck and pulling it out quickly with his right hand. When Darren removed the shank, blood squirted out violently from the wound and Cannon's eyes shot open, along with his mouth as he gasped for air. Darren stabbed Cannon in the neck seven more times in the same vicinity until the skin was torn apart. Then, Darren rapidly stabbed Cannon in his stomach and ribcage, although Cannon was already dead from being stabbed in the neck. Darren was consumed with murderous rage and stabbed Cannon fifteen more times with the toothbrush, until it broke off in Cannon's ribcage. Once Darren was satisfied with what he had done, he stepped back and looked at his work. Cannon's bunk was filled with blood, which looked black in the darkness. Darren wiped off Cannon's blood, which had spurted onto his own face during his murderous frenzy, with his hand. Darren knew that as soon as the guards looked into the cell and saw Cannon's body that there would be mayhem and they would then take him away and charge him with murder. Darren was at peace with himself, however, because he had avenged his brother's death. He jumped into his bunk and fell fast asleep for the first time since his brother's murder.

CHAPTER 13

Cannon was only thirty years old when he was murdered. His mother had died of a heroin overdose when he was twenty-five years old and his father had been absent from his life since his birth. His aunt, Pop's mother and Pop were his only family. Pop's mother, Miss Davidson, was his emergency contact for the jail. The morning after Cannon was murdered, Miss Davidson received a phone call from CFCF.

"Hello, this is Esther from the Curran-Fromhold Correctional Facility Administration Department. May I please speak with Cheryl Davidson?"

"This is Cheryl…"

"I'm calling in reference to Malik Davidson…," the woman from CFCF began.

"What, has he gotten into more trouble?" Miss Davidson interrupted. "Is he being transferred to a different jail?"

"No, ma'am," Esther hesitated. "I regret to inform you that Malik Davidson has been pronounced dead as a result of multiple stab wounds to his neck and torso. You can come to the facility and retrieve his property."

"W-What?" Miss Davidson gasped as tears formed in her eyes. "My nephew's dead? But who did it?"

"I can't get into that right now, ma'am. It's still under investigation, but we do have a suspect," Esther informed Miss Davidson. "Do you have any other questions?"

"When did it happen?"

"From what I'm aware of – sometime last night, ma'am."

"Thank you," a tearful Miss Davidson quietly replied before hanging up. She burst into tears after she hung up the phone. "Why, Lord, why?"

Miss Davidson sobbed for at least fifteen minutes before regaining her composure. Within thirty minutes she was dressed, out the door and on her way to the bus stop in order to catch the buses necessary to pick up her son, Pop, at the high school he attended – Murrell Dobbins Career and Technical Education High School at Twenty-Second Street and Lehigh Avenue in North Philadelphia. Pop was enrolled in the barbering program there and planned to open a barber shop as a front-business for his cocaine dealing within a few years of graduating high school.

When Miss Davidson arrived at her son's school, she entered and went directly to the principal's office and asked to speak with the principal. The principal was in a meeting at first, and Miss Davidson had to wait twenty-minutes to see her. Once they did meet, a tearful Miss Davidson informed the principal that Pop had a death in the family and needed to leave school immediately.

"My condolences, Miss Davidson," the principal offered her sympathy. "I know that's always difficult. I'll call Darryl over the loudspeaker and tell him to come to the office right away."

Fortunately for Pop, he had decided to attend his classes that day. He was surprised to hear his name being called over the loudspeaker, along with instructions to go "directly to the principal's office." The other youngsters in his class teased Pop about how he must be in trouble. He was somewhat nervous, however. He didn't know if perhaps word had reached the principal that he had been selling guns out of the Mustang to some of his associates after school, and he feared that the police would be waiting for him in the principal's office. He contemplated just leaving school without even going to the principal's office.

"It couldn't be that," Pop reasoned. "The cops would've just grabbed me before I came in this morning!" Pop reluctantly made his way to the principal's office. He was relieved, although confused, when he saw his mother standing inside the office speaking with the principal. "Hey Mom, what's going on?" Pop asked as he walked up to his mother and noticed the tears in her eyes.

"I'll tell you when we get home," Miss Davidson replied as they walked out of the office and she waved goodbye to Pop's principal, who waved in return.

"Thanks for getting me out of school early, Ma," Pop smiled as he walked his mother to the Mustang and helped her into the passenger's side seat. He started the car and began the drive back to the Hunting Park section of the city where they resided. "You look upset though…"

"Darryl," Miss Davidson began as Pop drove, "I need you to change your lifestyle! I don't want you to end up in jail, or even worse – dead!" Miss Davidson burst into tears and leaned against the passenger door, sobbing.

"Ma, it's okay," Pop held the steering wheel with his left hand and rubbed his mother's shoulder with his right hand. "I'll be fine. But I can't stop doing what I do. I need to pay these bills, you know? But I promise you I'm being careful."

"I don't even care about the money anymore," Miss Davidson sobbed. "I'm worried about my family!"

"You don't need to worry about me, Mom," Pop attempted to reassure his mother. "I know what I'm doing out here."

"Yeah, and I'm sure that's what Malik thought, too," Miss Davidson broke down.

"Yeah Ma, but he's innocent anyway," Pop lied. "Besides, I'm sure he'll be out soon."

"No, he won't, Darryl!" Miss Davidson screamed hysterically, not able to wait to reveal the bad news due to her emotional state. "Malik is dead!"

Pop turned the wheel immediately causing the vehicle to jerk, and pulled the car over on the side of Allegheny Avenue. He sat in the driver's seat for a minute, not saying a word, gripping the steering wheel with both hands and looked through the windshield, while his mother continued to cry. Then he took a deep breath and began to speak.

"Ma… Ma… Ma! I know you're not talking about my cousin, Malik!" Pop stated assertively. "Please tell me you're not talking about Cannon!"

"B-baby, I-I-I'm s-s-so s-sorry!" Miss Davidson was so worked up she began to hyperventilate. "H-H-He w-w-was s-s-stabbed!"

"Shit," Pop exclaimed and punched the steering wheel. His mother was too upset over her nephew's murder to reprimand her son for cursing as she typically would have. Pop burst into tears and his mother embraced him. After roughly five minutes, Pop regained his composure, which his mother had finally been able to do as well. She explained to her son that she had received a phone call from the jail informing her that Malik had been stabbed multiple times in his neck and abdomen during the night, he was dead, they had a suspect but could not reveal any more information other than the fact that she could come to the jail and retrieve Malik's personal effects.

Pop pulled away from the curb and drove his mother to CFCF, where she obtained the few personal belongings Cannon had brought with him into jail. She spoke with the same woman, Esther, with whom she had conversed over the phone that morning and who had been the one to inform her that her nephew had been brutally murdered as he slept in his jail cell.

"You just need to read and sign these papers, Miss Davidson," Esther informed her. "Then the belongings are all yours."

"Thank you." Miss Davidson signed the forms. "Is there anything else?"

"Um... yes," Esther hesitated. "Mister Davidson's body will be transferred to the County Morgue tomorrow, where you can identify the body and make arrangements for transport to whatever funeral home or church you are holding the funeral."

"Thank you," Miss Davidson said solemnly while holding back tears. "I'll do that."

"Good luck, ma'am," Esther watched as Miss Davidson walked away without a word, her head hung low on her shoulders.

Pop waited on Will's stoop for him to get home from school. He knew Will's routine was the same as his own – leave school, go to Twenty-First Street and Venango Street to retrieve the drugs from the stash-spot, come home and change clothes, then head out to the block to hustle until at least ten-o'clock at night.

Will pulled up in front of his house, saw Pop sitting on his stoop and wondered why Pop was waiting for him. Pop usually text-messaged Will while he was in school and Pop was cutting class, so this was out of the ordinary. Will exited his Cadillac and approached his house.

"What up, my nigga? What's good?" Will asked with a smile.

"Yo, what up?" Pop greeted Will without returning the smile. As Will approached, he could see that Pop's eyes were bloodshot and watery.

"You good, homey? It looks like you've been shedding some tears, dog," Will observed.

"They killed Cannon, man!"

"Wait – what? Cannon's locked up though," Will stated, confused.

"He got stabbed all in his neck and his stomach last night in jail," Pop explained. "He's dead, my nigga! Cannon's dead! My cousin's dead!" Pop burst into tears.

"Damn, my nigga. I'm so sorry," Will replied as he placed a hand on Pop's shoulder. "Damn, I can't believe my nigga's dead!"

"Aw shit," Pop inhaled deeply, attempting to stop crying. "I gotta stop this crying shit; especially out here on the block!"

"You're good, my nigga. Everybody knows you ain't soft," Will assured his friend. "I can't believe they killed a strong-ass nigga like Cannon, though. We need to put one in the air for him!"

"We sure do," Pop sniffled and laughed at the same time. He had finished crying. "One of my customers, Esteban, sells reggie." Will and Pop couldn't smoke anymore of the sour-diesel because they were only buying one pound at a time, which was enough for the four quarter-pounds they had been selling each week. They had decided that they would just buy dime-bags of "reggie," or regular marijuana, when they wanted to smoke.

"Yo, Es... what's good, cuz?" Pop said into the phone after Esteban answered.

"Ain't shit, homey," Esteban answered. "What's the deal?"

"Calling to see if you got tree…"

"You already know," Esteban replied.

"That's what's up. You need anything?" Pop asked.

"Yeah, I need four," Esteban answered.

"Well, we can trade two for two, and you can just pay for two," Pop calculated aloud. "Come over to Ninth Street."

"Alright, bet. I'll be there in a minute."

Will and Pop got into the Mustang, drove over to the corner of Ninth Street and Lycoming Street and waited for Esteban's arrival. A few minutes later, Esteban pulled up in an old Honda Accord and parked behind the Mustang. Esteban walked up to the driver's side window, which Pop had rolled down, and handed Pop two dime-bags of marijuana and a twenty-dollar bill. In return, Pop handed Esteban four dime-bags of cocaine. Esteban hopped back into his rusty, old Honda Accord and drove off.

"I'ma call Veronica and see what she's up to," Will informed Pop. "Maybe she'll wanna meet us at CeCe's crib. Do you mind? I know you've had a rough day."

"Naw, that's cool," Pop replied. "But let me call CeCe first and make sure she's down." Pop pulled out his phone, dialed CeCe's phone number and waited for her to answer.

"Hey, daddy," CeCe greeted Pop over the phone. "How are you?"

"To be honest, I'm fucked up in the head right now," Pop replied, his voice shaking as he tried to refrain from crying. "My cousin was stabbed to death in jail last night."

"Oh my God! I'm so sorry, *papi*," CeCe replied sympathetically. "Do you wanna come over? My parents are at their friend's house and my sister is out with her man."

"Yeah, that's what I was calling for. Me and Will just copped some tree and we wanted to see if you and Ronnie wanted to put it in the air with us."

"Sure, baby! Anything to make you feel better. When will you be over?"

"In like ten minutes. I'ma have Will call and see if Ronnie needs a ride to your crib."

"Oh, okay. See you soon baby. Bye."

"Yea, CeCe's down," Pop said as he turned to his friend. "Why don't you call and see if Veronica needs a ride over there?" Will nodded and dialed Veronica's phone number.

"What's up, ma?" Will greeted Veronica when she answered her phone.

"Hey Will! What's up, pop," she greeted him affectionately.

"Me and Pop are going over CeCe's to blow some tree," Will informed her. "You want me to come scoop you?"

"Um...," Veronica hesitated. "I would love to have you scoop me up in your Cadillac, but if Jasiel rode by and saw that, it would cause unnecessary beef, and I don't want that for you or me. I'll just walk. I'll leave now, okay, baby?"

"Alright, that's cool, I guess," Will sighed. "But I'm so tired of hearing about this nigga, Jasiel! You need to let me get rid of this nigga for you!"

Will had become much more eager to kill Jasiel since he had taken part in murdering Devin. Once he had eliminated that first person, his qualms about killing had subsided.

"Well, I'm sorry, baby, but it is what it is," Veronica replied softly. "And besides... you still have a girlfriend!"

"You're right, and I'll handle that eventually, but my girlfriend isn't abusive like Jasiel is! Plus, you know me and Pop have beef with Jasiel and his brother…"

"I'm sorry, babe, but I really don't wanna talk about it right now," Veronica sighed. "I just wanna come meet up with you and have a good time."

"You're right. I'll see you soon. We're headed over there in a minute. We just gotta stop and pick up the blunts," Will replied.

Pop drove over to the beer store on Hunting Park Avenue and bought two cigars before driving to CeCe's parents' house. As Will and Pop pulled up to the curb, they noticed Veronica walking up the street, so they waited for her before knocking on CeCe's door. They all went into CeCe's room. CeCe locked her bedroom door, turned on her radio and tuned it to the Hot 107.9 station while Will and Pop each crushed up the marijuana and rolled it into their respective cigars.

"So, how you guys doing?" Veronica asked, as she watched the teenagers skillfully manipulate the cigar paper.

"We're fucked up right now," Will sighed. "Pop's cousin just got stabbed to death in jail."

"Oh my God," Veronica gasped as she covered her mouth with her hands. "That's horrible! I didn't know stuff like that really happened! I thought it was just on TV. I'm so sorry for your loss, Pop!" She walked over and rubbed Pop's shoulders for a moment. Veronica wanted to give Pop a hug, but he was in the process of rolling the blunt so she didn't want to interfere.

"Thanks, Ronnie," Pop replied. "I appreciate the sympathy. I'm real fucked up about it."

"Well, then," Will interjected, "let's get fucked up off this tree in Cannon's memory!"

"No doubt," Pop smiled as he and Will finished rolling their marijuana cigars, lit them, inhaled several times and then passed them to the girls.

"Y'all want some Puerto Rican rum?" CeCe offered as she exhaled the marijuana smoke. "There's some downstairs in the refrigerator."

"Hell, yeah," Pop replied excitedly. "That one-fifty-one is the truth!"

CeCe went downstairs to the kitchen and quickly returned to the bedroom with the bottle of Puerto Rican rum in hand. While she was gone, the three others had continued smoking, but they weren't getting high.

"This weed is trash," Will blurted out all of a sudden.

"I wasn't gonna say anything," Veronica chimed in. "But I don't even smoke like that and I'm not getting high!"

"Leave it up to Esteban's coke-head-ass to give me some doodoo-ass smoke," Pop exclaimed, frustrated.

"It's okay, baby," CeCe comforted him. "At least we have this!" She held up the bottle of Puerto Rican rum. "This shit will get us all fucked up!"

Within thirty minutes, all four of the young people were highly intoxicated. They decided not to waste the marijuana, although it wasn't the best quality, so they smoked the rest of it. The four of them had finished drinking the whole bottle of rum within the hour. Will and Pop were just sitting down, relaxing and talking, although their speech was heavily slurred, while CeCe and Veronica were dancing around the room to the music playing on the radio.

"That's my shit!" Veronica screamed when "Pop That," a popular party song by a rapper named French Montana played. She danced over to Will, pulled him out of his seat, and began rapidly grinding her pelvis against his to the beat of the song. Pop and CeCe looked at each other and rolled their eyes.

"Ooh, girl! You like Will! What's going on with you two?" CeCe accused Veronica. A few hours had passed and the guys had drank water, sobered up some, and left CeCe's place before her parents came home.

"Nothing's going on! And no, I don't like him," Veronica objected, lying. "I'm just drunk! I was just messing around!" She still hadn't revealed her and Will's secret relationship to anybody, even CeCe, due to her fear that Jasiel would find out and do something drastic.

The next morning, Will was awoken by the sound of his phone ringing. He was hung-over, and the noise was excruciating. He had been so intoxicated the night before that he forgot to change the ringer on his phone to vibrate so that it wouldn't wake him.

"H-Hello?" Will's voice cracked into the phone.

"Yo, Will!" Pop hollered frantically into the phone. "Somebody stole the Mustang!"

"Yo… wait a minute… slow down," Will said slowly as he rose from his bed, his head pounding, trying to process what Pop was telling him.

"What did you say?"

"Somebody stole the Mustang, man! I looked out my window when I woke up and didn't see it! Then I came outside; it's nowhere on the block, my nigga! Somebody stole that shit!"

"Wait – was there broken glass on the ground near where you were parked?"

"Naw… I didn't see any," Pop replied.

"Have you been making the payments on the car-note, Pop?" Will asked.

"Naw, man," Pop replied, clueless. "Cannon never gave me any information for that. I thought that jawn was paid off!"

"Come on, man," Will laughed, "Cannon was getting bread, but not enough to buy a brand new Mustang, cash! I think that thing got repossessed, not stolen."

"Damn, man! I was loving that Mustang, too," Pop exclaimed. "Plus all my CDs were in there!"

"Yeah, that's salty," Will responded empathetically. "Not to be in your pockets or nothing, but can you afford another wheel?"

"With all this paper we've been making, you already know!"

"Well, since you woke my ass up all early, and the girls won't be ready for work yet, you want me to take you to the dealer where I got my car?" Will offered.

"Yeah, good looking out."

"Alright, let me just take a shower and get dressed, then I'll come through and we can go."

Between selling cocaine, selling sour-diesel and selling guns, and after paying bills and spending money on various miscellaneous items, Pop had saved around thirteen-thousand dollars over the previous two months. He decided he could afford to spend eleven thousand dollars on a vehicle. Will drove him to the same used-car dealership on Roosevelt Boulevard, where Will had purchased his Cadillac. The salesman and the manager remembered the two young men and were very helpful. Pop was able to acquire a navy blue, 2006 Dodge Magnum for ten-thousand dollars, and the dealer included taxes and tags. They made the process very easy for Pop and kept the price under the tax reporting limit so that there wouldn't be any problems for either party with the Internal Revenue Service, since Pop was paying with cash.

"Well, that's what's up," Pop said to Will as they exited their vehicles after they pulled up to the curb on Ninth Street. "Now I just have to hustle up some rims!"

CHAPTER 14

Time elapsed, over two months to be more specific. Pop had turned eighteen, and both he and Will had continued their routines of school, selling drugs and entertaining females. However, one major thing had changed in Will's routine – basketball season had started. Will had decided to discontinue smoking and drinking for the duration of the basketball season - something he did he each year, and he was lifting weights and running in addition to attending basketball practice and games. His performance on the team was stellar, as usual, and he stood out as the all-star he had always been. Will's team was winning games, and he was the leading scorer as point-guard, averaging twenty-three points per game. Will also maintained an average of five rebounds and eleven assists per game – he was no doubt his team's Most Valuable Player.

Will was growing extremely frustrated, however, with how much time basketball took out of his schedule. It seemed like every week he had less time for everything else, especially as the season progressed and his team advanced. He had less time for Stacy, less time for Veronica, and, most importantly, less time to sell drugs and make money. The problem was he actually needed *more* time to sell drugs.

What he would do was stay up all hours of the night, selling cocaine or driving with Pop to Southwest Philadelphia to meet up with Tommy and Jay and their associates in order to sell them their quarter-pounds of sour-diesel each week. The next day, however, Will would oversleep, or skip basketball practice that evening, due to being too tired to accomplish everything he had on his schedule for that day. Will hadn't even had the opportunity to talk to Pop about when they would speak with Cannon's gun connection, Amin – he had just been too busy. He thought it was probably too late now that Cannon had been dead for months and the connect hadn't heard from Cannon in so long. Pop hadn't mentioned anything about selling guns either, so Will figured that the general consensus was that they were both too busy to sell guns. But Will decided he needed to clear something off of his proverbial "plate" so that he wasn't so busy. As January came, Will's birthday approached, and as he planned to get his own apartment, Will had a talk with his mother about his plans.

"Hey Ma! Where you at?" Will yelled as he walked into the house after school. Misses Bonner rushed down the stairs with a concerned expression plastered across her face.

"Will, what is it baby?" she asked her son. "Is everything okay?"

"Yeah Ma... why are you looking so upset? I just wanna talk to you about some things," Will replied nonchalantly.

"Oh, okay. Well maybe I look like this because you were yelling like the house was on fire! But yeah, we can talk. Your brother's still at school. I didn't expect you home so early – aren't you supposed to be at basketball practice?"

"Well, Ma – that's what I wanted to talk to you about," Will started. "I'm about to quit basketball."

"What?" Misses Bonner exclaimed. "Why would you do something silly like that, baby? What about your dream of going to the NBA?"

"Truthfully, ain't none of these NBA scouts checking for me, Ma," Will replied, downtrodden. "I thought because I've been in the newspaper a lot that they would come around, but they haven't been."

"But baby, do you realize how rare it is for a kid to go straight from high school to the NBA?" Misses Bonner asked her son. "I know that was your goal... but you can still try to get a scholarship to college. I'm sure you'll get one! You said the college scouts have been at your games, right?"

"Ma, I'm not really feeling the whole college thing," Will admitted. "I'm kinda done with school. I'm trying hard not to drop out. This basketball thing is taking too much time away from me getting money, you know? I need to take care of you and Carl. You know your job doesn't pay enough, Ma. And I'm about to move out too, so I'm gonna have more bills."

"Oh Lord! Here we go with that moving out shit again!" Misses Bonner sighed. "I don't know what's so bad about living with us that you have to move as soon as you turn eighteen! And you better not drop out of school, boy! You know your ass needs to take one of those scholarships and go to college so you can get a good job! If you're so worried about me and Carl, you need to set a good example for your brother and go to school and get a good job so that he can see there's more to life than hustling in these North Philly streets!"

"Yeah, Ma, well, the only college I might go to is Saint Joe's so that I can stay in Philly and still do my thing, 'cause I won't be making any money going to college!"

"Well, you'll be eighteen in a couple weeks and you'll be legally grown, so I guess I can't tell you what to do anymore," Misses Bonner replied, defeated. "Just, please, reconsider. I think you'll go far with the basketball, Will. If you go to college on the scholarship you can still make it to the NBA, baby. You just gotta think long-term."

"I feel you, Ma... it's just that I don't have time to wait, you know? I need money now! With the money that I make now, I'll probably be able to sell weight within a year and be a boss," Will bragged. "I will be making so much money... I'll be able to open up a club by the time I'm twenty-one. I won't need school or basketball!"

"That's all well and good, but how are you going to know how to manage the club without going to school?" Misses Bonner objected.

"I'll do just fine, Ma. The old-head, Tiny, owns three bars and he didn't go to school for it!"

"You young people think you know everything," Misses Bonner snapped. "Well, I guess you have it all figured out, son. So go do what you wanna do!"

The next Monday, Will's first day back at school after skipping for several days in order to sell drugs, his basketball coach, Coach Anderson approached him and asked to speak with him in his office.

"What's up, Coach? What did you wanna talk to me about?"

"Will, where have you been?" Coach Anderson asked abruptly. "You've missed practice, you missed our game against Bartram, which we lost, and you haven't been in class! What the hell is up, kid?"

"Well, to be honest, coach – I'm not really feeling this whole scene anymore," Will admitted.

"What do you mean you're 'not feeling this whole scene?'"

"I love basketball," Will started, "but I think I've kinda outgrown it, na'mean?"

"No! I don't know what you mean," Coach Anderson exclaimed. "Look, Will – I've seen a lot of young guys with talent, and I've seen a lot of them throw it away for dumb shit. I don't want you to do the same thing…"

"Well, Coach," Will interrupted, "I ain't got no dumb shit going on… just real, grown-man shit," Will stated arrogantly.

"Will, I'm not naïve," Coach Anderson replied matter-of-factly. "I've seen you getting into your car after practice. What kind of kid your age has a car nicer than his teachers if he isn't doing something illegal? Will, what are you into? You can talk to me. I've been coaching you almost four years!"

"Don't worry about it, Coach – I'm good. I was thinking about quitting ball anyway…"

"Quitting basketball?" Coach Anderson roared. "Who gave you that dumb idea? Will, you have a gift! You shouldn't throw it away. I have some news that might change your mind…"

"I don't think you could say anything to change my mind, Coach," Will replied coldly.

"What about three college recruitment letters?" Smiling, the coach opened his desk-drawer, reached in, retrieved three envelopes and handed them to Will. "One from Georgetown, one from Syracuse and one from UNC! Huh, kid… what do you think about that? We did it!"

Will looked over the letters for a few moments, and then tossed them back on Coach Anderson's desk.

"I wanna go to the NBA," Will said, devoid of emotion.

"And you can," Coach Anderson stated emphatically, "but college is the first step."

"What about LeBron James? He went straight from high school to the pros…"

"Come on kid! That is so rare! That's like seeing a white tiger walking down Broad Street!"

"You don't think I'm good enough to go straight to the pros," Will huffed.

"Look, Will. You're definitely an all-star. But this is Philly," Coach Anderson explained. "We come from a tough city. You should be happy that you have not only one recruitment letter, but three! I believe you have the talent to make it to the pros, but they wanna see that you can play college ball and adjust to that. It's a big leap from high school ball to the pros, and college is the stepping-stone players need to get to the NBA, you understand? But if you're gonna go to college, you can't be skipping school. Besides, the NBA doesn't even allow players to go straight to the League from high school anymore."

"Man, Coach… you sound just like my mom," Will sighed. "I don't wanna go to college anyway. I don't have time for that! I barely have time for high school. My family has financial needs that college won't help with. The only college I was thinking about going to is Saint Joe's – but only if I get a scholarship, 'cause I can't afford to pay for it. Saint Joe's is close to home… I wanna stay close to home."

"But Will, these are great schools knocking down your door already. Why don't you consider one of them?"

"'Cause I don't want to," Will stated coolly. "May I please be excused?"

"Yeah," Coach Anderson huffed angrily as Will exited his office. Just be smart, son!"

Two weeks passed and Will attended school, basketball practice and his team's basketball games sporadically at best. He was more concerned with making money and dividing his extra time between Stacy and Veronica.

Will's birthday arrived and he and Pop decided to use their false identification so they could get into Tiny's bar on Hunting Park Avenue and enjoy themselves that Friday night following Will's birthday. Stacy was upset because she hadn't been invited, but Will blamed it on Pop, saying that Pop wanted to take him out for a "guy's night out." The real reason Will hadn't wanted Stacy along, however, was because of his plans to talk to females. He was going to sign his lease the next day on an apartment he had found on Rockland Street in the Logan section of the city, and he didn't want Stacy around in case he met a new girl who wanted to come over and help him christen his apartment. Will and Pop were drinking gin mixed with pineapple juice, getting quite intoxicated, talking to girls, obtaining phone numbers at the bar and having fun. They even spoke to Tiny for a short while. Everything was going well and Will was having a good time until Jasiel and Jose approached a couple hours after the night had progressed.

"Pop! What's up dog?" Jasiel greeted Pop with a smile and shook his hand. "What's the deal?"

"Ain't shit, Jasiel," Pop replied. "What's good with y'all?"

Will ignored Jasiel and Jose as he sat at the bar and kept drinking. Will was still unaware that Pop had formed a business relationship with Jasiel and Jose, so he was actually irritated that Pop was speaking with their enemies, especially on his birthday.

"What's going on, Will?" Jose asked Will as he extended his arm to Will for a handshake. Will looked at Jose's hand, looked away and took another sip of his drink.

"Hey, Pop, what's wrong with your boy?" Jose asked innocently.

"You wanna know what's wrong with me, motherfucker?" Will roared. "Y'all niggas always rolling up on us, talking about robbing somebody, and now you wanna shake my hand? I ain't shaking your motherfucking hand, nigga!"

"You disrespect my brother like that," Jasiel barked. "I'll kill you!" Jasiel threw his drink down to the floor, shattering his glass. The remainder of his drink splashed all over the young men's feet. Jasiel jumped at Will, but Pop jumped in between the two and his strong arms kept Jasiel's small frame at bay.

"Trust me, you don't want none of me, Jasiel," Will scorned Jasiel. "I'll whoop that ass without even trying, dog."

"Next time, I'll greet you with heat, my nigga!" Jasiel threatened.

"Chill, y'all! Chill," Pop yelled in the midst of the mayhem.

"Hey! Hey... fellas," Tiny interjected as he ran over. He had noticed the drama occurring from the deejay booth where he had been standing, conversing with the deejay. "I know y'all ain't beefing in my establishment!"

"Sorry, Unc," Jose answered as he grabbed Jasiel's shoulder to calm him down. "We're not tryna start nothing."

"*This* motherfucker...," Jasiel began, pointing at Will.

"Look, whatever it was, I can't afford any drama in my bar in front of my bar or anywhere near my bar," Tiny cut Jasiel off. "And I do business with Will and Pop and you and Jose are my blood, so I can't afford y'all to be beefing, so I suggest y'all just squash it now. Alright?"

"Alright," Jasiel reluctantly agreed.

"What about you Will?"

"Alright Tiny," Will also reluctantly agreed. "You're the boss."

"*Mami*! Give the four of them a drink on me so they can chill the fuck out!" Tiny instructed the female bartender. "Now, y'all young-boys be nice to each other," Tiny smirked as he walked away.

"Look, Pop," Jasiel addressed Pop as he put his arm around his shoulder. "Your homey's wiling out... you need to handle that!"

Will overheard Jasiel, turned and looked Jasiel directly in his face and stared at him for a while as he drank his free drink. Jasiel paid Will no mind and kept talking to Pop. Will turned away and kept drinking.

"But anyway, what I wanted to holler at you about is them hammers you got on deck," Jasiel continued. "Me and Jose need some more. When can we hook up?"

"Whenever… within the next few days is good for me," Pop replied, looking out of the corner of his eyes to see if Will was paying attention. Will was staring straight ahead, bobbing his head to the music, seemingly oblivious.

However, Will had overheard the conversation and he felt betrayed. How could Pop sell guns without him? Cannon had told them both that the gun connect was their reward for killing Devin. Besides, they made their money together. Will had brought Pop into the cocaine business years ago, and they sold sour-diesel together – why would he sell guns without him? Will had a feeling that since Pop had hidden the fact that he had met with the gun connect and started selling guns without letting him know, this meant that Pop could not be trusted to a certain extent.

Early the next morning, Will went to the new apartment in Logan, signed his lease and received his keys. After that, he went back to Ninth Street and picked up Pop so they could head over to Rick's spot and pick up two ounces of cocaine, then pick up CeCe and Veronica from CeCe's house.

"What's up, my nigga?" Pop said with a smile as he entered Will's Cadillac.

"What up?" Will said coolly, still upset about what he had heard Pop discussing with Jasiel at the bar the previous night. "I hope we can get up out of the spot fast today… I need to go furniture shopping for the new crib after we're finished."

"Oh yeah, that's right! You're moving out today," Pop recalled. "Let me know if you need help, homey."

"Naw, I'm good, but thanks," Will declined. "I just got a few bags of clothes, a box of CDs and DVDs that I'ma throw in my wheel, oh, and my TV. Everything else I'ma buy new from the store and get it delivered."

"Oh that's cool," Pop replied. "So where you moving to again? Loudon Street?"

"Naw," Will hesitated. "Rockland." Will was even hesitant to tell Pop where he was moving because of the breach of trust in their relationship. "Man, fuck it… I was ear-hustling last night – what's up with you selling guns to Jasiel? That's our enemy! And you were acting all cool with him and Jose…"

"W-what you mean?" Pop stuttered, caught off guard.

"Come on man! You know what I mean," Will snapped. "You went to the gun connect without even telling me and you've been getting money without me! You're supposed to be my nigga, man… I wouldn't do that to you! I wouldn't cut you out of a money-making opportunity! Plus, you've been selling guns to our enemies! What if they use them against us?"

"Well… I mean, my fault man," Pop forced an apology although he wasn't truly sorry. "I didn't think you would take it that way. I just didn't think you wanted to be down with that since you didn't bring it up after Cannon mentioned it at the jail and 'cause you weren't helping me sell the first batch we got out of Cannon's crib."

"Hell yeah, I wanted to be down, nigga!" Will replied harshly. "I wanna be down with anything that involves getting money! And why the fuck would you sell them to our enemies? What if they turn around and try to pop us with the same damn guns you sold to them?"

"Well, I'm cool with them now, so that ain't gonna happen," Pop replied matter-of-factly. "But I'm gonna have to squash that beef you caused last night. I'm glad Tiny stepped in!"

"Man… I don't give a fuck! Fuck Jasiel and Jose!"

The teenagers picked up their cocaine, then picked up CeCe and Veronica from CeCe's house, before Will drove the four of them to the room in the house at Twenty-First Street and Venango Street. As usual, Will and Pop smoked marijuana, played video games and listened to music while the girls bagged up the product. Four and a half hours passed before the girls finished.

"We're done," Veronica stated triumphantly.

"That's what's up," Will said excitedly as he got up and turned off the video game console. "Now I can go to the furniture store!"

"What you going to the furniture store for?" CeCe asked.

"Uh… to buy furniture," Will teased her.

"Shut up, Will! Furniture for what? Don't you live with your mom?"CeCe asked.

"Not anymore! I'm moving out. I just signed my lease and got my keys today," Will replied proudly as he handed the girls their payment for bagging up the cocaine.

"Aw shit! You got your own place now? Somebody's balling," CeCe smiled.

Pop cut his eyes at CeCe, but nobody noticed. He didn't appreciate her comment about Will making a lot of money. Why did she always have to compliment him? Pop could feel his blood boiling as his jealousy and resentment against Will built up.

The four young people left the house. Pop and Will had divided half of the bags of cocaine between the two of them as they usually did, placed them in their book bags and placed the other half in the safe in the room. They entered the Cadillac and Will dropped everybody off at home so he could go furniture shopping. Will drove to the Raymour and Flanigan furniture store on Adams Avenue and Roosevelt Boulevard and purchased an expensive bedroom set, living room set and dining room set and had them delivered to his apartment the next day. Once everything was delivered, he settled into his new place.

The day after Will had moved into his apartment, it was time to re-up, or buy more drugs, again. It was a Monday and Will had decided to skip school so that he could see Rick, buy the cocaine, and pick up Veronica and CeCe so they could bag up the cocaine. Will was irritated with Pop because Pop said he wasn't able to make it because he had missed too much school and needed to attend all of his classes that day. In actuality, Pop did in fact skip school, and he was meeting up with Jasiel and Jose to sell them some guns. When Will arrived at CeCe's house after buying the cocaine from Rick, she was already waiting on the stoop for him. When she saw Will pull up, she approached Will's car and got in.

"What's up, CeCe? Where's Ronnie?" Will asked.

"Hey, Will," CeCe replied. "She has the flu. She can't make it today. She said she was gonna call you, but she's been sleeping a lot. I called and accidentally woke her up. Where's Pop?"

"Pop's at school, so I guess it's just me and you today," Will replied as he pulled away from the curb.

"That's what's up!"

"It is?" Will asked, confused. "Aren't you gonna be pissed that it's gonna take you longer to bag up the soft?"

"No, 'cause that means it's more time I get to spend alone with you, *papi chulo*," CeCe smiled and batted her eyelashes as she rubbed her hand on Will's leg.

"Uh, for real?" Will hesitated. "Don't you mess with Pop, though?"

"Uh well, yeah kinda," CeCe stuttered. "But I've always wanted you. You're so sexy, Will. Besides, Pop won't claim me! I've been trying to be his girlfriend for a while, but he won't call me his girlfriend, so that makes me think he's fucking around. So, I figure I wanna fuck around, too! And since you're the full package – you're very handsome, you got a nice car, you got money, you're cool, you got your own place now and you're athletic, I wanna mess with you!"

"But that's my nigga though…"

"Don't worry about Pop! He'll get over it! On some real shit… he doesn't even have to find out," CeCe replied coldly.

"I don't know, ma…"

Shortly thereafter, Will and CeCe arrived at the house where Will and Pop had rented a room to use as a stash-spot. Will played some music and sat on the futon smoking while CeCe bagged up the cocaine. It took her much longer than usual because she didn't have any help from Veronica. Will wasn't in the mood to play any video games. His mind was racing. Will couldn't stop thinking about CeCe's proposition. The fact that she kept staring at him and flirting with him throughout the day didn't help the situation either.

Will thought about Pop, and the fact that he had been so upset when he had felt Pop betrayed him and sold guns without telling him. Imagine how betrayed Pop would feel if Will had sex with CeCe, even though Pop claimed she wasn't his girlfriend. Will also thought about Stacy – he hadn't called her since his birthday. She had been calling him, but he was too busy hustling and seeing Veronica to return her phone calls and he felt badly about that. And Veronica – she and CeCe were best friends. Will realized that if he slept with CeCe and Veronica found out, he and Veronica would be finished, and CeCe and Veronica's friendship would also be over. The thoughts were overwhelming to Will. He was becoming stressed, so he decided it was time to roll another blunt and smoke some more.

Will weighed all the negative aspects of having sex with CeCe as he smoked. He didn't want to hurt Stacy, but that had never stopped him from having sex with other girls before. Will didn't want to betray Pop's trust, but Pop had already betrayed his. He didn't want to break-up CeCe and Veronica's friendship and hurt Veronica at the same time, but Veronica was still dating Jasiel.

Will looked up at CeCe. There she was, sitting there working diligently, looking beautiful; with her curly, black hair cascading halfway down her back; her light brown skin and her big, brown eyes, framed perfectly by long, dark eyelashes. He had to admit –she was very sexy. And she was built perfectly as well. The more he looked and the more he smoked, (he was smoking his third blunt at this point), the less he cared about everything else and the more he wanted to have sex with CeCe.

"I'm finally finished, Will," CeCe sighed as she placed the last bit of cocaine into a dime-bag.

"Cool," Will replied lazily as he lounged on the futon. He was extremely high after smoking two and a half cigars full of marijuana by himself.

"You ready to roll out?"

"Yes, *papi*," CeCe smiled.

Will paid CeCe double what he normally paid her since she had worked alone and then placed half of the dime bags of cocaine in his bookbag for when he went out to the corner later to sell them. He placed the rest in the safe in the room.

"Yo, CeCe... I was thinking," Will said deliberately so as not to slur his words due to how high he was. "You wanna come see my apartment?"

"Sure! I would love to!"

The two left Nicetown and Will drove to the Logan section of the city. Will parked in front of the building on Rockland Street and he and CeCe exited the Cadillac. They entered his building and walked into his apartment. Will made a vain attempt to give CeCe a tour of his apartment, but as soon as they made their way to the bedroom, they attached themselves to each other and fell on the bed, kissing and groping each other. CeCe straddled Will, removing his shirt, but her knee pressed against his phone in his pocket several times, dialing Stacy's phone number in Will's phone's "Call Log."

Stacy was very happy to see her man's name appear on her "Caller ID" on her phone. She smiled excitedly as she answered the phone.

"Hey baby!" There was no response. "Hey baby... Hello. Hello!"

CeCe then removed Will's pants and boxers, placed them next to Will and began kissing and licking his chest and his stomach, then further down she went.

"Oh my God, CeCe," Will moaned. "Do it just like that!"

"What the hell? Oh my God! Oh no!" Stacy hung up the phone and burst into tears.

CHAPTER 15

Stacy was devastated and she didn't know what to do. She needed someone to talk to; somebody to confide in. An emotional wreck, she decided the best person for her to confide in would be Will's best friend, Pop. Stacy didn't have Pop's phone number, but they were friends on Facebook™, a popular social networking site. She turned on her computer and logged onto the site and sent a message to Pop.

"Pop, I'm going through it right now and I need to talk to you. Can you please come over ASAP? Don't tell Will…"

The message went directly to Pop's "Facebook Messenger™" feature on his phone. He had been sitting in his car, hustling on the corner of Ninth Street and Lycoming Street with the few bags of cocaine he had left when the message had come through. After he had finished selling a couple guns to Jose and Jasiel, he had hung out with them for a while and smoked wet with them for the first time in his life, and he wasn't feeling well. He was extremely high and extremely paranoid. He attempted to contact Will, but Will hadn't answered his phone, which had Pop suspicious. When he finished exchanging money for his last three bags of powder with a customer, he checked his message. Pop replied within five minutes of Stacy sending the message.

"Sorry to hear that, Stacy. I'll be right over. And I won't tell Will."

When Pop pulled up in front of Stacy's building on Twentieth Street and Hunting Park Avenue, she was already waiting outside in the cold to let him in. He parked and exited his vehicle. As Pop approached, he noticed that Stacy was crying.

"Damn, Stacy. What's all that for, sis?" Pop asked, perplexed. "What you crying for, ma?"

"I'll tell you when we get inside," Stacy sniffled.

Pop followed Stacy into the house, which was subdivided into apartments, and then followed her into her apartment. Stacy's mother was sitting on the sofa watching television.

"Who's this nigga?" Stacy's mother abruptly asked.

"Mom! Please be nice," Stacy pleaded. "This is me and Will's friend, Pop. We're gonna talk in my room."

"Talk? In your room?" Stacy's mother asked incredulously. "Oh, so you're fucking him, too? I always knew you were a smut!"

"Mom... I don't need this right now!"

"Well, then, go 'talk,' bitch!"

Stacy stormed off to her room in tears as Pop followed, shaking his head in disgust. Stacy closed her bedroom door behind Pop and locked it.

"So is that what's wrong Stacy," Pop asked. "Is it your mother?"

"Oh Pop," Stacy ran over to Pop and embraced him tightly as she cried on his shoulder. "I wish she was the problem! I'm used to her acting like that! It's Will..."

"What happened? Did he break up with you or something?"

"No," Stacy said as she released her embrace and paced the room as she began to explain. "This motherfucker cheated on me! After all we've been through!"

"But Stacy, how do you know Will cheated on you?"

"Because he just accidentally called me while he was fucking some hoe, like twenty minutes ago," Stacy sobbed.

"Slow down, Stace...," Pop replied. "Tell me exactly what happened."

"Well, I saw his number pop up on my phone, and I was all happy 'cause I haven't been able to reach him since his birthday, but I just figured he was busy hustling with you. Now I know he's been fucking this hoodrat!"

"But please finish, Stacy..."

"Well, anyway," Stacy continued, "I answered the phone like, 'hey baby,' and he didn't say anything and then I said 'hello' a few times until I heard him say, 'Oh my God, CeCe... just like that!' Then I hung up and started crying!"

"CeCe? Did you say 'CeCe?'" Pop asked in disbelief.

"Yeah, that's what I heard," Stacy sniffled. "He's cheating on me with a bitch named CeCe!"

"Look, I'm really sorry he did that to you, Stace," Pop apologized on Will's behalf. "What are you gonna do?"

"I gotta talk to him and find out what the fuck is going on."

"What do you mean 'find out what's going on?' You know *exactly* what's going on, ma – he's fucking the bitch, CeCe," Pop stated matter-of-factly.

"Yeah, I know," Stacy replied, disheartened. "I just love him so much though. I don't want to lose him."

"Honestly, Stacy, I hate to say it, but it sounds like you already have," Pop was brutally honest. "But you know... I would never treat you like that, ma."

"What are you saying, Pop?" Stacy asked warily.

"I'm saying, why don't you quit Will and get with me? I think you should break up with him for what he did to you."

"Yeah, but y'all are boys, plus you do business together – I can't come between that!"

"But Will did you dirty and I can't be his friend anymore after what he did to you. I consider you my friend, too. And I've always had a little crush on you."

"Aw, that's sweet Pop, but I can't do it. I just can't jump from one relationship into another, you know?" Stacy declined. She didn't want to hurt Pop's feelings by telling him that she was in no way, shape or form attracted to him anyway.

"Well, at least think about it ma, okay?"

"Alright, Pop."

"I'm about to get outta here," Pop informed Stacy. "Do you mind? Are you good?"

"Yeah, I'm better, thanks. Thanks for coming over and talking to me and helping me out."

"Anytime, sis," Pop replied. "But whatever you do, don't tell Will that we had this conversation, okay?"

"Okay, I promise."

Pop left, his head spinning. How could Will betray him like that and have sex with CeCe? He was already having sex with Veronica – why was he being greedy? Why did he need them both? Pop was infuriated. The fact that he was high off the PCP didn't help either. It heightened his murderous rage. Pop began to plot against Will, and he knew just who to talk to in order to help him carry out his plan.

"Yo, Jasiel, what up?" Pop greeted Jasiel when he answered his phone.

"Yo, what up, gun-runner?"

"Can you meet up with me in like ten minutes at Old York Road and Lycoming?" Pop asked. "I got a proposition for you and Jose."

"Yeah, we'll be there in ten," Jasiel said and then hung up.

In less than ten minutes Jasiel and Jose drove up in Jasiel's Pontiac Bonneville, exited their vehicle and entered Pop's Dodge Magnum.

"Yo, Pop, this jawn is nice man," Jose exclaimed. "I meant to tell you earlier... I see you got the twenty-inch rims and the system and all that! You and Will are getting money together!"

"Fuck that nigga!" Pop roared.

"Whoa," Jasiel laughed. "What's up with that? I thought that was your man!"

"Not anymore! That nigga fucked my bitch," Pop complained.

"You're gonna let a bitch come between y'all?" Jose asked, surprised. "You're supposed to be running trains on these bitches together!"

"It's a trust thing, na'mean?" Pop stated. "Plus, Jasiel, Will told me he's fucking your girl, Veronica!"

"What?" Jasiel barked. "That high-yellow nigga is fucking my bitch? I'll merck that *maricon*! When did you find out?"

"He just told me earlier today," Pop lied, not wanting to reveal the fact that he had known about the affair for months.

"Man, that's fucked up," Jose sighed.

"Yeah, it is fucked up," Pop concurred. "I told Will that I thought she was your girl but he said, 'Fuck that nigga, Jasiel, and his bitch-ass brother, too,'" in an attempt to make the twins even angrier and prime them for his scheme.

"Oh yeah? That motherfucker said that?" Jasiel roared. "Wait... how did you know Veronica was my bitch?"

"Oh, uh, how did I know?" Pop stuttered, not wanting Jasiel to know that he had been dealing with Jasiel's and Jose's cousin, CeCe. "I think Tiny or Rick mentioned something a while ago. Plus I've seen y'all riding together around the hood..."

"Oh okay... if you say so," Jasiel replied suspiciously.

"So, anyway," Pop continued, "were you serious when you said you wanted to merck Will?"

"You're motherfucking right! I've *been* wanting to kill that motherfucker," Jasiel grinned maniacally with a devilish look in his eyes. "And now he's fucking my bitch! Ooh, I wanna do that nigga so dirty!"

"What about you, Jose?" Pop turned to Jose in the backseat and asked.

"Shit, I'm down for whatever, yo," Jose replied nonchalantly. "He's fucking my brother's girl, calling me a bitch... I'll show him I ain't no bitch!"

"Well, the nigga fucked my girl, too," Pop began. "Plus he's being greedy with the bread and tryna keep it all to himself," Pop lied to try to justify what he was about to say. "So I agree – Will needs to die..."

"Damn, dog! You a cutthroat motherfucker," Jasiel laughed.

"You're gonna kill your own homey?"

"No, I was thinking y'all would," Pop replied. "Besides, that nigga is shady! He's not my homey anymore! I can help y'all set it up. I'll pay y'all five-hundred each. Plus, we could do it in two nights from tonight after we get our weight from Rick, so y'all can get an ounce of coke from him, too. And he carries mad cash on him so you can take what he has on him. What I'll do is I'll convince him to come with me and hustle on Ninth and Lycoming. Y'all can creep up, I'll roll down his window and one of y'all can pop him, then we'll be out! What you think? Y'all down?"

"No doubt," Jasiel enthusiastically replied.

"Fuck it... I'll do it," Jose replied casually. "But you should let Will drive so you don't have a dead motherfucker and blood all in your car, na'mean?"

"Good thinking," Pop agreed. "Alright y'all. I'll text Jasiel on Wednesday night when I'm ready for y'all to come through Ninth and Lycoming – probably around midnight."

"Alright cool, just let me know and we'll be here."

The young men exchanged handshakes and then Jasiel and Jose exited Pop's vehicle, entered Jasiel's vehicle and drove away.

The next day Pop met up with Will in the early afternoon (they had both skipped school again) and went to the stash-spot to get Pop's half of the cocaine to sell. It was awkward for Pop, seeing Will for the first time after finding out Will had sex with CeCe and after plotting his murder with Jasiel and Jose. The plot was to be carried out the very next night and it was all Pop could think about. He tried to act normal around Will, but it was difficult. He had built up so much resentment and jealousy towards his former friend that he had become consumed by it.

"Pop... Pop... *Pop!*" Will shouted Pop's name the third time as he tried to get Pop's attention.

"Huh? Yo, what's up?" Pop's finally responded. He had been deep in thought.

"I said are you tryna smoke?" Will repeated his initial question. "I got some weed."

"Uh... naw, not really, man," Pop declined. "I gotta get out on the block, na'mean?" Although Pop really did need to go out and hustle, he passed up on Will's offer because he didn't want to spend any more time around him than he needed to.

"Yeah, I feel you," Will replied. "I'm about to do the same thing after I blow this tree!"

"Alright Will... I'ma get up outta here..."

"Okay, my nigga. But don't forget we gotta go meet with Jeremiah in a few hours then go see Tommy and Jay and them tonight."

"Alright bet, just hit me up, Will. I'll be on the block."

Pop left the stash-spot at Twenty-First Street and Venango Street and drove to the corner of Ninth Street and Lycoming Street to sell his dime-bags of cocaine.

"This back-stabbing nigga, Will," Pop thought to himself. "He's smiling in my face, knowing he just fucked CeCe! He'll get his tomorrow night! And that's good that we're selling to Tommy and his homeys tonight 'cause that means he might have that bread on him tomorrow night. Maybe I can convince Jasiel and Jose to split that money with me!"

Pop's mind was racing with anticipation. Pop was actually growing excited about killing his best friend, the guy he had grown up with and the person who had brought him into the drug business and had shown him how to make more money than he had ever made in his life. Their illegal way of living had torn them apart.

Wednesday morning, the two eighteen-year-olds skipped school again in order to meet up with Rick and buy their usual two ounces of cocaine.

As was their routine, once they bought the powder from Rick, they would go to CeCe's house and pick her up, along with Veronica, in order to take them to the stash-spot so that they could bag up the product. Veronica was feeling better and no longer had the flu, so she would be working alongside CeCe that day. Pop had a very hard time maintaining his composure around CeCe and Will, but he had to continue to act normal for the time being.

In any event, the four youngsters pulled up to the stash-spot on Twenty-First Street in Nicetown and exited Will's Cadillac. However, that very same morning, Jasiel and Jose were out early, at around eleven-o'clock in the morning looking for a "come-up" – somebody or someplace to rob at a later date. They had decided that they had robbed most of the drug-houses and stash-spots they had found in Hunting Park and that they would go to the other side of Broad Street and scout the Nicetown section of the city for probable drug-houses they could rob. Coincidentally, as Will, Pop, CeCe and Veronica walked from Will's Cadillac to the house, Jasiel and Jose happened to be driving down Twenty-First Street in Jose's Chevrolet Impala with dark-tinted windows, and Jasiel spotted the four young people walking into the house.

"What the fuck? Do you see what I'm seeing, Jose?" Jasiel roared as he pointed past Jose's face towards the driver's side window.

"Oh shit! Is that our cousin?"

"Yeah! That's Cyndal with that motherfucking liar, Pop, that cheating-ass bitch, Ronnie, and that high-yellow nigga, Will!" Jasiel growled.

"What is Cyndal doing with those Black motherfuckers?" Jose asked, dumbfounded.

"Fuck it… pull over so I can bust at them," Jasiel blurted out.

"Jasiel, are you crazy? You might hit Cyndal!" Jose yelled as his foot slammed the car's gas pedal and the vehicle sped past the house so Jasiel could not act on his impulse.

"That motherfucker, Pop, has been hanging out with Will while Will's been fucking my bitch!" Jasiel roared. "And he's fucking our cousin too? That lying motherfucker!"

That evening after the girls finished bagging up the cocaine, Will dropped them back off at CeCe's house and then went back to Ninth Street to drop Pop off and visit his mother in order to give her some money and have dinner with her and Carl.

"Yo, Will, what you up to later, dog?" Pop asked.

"My mother called me while we were at the spot and said she wanted to have dinner as a family so I'ma go to the crib now. She said she wants to talk to me about something," Will replied, shrugging his shoulders.

"Oh alright, have fun. But um… why don't I go with you to the old corner to hustle tonight?"

"That's cool with me," Will agreed. "Maybe we can blow some tree!"

"Bet," Pop responded with false enthusiasm and a forced smile. "Just hit me up when you're finished dinner."

"Hey baby," Will's mother greeted him with a hug and kiss as he walked through the front door.

"Hey, mom. What's up, Carl?" Will greeted his family, "What's for dinner, Ma?"

"I'm making fried fish, greens, potato salad and cornbread. It should be ready in about twenty minutes."

"My favorite," Will said excitedly. "Thanks, Ma! That's what's up! Oh, and here you go." Will handed his mother a roll of money – seven-hundred and fifty dollars, the amount he gave her every two weeks.

"Thanks, baby," Misses Bonner sighed as she placed the money in her bra. "I really wish I didn't need this money. I wish I could've gone to college so that I didn't have to work at this nursing home making seven dollars an hour doing laundry."

"Yeah, but don't worry, Ma, I got you!"

"And I appreciate that, son, but I don't want you to have to take care of me. I'm your mother," Misses Bonner explained, "and you've been doing this for too long. You've been selling drugs since you were how old – fourteen?"

"That's when you found out about it, Ma," Will chuckled. "I started when I was thirteen, but had enough money to start helping out around here by the time I was fourteen."

"Oh, well, excuse me! Well, I know you're grown now and have your own place and bills of your own, but I just wish you didn't have to go out there and risk your life anymore."

"Don't worry about me, Ma," Will attempted to reassure his mother. "I'm good. Nobody messes with me. Plus, Pop has my back."

"Well, you know I wanted to talk to you about something," Misses Bonner changed the subject. "Your coach called me today. He says you have hardly been in school or at basketball games or practice…"

"Well, Ma, I told you I was thinking about quitting and I told Coach Anderson, too."

"Well he says he has some good news that might change your mind, but he wants to tell you in person, tomorrow, before basketball practice. Please promise me you'll go, Will…"

"Oh, for real? Well, I really don't think he'll change my mind, but I do kind of miss basketball. I guess I can go tomorrow."

"He already told me the news," Misses Bonner said excitedly. "I'm so happy for you! I know you'll be happy, too! But you have to go back to school to make it happen."

"What is it, Ma?"

"Coach Anderson made me promise not to tell! You're just gonna have to go to school and basketball practice tomorrow," Misses Bonner smiled. "You really should be happy. He's giving you so many chances. Most kids would've been kicked off the team by now. Anyway… time to eat! Come on, Carl!"

The small family enjoyed their dinner and, when they were finished, went into the living room and, ironically, watched a movie from the 1990s called "Soul Food," a movie that the Bonner family watched together often. Once the movie was finished, Will said his goodbyes to his family and went outside to call Pop. It was about ten-o'clock when Will finally called Pop and told him he was ready to go to the corner to hustle.

"Are you finally ready to trap, nigga?" Pop's husky voice asked as he answered the phone. "That was a long-ass dinner, man!"

"My fault, dog," Will apologized. "My mom wanted to watch a movie, too. I'm in the wheel now though. You ready?"

"Yeah, here I come. I've had customers calling me already."

Pop walked down the block to Will's Cadillac and hopped in. Will pulled off, drove down the block to the corner of Ninth Street and Lycoming Street and pulled over. Pop called his customers back, and within ten minutes a steady stream of his regulars were coming up to the Cadillac to buy cocaine. Will's customers stopped by as well, so for an hour and a half there was a constant flow of traffic on Ninth Street for the two young hustlers.

Pop looked at the time on Will's stereo – it was now eleven-thirty. He waited another fifteen minutes to see if the flow of customers would continue. When it seemed like business was slowing down, Pop assumed it was safe to text Jasiel. He was having second thoughts about killing Will, but he had already put the plan in motion – he was in too deep to quit now. Pop sent a text message to Jasiel telling him it was the right time for him and Jose to come to the corner of Ninth Street and Lycoming Street and carry out their plot.

Within five minutes Jasiel and Jose had pulled up on Ninth Street in Jasiel's Pontiac Bonneville, about a half-block behind Will's vehicle. Jasiel had turned his headlights out so as not to be spotted by Will. Jasiel and Jose exited the Bonneville, crouched down, and slowly crept up the block towards Will's Cadillac. As they neared the vehicle, Jasiel crossed over to the passenger's side of the car where Pop was seated and Jose approached the driver's side, where Will was seated. Jasiel and Jose popped up on either side of the vehicle, surprising both Will and Pop.

"Oh shit!" Will exclaimed. He frantically reached down under his seat for his gun as two bullets from Jose's forty-five caliber handgun, (which he had purchased from Pop), burst through the driver's side window, shattering the glass and hitting Will in the back of his neck. Jose intended for the shots to hit Will in his head, but since he had ducked down to reach for his gun and it was difficult for Jose to see through the tinted windows before the glass shattered, he missed Will's head ever so slightly. He looked at Will through the shattered glass and saw that he was slumped over in his seat awkwardly, gasping for air, blood seeping from the back of his neck, and realized that Will was dying. Jose opened the door and reached into Will's pockets, pulling out a large wad of cash, then ran over to the passenger's side of the car alongside Jasiel. Both young men had their guns drawn.

"Damn, Jose! That was reckless as hell!" Pop exclaimed as he got out of the vehicle in front of Jose and Jasiel with both his and Will's book bags in hand. "You almost shot me, too, dammit! It's cool though. Let's be out!"

"You ain't going nowhere, motherfucker!" Jasiel barked.

"What?" a confused Pop asked.

Crack! Crack! Crack!

The shots echoed in the darkness and Pop fell to his knees, then onto his face, holding his chest and gasping for air. Jasiel emptied Pop's pockets while Jose grabbed the two book bags. As Jasiel scurried past Pop, who was lying face down in the grass, Pop made a weak attempt to grab Jasiel's leg.

"Get the fuck off me, *puta*," Jasiel growled as he viciously kicked Pop in the side of the head. "You shouldn't have fucked with my family!"

Then Jasiel and Jose ran to their car and sped off.

CHAPTER 16

Minutes after Jasiel and Jose fled the scene of the crime, the police arrived. A few minutes later, an ambulance arrived. The emergency medical technicians pronounced Pop dead at the scene. Will, however, was still clinging to life. He was rushed to Temple Hospital and the doctors there performed emergency surgery and transferred him to the Intensive Care Unit. Misses Bonner was notified and she and Carl rushed to the hospital.

"The operation was a success, Misses Bonner... your son is going to live," the surgeon informed Will's mother as she and Carl sat in the waiting room.

"Oh, thank you, Lord!" Misses Bonner exclaimed.

"However," the surgeon continued, "Will is not able to control his bowels and he is having difficulty breathing, which are both signs of severe spinal-cord injury."

"So, what are you saying, sir?" Misses Bonner asked in horror.

"I'm saying that we need to run some tests within the next twenty-four hours to see if your son has feeling in his extremities and run some CAT scans and ultrasounds."

"Are you saying that my boy is paralyzed?"

"Well, ma'am... there was severe trauma to his cervical vertebrae. My initial diagnosis is that he now suffers from quadriplegia, which is paralysis of the chest, arms and legs. I'm so sorry, ma'am. I'll keep you up-to-date as to the findings of my subsequent tests."

"Oh God! No!" Misses Bonner let out a blood-curdling scream as she broke out in tears and fell to her knees at her son, Carl's, feet.

"Ma, don't cry," Carl consoled his mother as he picked her up and walked her back over to the chairs in the waiting room. "Hey, doc, can we see my brother now?"

"Well, he's sleeping, but I don't see why not. I'll show you to his room."

Meanwhile, in Hunting Park, Tiny was furious when he heard the news about the shootings. Word traveled fast in the neighborhood. Rick had been driving down Ninth Street and saw the crime scene with the police and the ambulance taking Will away. He saw Will's car with the window shot out and noticed Pop's dead body being zipped up and carried away on a gurney. Rick immediately drove to Tiny's bar on Hunting Park Avenue to speak with his boss.

"Goddammit! I know my crazy-ass nephews did that shit!" Tiny vented as he and Rick sat in Tiny's office in the back of the bar. "They're fucking up my money! Will and Pop weren't my biggest customers, but they were consistent as hell and they had mad potential!"

"I know, right?" Rick agreed. "What makes you think Jasiel and Jose did it, though?"

"Jasiel was always talking about killing Will and Pop and I kept telling him not to," Tiny explained. "Then I had to break up a fight between the four of them in here last week!"

"Oh, shit."

"And my nephews are wiling out," Tiny continued. "You know they're the ones who robbed and killed Chris Martinez?"

"For real?" Rick gasped. "Oh shit! How'd you find out?"

"I already knew it – I just knew it! But when I confronted them about it, Jasiel swore on my sister's grave that they didn't do it. Then I ran into Tito, you know, the guy down the Badlands who has the chop-shop? He was running his mouth, talking about how he gets the best cars in and if I ever want something to let him know 'cause he can switch the VINs. He told me Jasiel and Jose sold him a white Yukon Denali that was rimmed up and all hooked up. That was Chris's truck, Rick! He even sold me this gun he said he found inside the truck!" Tiny retrieved a shiny gold and silver forty-five caliber handgun from his desk and showed it to Rick. "So then I *knew* them motherfuckers killed my nigga, Chris! And Jasiel swore on his own mother's grave. That sick motherfucker!"

"That's crazy as hell, man," Rick replied in shock. "I can't believe that! Chris was a good dude too, man. Your nephews are out of control, Tiny! What are you gonna do about that?"

"I've got it all figured it out. Matter-of-fact, please excuse me, I gotta handle some business."

"Alright, man," Rick said as he stood up and shook Tiny's hand. "I'ma get up outta here and let you handle your business."

"Alright man, I'll get with you later," Tiny replied. After Rick had left and closed the door to the office, Tiny locked the door and returned to his desk. He took out his second cellular phone, a pre-paid, and called a police officer in the Twenty-Fifth District named Vincent, who he had on his payroll.

"Yo, what's up?" Tiny said into the phone. "You know who this is. Come through the bar at one-forty-five. Come in plain clothes. I'll be waiting at the door."

At one-forty-five in the morning the corrupt police officer, along with his equally corrupt partner, arrived at the entrance of Tiny's bar. Tiny was waiting there for them, as he said he would be, and led them to his back office.

"So, Vincent, Earl... how have you two been?" Tiny asked as he poured them both a drink.

"We've been doing pretty good, Tiny," Vincent replied with a smile.

"Yeah, we can't complain," Earl added. "Especially with the way those young-boys are moving those keys you've been fronting us!"

"Good... good! I'm glad to hear that," Tiny nodded. "Tonight I have something different for y'all. I'll pay you ten-thousand dollars each if you kill my nephews for me."

"Your nephews, Tiny?" Vincent asked in shock as he and Earl looked at each other in disbelief. "You mean Jose and Jasiel? But why?"

"I won't tell you anything other than the fact that they're out of control and they're bad for business. So will you do it or not?"

"Yeah, if you say so and if you're paying ten stacks," Vincent answered eagerly.

"But we gotta make it look like they tried to shoot us first so it doesn't draw any suspicion from the Department," Earl interjected.

"Whatever you do is fine with me," Tiny said. "Just get it done within the next twenty-four hours. They live on Marshall Street near Hunting Park. Jasiel drives a silver Bonneville and Jose drives a black Impala, both with dark tints. They usually ride together, though. You already know they're stick-up kids and they stay strapped. Here's half the money now. I'll give you the other half when they're gone."

The next evening, at around nine-o'clock, while Vincent and Earl were out on patrol, they parked on Marshall Street near Jasiel and Jose's cars, waiting for the twins to exit their home and drive off in one of their vehicles. The corrupt cops planned to pull the twins over for having illegal tints on their windows. In Pennsylvania, it is technically illegal to have any tints on a car other than that which is issued by the manufacturer.

"Hold up," Earl tapped his partner on the shoulder. "Isn't that one of the twins coming out of that house right there?"

"Yeah, and there goes the other one behind him," Vincent added.

"Let's get ready!"

The two corrupt cops watched as the young men walked down the steps, talking and laughing, unaware of what was about to occur. The twins entered Jose's Impala and pulled off. The police officers pulled off behind them, followed for a half-block, and then turned on their blue and red lights. Jose pulled over.

"What the fuck are you pulling over for?" Jasiel screamed at his brother. "We're both dirty in this motherfucker. We both got guns. We're gonna go to jail, *stupid*! You should've bounced on them!"

"Don't worry, Jasiel," Jose reassured his twin, "it's probably just a routine stop or something stupid."

Although they had bullet-proof vests, they rarely remembered to put them on before they went out unless they were going on a mission to rob somebody. Now, Jasiel was wishing they had. He did not have a good feeling about getting pulled over. The police exited their vehicle and drew their weapons.

"Oh, fuck that, Jose!" Jasiel yelled as he looked in the side mirror. "This motherfucker's got his gun out!"

Jasiel quickly stepped out the Impala with his gun drawn. He raised his gun and...

Pop! Pop! Pop! Pop! Pop!

Earl sent five shots directly into Jasiel's body. Jasiel immediately dropped to the ground. No sooner had the shots rang out than Jose turned around in his the driver's seat to see what was transpiring and...

Pop! Pop! Pop!

Vincent fired into the driver's side of the rear window and hit Jose in the forehead, in the nose and in the jaw. The two officers rushed over to the vehicle. Earl kicked Jasiel's gun, which was lying on the ground next to him, away from his hand; but by that time Jasiel was already dying. Vincent searched Jose's body, found his revolver, and placed it in Jose's hand.

"Well, look at that," Vincent chuckled. "I didn't even have to use my throwaway gun!"

Over the next two days at the hospital, tests were run to confirm that Will was a quadriplegic. His mother was devastated. They still hadn't broken the news to Will, however. On Saturday morning when Misses Bonner and Carl came to visit Will, she decided it was finally time to tell him.

"Will, baby... there's something I need to tell you," Misses Bonner began as she sat next to her son's hospital bed.

"What is it, Ma?" Will struggled to speak. His once strong voice was weak now.

"You're a quadriplegic now, Will," Misses Bonner broke down into tears as she held Will's hand. "That means you won't be able to move your chest, arms or legs, baby."

"I know... I can tell 'cause I can't feel them." Will was strong, though. He didn't cry or complain about his lot in life. He knew that as a hustler he could be shot or killed one day, and he was happy to still be able to breathe, although even breathing was proving difficult for him.

Just then Coach Anderson walked in, looking very melancholy. He hugged Misses Bonner, shook Carl's hand, and commented that he hoped Carl would play basketball for him one day. Then the coach walked over to the opposite side of Will's hospital bed.

"Will, Will, Will. My God, son! What did they do to you?"

"They paralyzed me, Coach," Will forced a smile as he struggled to utter the words.

"I wish you would have listened, Will," Coach Anderson shook his head. "But I'm so, so sorry for you and your family."

"C-C-Coach," Will struggled to speak. "What did you wanna talk to me about?"

Misses Bonner looked up at Coach Anderson and shook her head "no." Coach Anderson nodded in agreement.

"Will, son, it's not important anymore."

"But, Coach, please! I need to know," Will pleaded with shallow breath. "I was going to come to school and practice on Thursday. I promised my mom."

"Well, son," Coach Anderson hesitated. "It was about your future...," Coach Anderson decided to give Will what would have been good news. He continued while avoiding making eye-contact with Will's mother. "You finally received a full scholarship offer from Saint Joe's. On top of that, you got an offer to try out to play ball overseas next year in the EuroLeague, playing for FC Barcelona Regal, if you finished out your high school season with the same performance you've had all year." Coach

Anderson paused. "But, you see, Will, because of what happened to you, it doesn't matter now. I'm so sorry, son."

Misses Bonner burst into tears. And to everyone's surprise, so did Will. He cried profusely – so heavily that he began to choke badly. Coach Anderson frantically called a nurse into the room who then cleared him, Carl and Misses Bonner out of the room so that she and the other staff could assist Will. Then suddenly, Will went into cardiac arrest. Within minutes, Will Bonner was no more.

It's a story about money, drugs, robbery, murder, lust and betrayal. It ends on a sour note. It is somewhat of a sad story. But that's just one North Philly story. And that's life – an illegal life.

OUTRO: (SUMMER 2014)

Misses Bonner and Miss Davidson had never developed a tight-knit relationship like their sons Will and Pop had. However, the fact that both young men's fatal shootings occurred at the same time drew them together for the purpose of planning their son's funerals. The emotionally devastated women decided to hold the boys' funerals simultaneously the following weekend. Coach Anderson was gracious enough to go about the business of making the funeral arrangements so the mothers could grieve in relative peace.

Carl's mood had been stoic ever since his brother passed away in the hospital. Other than attempting to comfort his inconsolable mother, Carl hadn't really spoken to anybody since the doctor informed them that Will had been pronounced dead on that fateful day after Coach Anderson delivered the devastating news to Will about his missed opportunity to play professional basketball. Carl was devastated not only by the loss of his older brother and only sibling, but also by the deaths of Pop and Cannon. Carl had lost all three of his male role models in a short period of time and the trauma to his young psyche was more than he could handle emotionally.

The relatively small funeral home was filled to capacity and Misses Bonner was overwhelmed by the number of people who showed up to offer emotional support after learning of Will's death. Dozens of students from Will's school were in attendance, along with Coach Anderson, the entire basketball team, the school's principal and several of Will's teachers.

Of course, Stacy was in attendance. After embracing Carl and Misses Bonner and offering her sincere condolences, the emotionally damaged young woman entered the funeral home and sat silently next to Will's mother, not revealing what she learned about the breach in her and Will's relationship shortly before he was murdered. Stacy also kept the conversation she had with Pop after learning of Will's affair with CeCe to herself. She had absolutely no desire to tarnish either of the young men's reputations post-mortem.

Rick and Tiny also attended the young men's funeral. They stayed in the back of the funeral home, however. Neither of them had officially met the boys' mothers and they concluded that the young men's funeral would be a bad time to introduce themselves.

"Coach Anderson... thank you so much for your help with organizing this," a tearful Misses Bonner thanked the man as she stood up and hugged him when he approached before the funeral proceedings began. "I don't know what I would have done without you."

"It was the least I could do ma'am," Coach Anderson sincerely addressed his attractive female peer. "I'm so sorry for your loss. Will was a fine young man. I wish I could have saved him."

"Well, I appreciate everything you did for him over the years..."

"It was my pleasure working with Will," Coach Anderson replied with tears in his eyes. "Carl, I heard you'll be attending Gratz this fall. Please don't hesitate to reach out to me if you need anything."

"Thanks. I'll be good, though," Carl concisely replied without making eye-contact with the older man. "I don't play basketball so I don't see how you could help me."

"Well, I hear you play a mean game of chess, son," Coach Anderson replied with a smile. "Maybe you can show me what you got after you start school in September."

"I don't really play like that now," Carl abruptly informed the coach. "Will taught me how to play when I was a young-boy. We haven't played as much since he moved out and I'm not playing anymore now."

"Well, I'm sorry, son," the coach empathetically replied. "I can't imagine how difficult this whole situation must be for you. Please feel free to reach out if you need anything at all..."

"Yeah, alright."

Stacy cut her eyes at Carl, sensing the dismissive tone in his young, raspy voice. She intuitively sensed Carl held some animosity towards Coach Anderson although Carl had not confided in her. Carl subconsciously did blame the coach for his older brother's death and wanted nothing to do with him. Stacy struggled with whether or not she should share the information about her conversation with Pop and how he had propositioned her. She did not want Carl's anger to be misdirected, but she also didn't want the information she shared to cause people to speculate about the potential circumstances of the young men's deaths and tarnish their reputations now that they had passed. Stacy decided to keep the information to herself and sat in silence.

Moments later, two young, attractive Puerto Rican women and a teenaged boy around Carl's age entered the funeral home, approached the area where Carl, Misses Bonner and Miss Davidson were seated and approached the women.

"Hi, my name is CeCe, this is my girl, Veronica and my cousin Mannie," CeCe began as she approached the middle-aged women. "We were close with your sons. We just wanted to pay our respects and tell you we're so sorry for your loss."

"Thank you dear," Misses Bonner replied as she stood up halfway and embraced the two young women. "That's sweet of you. Thanks for coming."

"CeCe? Darryl mentioned you plenty of times before," Miss Davidson began as she stood up and hugged the young woman tightly. "Thank you so much for coming! He would be so happy to know you are here."

Stacy quickly looked up upon hearing the name "CeCe." She instantly had a flashback of the phone call Will had made to her in error when she heard him being intimate with another woman. The tears she had been attempting to hold back, which already filled her eyes to the brink, were forced out when she became overwhelmed with emotion upon seeing the young woman who had "stolen" her man and had been intimate with him more recently than she had.

"There is no way this isn't the same CeCe," Stacy thought as she burst into tears, rose from her seat and ran to the bathroom. She sobbed for five consecutive minutes before regaining her composure, blowing her nose and reapplying her makeup. Before exiting the bathroom, Stacy stared at herself in the mirror, more tears welling up in her eyes, and rubbed her mostly flat stomach which had begun to protrude slightly over the previous few weeks. "I wonder what I'm gonna do now," the devastated young woman said to her reflection. "I wonder if he got that bitch pregnant too."

After the funeral, dozens of mourners attended the repast Coach Anderson hosted in the spacious basement of his large, three-story Nicetown home. Stacy attended with Carl and Misses Bonner and sat at the table with the two of them, along with Misses Davidson. The women forced themselves to make casual conversation, but Carl was not in the mood to act like he had anything to say.

"CeCe! Come here girl!" Misses Davidson called out to CeCe when she, Veronica and Mannie entered the crowded basement. "Come sit over here with us."

"Oh, okay. Thank you," CeCe bashfully accepted as she led the way across the basement to the table where the deceased's family members were seated. "Are you sure you want us to sit here? Isn't this table only for family?"

"Girl, please," Misses Davidson waved her hand dismissively. "We're the only family the boys had, so if we say it's okay, then it's okay! We just need to pull up another chair."

"Carl, go grab another chair and bring it over here," Misses Bonner instructed her son.

"No, it's okay," Stacy tensely interjected. "I should leave. I'm not feeling well. I need to go home and lie down..."

"Oh no! Are you okay honey?" Misses Bonner asked Stacy, her brow wrinkled with concern. "I know this must be rough on you..."

"Oh, don't worry about me, Mom," Stacy nervously replied, trying to keep herself from staring at the young woman Will had cheated on her with shortly before he died. Stacy had been overcome with anxiety at the thought of sitting and eating a meal in the same room as CeCe, let alone at the same table. Her eyes were filled with tears as she rose from her seat. "I'll be okay. I'm sorry I can't stay and be here for you right now, but I gotta go."

"No problem sweetie," Misses Bonner empathetically replied as she rose and hugged Stacy. "You just go home, try to clear your head and get some rest."

"Okay, thanks Mom," Stacy whined. "See y'all later. I'm sorry again Misses Davidson. Stay strong, Carl."

"Thanks Stace," Carl replied, devoid of emotion.

Stacy quickly exited Coach Anderson's basement as CeCe, Veronica and Mannie joined Will and Pop's family at their table. Carl looked over at Mannie and nodded.

"Hey man," Mannie began as he extended his hand to shake Carl's. "I'm Mannie. I'm sorry about your brother, man."

"I'm Carl, but you can call me 'C.' You don't have to be sorry though... you didn't do it," Carl solemnly replied as he shook the teenager's hand. "Where are you from? I never saw you in the hood or at school before."

"I'm from P.R. – San Juan," Mannie informed his peer. "I just moved here last week. How old are you?"

"I just turned fourteen," Carl informed Mannie. "What about you?"

"I'll be sixteen in a few months," Mannie replied.

"I'm getting claustrophobia in here," Carl huffed. "You tryna go chill outside?"

"Yeah, we can do that." Mannie shrugged his shoulders and followed Carl's lead in rising from his seat and pushing his chair under the table.

"Ma... me and Mannie are about to go get some fresh air," Carl informed his mother matter-of-factly as he briskly walked away from the table and up the basement stairs without waiting for his mother's response. Mannie quickly followed suit. "Do you smoke weed?" Carl asked his new associate once they were outside and halfway down the block from Coach Anderson's home.

"*Si*! I fuck with Mary Jane *heavy*, bro," Mannie smiled.

"Let's walk to my house so we can grab some of this weed I have and smoke," Carl suggested. Carl had found his brother's personal stash when cleaning out Will's apartment after his death and had been smoking heavily ever since. "I'm not trying to be around all these fake motherfuckers right now."

"I understand, bro," Mannie acknowledged as he reached into his pocket and retrieved a small, plastic jar. "We don't have to walk to your crib, though. I got that *fuego gasolina* right here!"

"Oh, shit!" Carl smiled. His eyes grew large when he saw the multi-colored marijuana buds Mannie held in the clear, plastic tube. "That's what's up! You got a wrap?"

"Yeah, I got Fanta-leaf. Where can we go roll up and smoke?"

"I know a ducky spot around the corner," Carl replied as he began walking. "Follow me!" Carl led the way until the two teenagers reached a relatively secluded area around the corner from Simon Gratz High School. Mannie rolled the marijuana into the natural-leaf wrap, lit the marijuana and passed it to Carl. "Good looking," Carl thanked Mannie as he exhaled and began to cough profusely. "This is that shit!"

"Yeah, bro... I only smoke fire," Mannie confidently replied with his thick Spanish accent as Carl passed the blunt back to his newfound friend. "Hang with me if you wanna smoke good. I can hook you up."

"Oh, yeah?" Carl was intrigued by his young associate and how mature he seemed to be for a fifteen-year-old. "So, what made you move here from Puerto Rico anyway?"

"I was getting into too much trouble in P.R.," Mannie admitted. "My mom went to prison last year for stabbing my father to death. My old-ass, alcoholic uncle says he 'can't control' me. I just got into it with these older niggas and hit one of them with the machete. Now everybody's mad 'cause it took his hand off and his people say they 'got something for' me! I'm not worried about them but everybody was acting like I needed to leave the island, so they sent me up here to live with my cousin, CeCe, 'cause her dad is mad strict. I guess they figure he's gonna put me on lock down or some shit!"

"That's corny," Carl sighed.

"*Esta' bien*, though," Mannie replied as he took another drag of the marijuana. "I'm real sorry about your bro, though. My cousin, CeCe, told me he got killed. That's real fucked up. I would be ready to kill somebody if they killed my brother. On some real shit, if I find out who killed my cousins, I'ma get him! They were twins and the cops shot them the other night but the story I heard seems suspect to me."

"Shit...," Carl groaned as Mannie passed the marijuana back to him. "If I find out who killed my brother or his homey, Pop, I'ma kill him! Real rap! I'm not letting a nigga slide for killing my bro! I don't give a fuck who it is!"

"Oh, you get down like that?"

"Naw," Carl reluctantly admitted. "I'm about to, though. Fuck all that being good shit. You know my mom is already behind on bills since my brother died. She was already having issues with her health before and she hasn't worked in a few weeks. I'm gonna have to go out and get some money..."

"You need money, bro?" Mannie quickly stood up from the makeshift bench the boys sat on as they smoked. "I can help you get some money. Let's go!"

Carl followed Mannie as the two teenagers briskly walked down Hunting Park Avenue towards Broad Street – leaving Nicetown, headed back towards the Hunting Park section of the city. Mannie continued to lead the way as they crossed the intersection of Broad Street and Hunting Park Avenue. Without warning, Mannie darted towards a car idling at the red light in the intersection, pulled a large revolver from his waist and opened the driver's side door, leveling the firearm at the terrified driver's head.

"Get out the car, *maricon*," the reckless teenager commanded the middle-aged male driver, who sat motionless, paralyzed by fear, his eyes and mouth frozen wide open. "Did you hear what I said, motherfucker? Get out before I pop the shit out you!"

"Yo, bro! What the fuck?" Carl screamed as he stood in the middle of the intersection. "It's the middle of the day, nigga! This ain't Puerto Rico... You can't get away with that shit up here!"

"Fuck that! Help me get this *puto* out the fucking car so we can get some money for this shit!" Mannie argued with Carl in the middle of the crowded intersection as they drew attention from dozens of onlookers who were walking and driving by.

"Naw, dog! This is a dummy mission," Carl objected. "Let's get the fuck outta here before the cops come!"

Before Mannie could even think to act on Carl's suggestion, a passing policed squad car screeched to a halt, activated its emergency flashing lights. The two officers in the vehicle jumped out and aimed their guns at Mannie.

"Drop your weapon," one of the officers screamed as the other used the vehicle's radio to call for backup. "Put your hands in the air and get on the fucking ground!"

"Oh shit!" Mannie looked up in shock. "These cops really show up fast as shit around here, huh?" The reckless young man laughed maniacally. He swiftly struck the driver of the vehicle in the forehead with the butt of his gun, splitting the innocent man's forehead open, spit in the man's face and laughed before turning to face the officers; slowly raising his arms in surrender and kneeling to the ground in the middle of the intersection next to his target vehicle.

The two responding officers and an additional two officers who arrived on the scene just as Mannie surrendered ran across the intersection and converged on the teenager, kicking his gun away from him and handcuffing his hands behind his back. Carl stood motionless, his mouth wide in shock. He could not believe what had just occurred. Carl thought to himself that Mannie seemed like a cool friend, but he was obviously mentally imbalanced! As the police officers hoisted a handcuffed Mannie up from the ground, they walked towards Carl as they made their way to the patrol car they intended to use to transport Mannie to the police district building for processing.

"You were with this guy?" One of the police officers aggressively questioned Carl as he shoved Mannie into the back of the squad-car.

"Uh... um...," Carl stuttered.

"Man, I don't know that motherfucker! I do my dirt by my fucking self," Mannie boasted, laughing. "I don't need any new friends anyway, so just take me to jail, motherfuckers!"

"Please clear the area, son," the officer firmly but politely addressed Carl after hearing Mannie's confession. "This is an active crime scene."

The next afternoon, Tiny broke his regular routine and made a special trip to Ninth Street and Lycoming Street to introduce himself to Will's mother. He brought Rick along with him so they could both offer their condolences. There was another, less sentimental reason Tiny decided to pay the Bonner family a visit that afternoon, however.

Tiny had almost immediately learned of his nephew's arrest and had also learned that Carl had been present but was not apprehended by the officers. Tiny wanted to discuss the events of the previous day with Carl.

"Hello, Misses Bonner," Tiny greeted the woman when she answered the door. "My name is Luis and this is my associate, Rick. We never officially met, but I have heard so much about you. We were something like mentors to Will over the years. We just wanted to stop by and formally introduce ourselves. I'm sorry it wasn't under better circumstances…"

"Oh, thanks for stopping by. Come on in," Misses Bonner winced in pain as she held the screen door open to allow the men to enter.

"Are you okay ma'am?" Rick interjected. "You look like you're in pain."

"It's this damn gout," Misses Bonner complained as she limped over to the kitchen table. "My diabetes and my gout have both been kicking my ass the past few weeks, as if I didn't already have enough to deal with!"

"Well, thank you for letting us come in, but we won't keep you long Misses Bonner," Tiny replied. "I know you have a lot going on. I just wanted to introduce myself and let you know that you can reach out to me if you need help with anything at all."

"Oh, well I appreciate that Mister Luis," Misses Bonner thanked Tiny. "I'll be sure to keep that in mind. I don't know if you could mentor my younger son. I just don't want him to get involved in the streets like his brother did. He needs an intelligent, well-groomed male role model in his life." Misses Bonner smiled naively at the multiple kilogram drug dealer who did everything in his power to pass as a legitimate businessman. "Carl! Come down here and say hi to your brother's mentors!"

"Yeah, ma?" Carl walked downstairs and entered the kitchen a few short moments later. "What's going on?"

"I want you to meet your brother's mentor, Mister Luis and Mister Rick," Misses Bonner began. "They stopped by to offer their condolences and said they would help us if we need anything. Maybe you should see if he can teach you some work skills so you can find a job and keep yourself busy so you can stay out of trouble."

"Oh… hey," Carl hesitated before greeting Tiny and Rick. Carl was fully aware of who Tiny was – his reputation preceded him in the neighborhood and he had met Tiny in passing on a few occasions over the years since Will had been working closely with Rick.

"Yo, what's up, pop," Tiny warmly greeted Carl. "You been keeping yourself out of trouble?"

"Yeah… I'm cool," Carl passively replied.

"That's what's up," Tiny nodded his head. "Misses Bonner… I'm about to walk to the corner store. Do you need anything?"

"Um, well, I could use some paper towels and flour, but I was just about to give Carl my last couple dollars and send him over there to get it…," Misses Bonner reached for her purse and retrieved her wallet.

"Don't worry about it ma'am," Tiny objected. "I got you. Carl, why don't you take a walk with us to the store?"

"Alright."

"We'll be back in a minute Misses Bonner. Are you sure you don't need anything else?" Tiny asked the woman.

"No, that's it for now. Thank you," Misses Bonner replied with a smile.

"Carl," Tiny began as the three men stepped outside, closed the door behind them and made the short trip down the block to the corner store. "You good, pop?"

"Yeah, I'm chilling," Carl concisely replied. He didn't know why, but he felt somewhat nervous and slightly uneasy around Tiny.

"I heard you were with my crazy-ass nephew yesterday when he tried to jack somebody's car in broad daylight after the funeral!"

"Uh… um, well," Carl stuttered.

"Listen," Tiny began. "I don't blame you for any of that. Manuel has been crazy since he was a little kid. He just got here from P.R. last week and now that he got booked for that dumb shit he's going to get sent back. I'm just glad you didn't get caught up. I'm sure your mother would be devastated and wouldn't be able to cope if something happened to you now. You're all she has left, right?"

"Yeah…," Carl acknowledged as a solemn look spread across his face. The teenager was already aware that he was his mother's only surviving family member now that Will had been killed, but hearing somebody else say it aloud had a sobering effect on the young man.

"So, you know that means you gotta stay around for her, right?" Tiny continued. "I spoke to my dumb-ass nephew this morning. He told me he was trying to jack that car to help you with money, even though it was his idea. Ya'll need money that bad, pop?"

"I mean… yeah," Carl reluctantly admitted. "We've been messed up since Will got killed. He paid most of my mom's bills since she's been sick and working even less than she usually does."

"You want to make some money?" Tiny asked with his eyebrow raised, staring Carl directly in his eyes. They stood at the counter of the corner store as Tiny paid for Misses Bonner's groceries and his own pack of cigarettes.

"I mean… yeah, sure," Carl answered. "What you want me to do? The same shit Will did?"

"Don't even worry about it right now," Tiny smugly instructed the teenager as they exited the bodega and walked back up the block towards the Bonner residence. "Tomorrow afternoon at two-o'clock, Rick here is gonna come scoop you and teach you everything you need to know. You with it?"

"Yeah," Carl nodded his head excitedly. "I'm with it!"

"Okay, cool," Tiny smiled as he pulled out a wad of cash and placed it in Carl's hand along with the grocery bag. "Now go in and give the groceries and half the money to your mother. Have fun today and make sure you get enough rest tonight. You're about to become a working man tomorrow!"

"Okay, thanks Tiny!" Carl shook Tiny's hand vigorously before quickly turning and running up the steps leading to the front door of the house. "See y'all tomorrow!"

"Good shit, boss," Rick commented as the men walked across the street and entered Tiny's Cadillac truck. "Hopefully he's as good of a worker as his brother was. Once he gets used to the routine, you'll be able to recoup all that bread you're losing from Will and Pop not hustling on this block anymore."

"Yeah, real shit," Tiny concurred as he placed the key in the ignition and started the truck. "Oh yeah," Tiny turned to Rick before pulling off. "I don't know the young-boy like that, so we gotta be careful until we see what type time he's really on."

"Yeah, I got you, boss," Rick sighed and rolled his eyes as he grinned. "I already know what you're about to say…"

"Yeah, well, I'll say it anyway," Tiny interrupted as he lit a cigarette and drove away from the curb. "Just make sure that young-boy doesn't fuck up!"

TO BE CONTINUED…

ALSO AVAILABLE FROM
PAPER-CHASE PUBLICATIONS:

-Suicide Tuesday by J. Cerrone
-The Prodigal Son: Book One by J. Cerrone
-Tears Behind the Veil by Shannon Jihan Smith & J. Cerrone

Available at: www.paperchasepublications.com

Coming Soon:

-Jewels For Your Crown by J. Cerrone
- Illegal Life II: Carl's Revenge by J. Cerrone
- Hood Politics by Jermaine Crews & J. Cerrone

*For information on writing services, voice-over/narration services and speaking engagements, contact J. Cerrone Smith, owner and founder of Paper-Chase Publications, directly.

Phone: 1(888)399-0365
E-Mail: jaycerrone@paperchasepublications.com
Alternate: paperchasepublications@gmail.com

**If you aren't already doing so, please follow Paper-Chase Publications on social media to stay up-to-date with availability of products, events and new releases.

Instagram: @paperchasepublications
Facebook & YouTube: Paper-Chase Publications